WHISPERS THROUGH
A MEGAPHONE

WHISPERS THROUGH
A MEGAPHONE

Rachel Elliott

AN IMPRINT OF PUSHKIN PRESS

ONE

an imprint of Pushkin Press

71–75 Shelton Street, London WC2H 9JQ

First published by ONE in 2015

ISBN 978 0 992918 22 4

Text designed and set in FF Scala by Tetragon, London
Printed and bound by CPI Group (UK) Ltd,
Croydon CRO 4YY

www.pushkinpress.com/one

To my family, shore to my sea

———————

"When you decide to live, to finally live, a world of possibility opens, maddening and vast, but where is the bridge across to that world, can anyone see a bridge?"

MIRIAM DELANEY

1

THE SUPERABUNDANT OUTSIDE WORLD

M iriam Delaney sits at her kitchen table and watches
the radio. She is mesmerized, transfixed.

Inside a studio somewhere—somewhere in the *outside world*—a woman is speaking in the fullest of voices about her extraordinary life: the adventures, the flings, the lessons she mined from her mistakes. Her stories are punctuated by music, carefully chosen to reveal *even more life*.

Miriam takes a deep breath in, because maybe what's on the air is also in the air, maybe something of this woman's superabundant presence will transmit through the broadcast.

Fancy being able to speak like that.

Fancy being able to speak properly.

It's three years today since Miriam last stepped out of this house.

No, that's not quite true. She has stepped into the back garden to feed the koi carp, stepped into the porch to collect the milk and leave a bin bag for her neighbour to place at the end of the drive. But step out into the street? No chance. Risk collision and a potentially catastrophic exchange with a stranger? You must be joking. Not after what happened. *Not after what she did.* Inside the cutesy slipper-heads of two West Highland terriers, her feet have paced the rooms of 7 Beckford Gardens, a three-bed semi with a white cuckoo clock, brown and orange carpets, a life-size cut-out of Neil Armstrong.

Miriam's hibernation is three years old today, but numbers can be deceptive, three years can feel like three decades. Hibernation ages like a dog, so three is about twenty-eight, depending on the breed, and this one is kind, protective, it keeps the world at bay.

The *world*—now there's an interesting concept. Miriam rests her chin on her hands. Where is the world exactly? Is it inside or outside? Where is the dividing line? Am I in or am I out?

She tosses a coin. *Heads I could be part of the world, tails I'll always be outside it.*

The ten-pence piece, flat on her palm, says heads. *Best out of three?*

Three hopeful heads, one after the other.

Miriam smiles. It's time. She knows it and the coin knows it. Show me the money. Money talks. It's time to *get a life.*

The main problem? Other people. They have *always* been the problem. Other people seem to know things. They know what a life should contain, all the simple and complicated things like shopping and Zumba and being physically intimate with another body. They know the rules, the way it's supposed to go. Miriam is thirty-five and when she looks out of the window all she sees is a world full of people who know things she will never know.

The *world* again. After years of not looking it's all she can see. She would like to be part of it, to somehow join in.

She writes a plan on a Post-it and sticks it to the radio:

1. Do something I am afraid of. Apparently this builds confidence (have yet to see evidence of this—will be an interesting experiment)
2. Spend next few days clearing out house—get rid of mother's things
3. Leave house next week

The trouble with number one is what to pick from the enormous list? The task of actually *making* the list of things she is afraid of could take another month, and four more weeks inside this house? Four weeks that will feel like ten months? That thought is unbearable, it makes Miriam shiver and run upstairs to fetch one of her many cardigans.

But lists are good, remember? You can add things and take them away. Adding makes you feel like a person with clear intentions, subtracting feels like a small victory. What else? Well, a list is a personal map. It's a ladder that you can move up and down at your leisure. When you cross things off it feels like you're moving, you're getting somewhere, there is some purpose to all this—something is finally happening.

Back in the front room, she begins the list.

Write fast, Miriam. You can do this. Lists are good. Write until you land on something you could tackle tonight. No, not tomorrow. Tonight.

THINGS I AM AFRAID OF

1. Idea that my mother is still alive somewhere and I am not alone
2. Idea that my mother is definitely dead and I am alone
3. Going back to where it happened
4. Love

5. No love
6. Clothes shopping
7. Thought that I might do it again if I go back outside
8. Being stuck in a lift with a group of talkative people
9. Never being able to write a list or letter due to major accident involving hands
10. Turning into my mother
11. Having no capacity to know that I'm already just like my mother
12. Fingerless gloves
13. Naked cleaning

There it is, number thirteen on the list (unlucky for some). Naked cleaning—all it actually requires is removing this cardigan, this T-shirt, these jeans, pulling Henry the hoover from the cupboard and plugging it in. How scary can it be?

Answer: that depends on your childhood.

It depends on whether, at the age of eight, you found your mother sweeping the floor of the school corridor wearing nothing but a pair of trainer socks. (Had she planned to go for a run and slipped into insanity seconds after putting on her socks? Can madness descend that quickly, like thunder, like a storm?) There she was, Mrs Frances Delaney, quietly sweeping her way through a turbulent sea of hysterical children, the waves of laughter rising up and up and—

Miriam was drenched. She had wet feet, wet hands, wet eyes.

Mother here at school. Mother naked. Other children cackling, jeering. Poor mother. I love mother and hate mother.

The headmaster appeared. He walked on water. He took off his suit jacket and smothered Mrs Delaney's nakedness. He was gallant, unfazed. Perhaps he had seen it all before. (Miriam hoped not.) Frances carried on sweeping—she was thorough, if nothing else. She had always valued cleanliness and order. Perhaps the headmaster understood this, hence his sensitivity. Perhaps he respected it.

What made the situation worse, even harder for Miriam to comprehend, was the fact that her mother didn't even work as a cleaner. Turning up at your own workplace without any clothes on is a rupture of social etiquette, a glitch in mental health, forgetfulness at its most perverse, but at least it contains a thread of continuity: *I have done what I normally do, I have come to the right place, but something is amiss. I wonder what it could be?* Turning up at someone else's workplace—your daughter's school—in the nude, in the buff, apart from tiny socks, is unbearably nonsensical.

Miriam's mother was mad as a spoon.

Was it catching?

(Miriam hoped not.)

Fast-forward twenty-seven years and what do we see? We see a woman, carefully folding her clothes and placing them on the sofa. She walks to the cupboard in the hallway and pulls Henry the hoover out into the light, plugs it in, switches it on. Now she is vacuuming the brown and orange carpet in her front room wearing nothing but knickers and Westie slippers. A cuckoo springs from its house, making her jump. It's ten o'clock. Only two hours left until Wednesday becomes Thursday, until the first day of August is over, and then it will be three years and a day since she ran all the way home, whispering *oh my God, oh my God.* Anniversaries come and go. Important dates get sucked into the vortex and life rolls on, taking us with it, perpetual tourists who pretend to be at home.

Steady on, Miriam. There's no need to start brooding over the nature of existence. You've got to stay focused, just for once, otherwise you'll *never* leave this house. Self-soothe, remember?

Remember what the book said, the one Fenella lent you, the one about staying sane in a mad world.

Fenella Price. Chief supplier of objects from the outside world: food, pens, knickers, etc. Fenella is no ordinary friend. She is a Beacon of Sanity, forever glowing, her equanimity unshakeable. She is proof that people can be sensible, rational, consistent. But more importantly, she is proof that Miriam isn't contagious. Her mother's madness is in her blood and her bones—it has to be, doesn't it? But Fenella has been there and seen it all, the highs and lows, the dramas and trips, ever since they were at primary school, and *still* she is sane. She wears smart clothes, works as a cashier in the local branch of Barclays, goes to evening classes three times a week: Pilates, Tango, How to Make Your Own Lampshades. As sane as they come, surely?

"Stay sane in this mad world," Fenella said. "When your thoughts race off into historical territories, talk softly to yourself. That's what I do. I don't care where I am. I say *just you settle down, Fenella Price. Everything is fine.*"

Miriam sighs. Thank goodness for Fenella. If only she could tell her the truth about the thing that happened, the thing she did, three years ago today.

It happened like this.

Oblivious footsteps along the woodland path.

Oblivious footsteps across the field and all the way to the pub.

Lunch with Fenella (a cheddar and onion-marmalade sandwich, a few French fries, half a cider).

A hug and a goodbye, nice to see you, give me a ring soon.

Now we travel in reverse.

Oblivious footsteps across the field.

Oblivious footsteps along the woodland path. Disgustingly ignorant, outrageously unaware, until—

The world is a safe place until it isn't.

People are good until they're not.

Miriam wishes she had taken a final look at the buildings, the trees, the dogs playing in the field, but you never know what's coming, you walk small and blind, the world simply an echo of your own concerns.

2

MOVE OVER DARLING

Ralph has Treacle all over his legs, his arms, his stomach. Treacle the ginger cat, bored with Ralph's inactivity, hungry for breakfast. She pads up and down the sleeping bag, treads over the lumps and bumps of her new owner, searching for signs of life.

Treacle had been lost and alone, a stray cat in the woods, patchy and thin. Then she met Ralph Swoon, who was also lost and alone. Now they had each other, and a rickety old shed in the middle of the woods, full of slatted light.

He bought her a can of pilchards.

It was a fishy kind of love, but it was real.

Still wearing yesterday's clothes, Ralph steps out of his sleeping bag. He runs his fingers through his hair and opens the door, heading for the pile of leaves that has become his outside toilet. Treacle sits in the doorway, waiting. She is already used to this part of their daily routine. She knows that Ralph will stumble back in, tip some food onto that cracked blue plate on the floor, then return to his sleeping bag and invite her inside it. Yesterday they fell asleep like that for three hours, with Treacle opening her eyes every now and then to make sure Ralph was still breathing.

Feline logic told her that he had dragged himself here to die. Why else would he have turned up in the woods at 11.30 p.m. on 4th August with no bag, no possessions, just a wallet, a phone and a guitar?

But the cat was wrong.

He hadn't come here to die.

Last week, Ralph was sitting at the breakfast bar in his kitchen, listening to his wife and their two teenage sons out in the garden. Sadie and Arthur were hosing the legs of their new puppy while Stanley watched.

"This dog stinks," said Arthur.

"It's just mud. Help me hose it off," said Sadie.

"He's your dog, Mum."

"Don't start this again."

"Who went and got him?"

"I bought him for you and Stan. You always wanted a dog."

"I wanted a dog when I was six. You're ten years late."

"Oh fuck off."

Arthur smirked. The puppy wriggled about, trying to escape the cold water, trying to play.

Ralph had been against the idea of a dog. Didn't they have enough problems, without attending to the needs of what was effectively a furry baby? As usual, Sadie won. She said it would be good for Arthur, who was showing signs of excessive boredom. It would relax him, teach him responsibility, get him outdoors. A teenager needs a reason to climb out of bed in the morning, she said, otherwise he will sleep all day and all night and life will pass him by like an unremarkable dream. Sounds familiar, thought Ralph.

"Don't get water in his ears," said Sadie. "Dogs hate water in their ears."

"So why does he keep jumping in the river?"

"Spaniels like to swim. They don't swim *underwater*."

Arthur dropped the hose on the floor. "He's clean now, I'm going in."

"He's not clean. Look at him, he's filthy."

While the puppy shivered between them, Arthur and Sadie glared at each other. Stanley was an absent bystander, his thoughts elsewhere. These departures had been happening since last Friday, when Joe Schwartz kissed him hard, led him upstairs, sat beside him on the bed, kicked off his Converse trainers, flicked the hair out of his eyes and said you're wonderful, Stan, I really think you're wonderful.

Canadian Joe. An Adonis. He was a magician too—he had turned down the bickering voices of Arthur and his mother so that Stanley could barely hear them. Something about a filthy dog. Something about his brother having a problem.

"I'm not impressed with you right now," said Sadie.

"Oh really," said Arthur.

"You talk to me like I'm a piece of shit. What's your problem?"

"I don't have a *problem*."

"Just go and make me a coffee, Stan can help me finish. Stan, are you with us?"

Arthur marched through the kitchen in muddy boots, tapping on his iPhone.

Arthur Swoon @artswoon
Mum drowning new dog in garden call RSPCA

Mark Williams @markwills249
@artswoon Really? Not the LOVELY Sadie? Don't believe you

Arthur Swoon @artswoon
@markwills249 Enough SICKO BOY thats my mother!
My dad wearing hoodie not cool at his age

Mark Williams @markwills249
@artswoon Maybe he's in midlife crisis? One word for
you: MILF

When the twins were born, Ralph was still an undergraduate.
He was twenty years old, passive and unworldly. He hadn't
wanted to call his sons Arthur and Stanley. He preferred Mark,
Michael or Christopher, but he would never have risked arguing with Sadie about such crucial matters. They were fine,
they were happy, he could lose her at any moment. This was
the wordless core of their relationship, known and unknown.
Sixteen years later they argued all the time and the sight of
her Mini pulling into the driveway, its back seat covered with
newspapers and unopened poetry anthologies, had begun to
make him queasy.

Should your own wife make you feel queasy? Perhaps at the
beginning, with the anticipatory fizzing, the urgent desire. But
after sixteen years? What would she say if she knew?

"You make me feel queasy, dear."

"You make me feel queasy too."

"What now? A dry biscuit, a cracker, Alka-Seltzer?"

He took a digestive biscuit from the packet and put the kettle
on. He listened to Sadie telling Stanley about an exhibition she
wanted him to see—maybe they could go this afternoon, she
said. There was a pause before the inevitable rejection: I'm
sorry, Mum, but *no can do*.

"Why not?"

"I'm taking someone to the cinema this afternoon."

"Can't you go to the cinema another time?"

"Maybe you could see the exhibition with Kristin."

"I don't want to see it with Kristin, I want to take you."

"But Kristin's into art."

"Will you shut up about Kristin?"

Kristin Hart. The boys' godmother. She and her partner Carol were the paragons of contentment, which made them mesmerizing and annoying, even more so since Sadie found herself preoccupied with thoughts of Kristin in bed, Kristin in the shower, Kristin doing stretches before her morning run. Discombobulating, that's what it was—the sexualization of an old friend. Really quite *distracting*.

Ralph closed his eyes.

He saw flickering lights, blocks of colour.

Yellow, black, reddish brown.

The talking had stopped. There was a moment of silence. Yes, *silence*.

He exhaled into it, feeling his shoulders drop.

He noticed his fingers, the way they had curled into fists.

"I'm in such a foul mood," said Sadie, marching into the kitchen with a cocker spaniel attached to her leg. "I need a coffee."

"I'll make it."

"This bloody dog's driving me insane. You can take him out this afternoon."

"I don't think so."

"Why not? I need to get the food and drink for tomorrow. It'll take me ages."

His birthday party—something else he hadn't wanted. But it wasn't really for him. Sadie liked to surround herself with as many people as possible on a regular basis, otherwise his continued presence came as a shock.

"What do you know about Stan's girlfriend?" she said, finishing her coffee while the spaniel licked her face.

"Are you sure he has a girlfriend?"

"I hope she's not dull, like that girl he brought to the barbecue last month."

"I thought she was perfectly nice."

"He can do better than *perfectly nice*. She had no ambition."

"Sadie, she's a teenager."

"When I asked where she wanted to be in five years' time, do you know what she said?"

Ralph stood up, trying to decide whether to wash the dishes or go upstairs. "What?" he said, running the hot tap.

"In a swimming pool."

"Maybe she loves swimming."

"In five years' time she wants to be in a fucking swimming pool? She could be in one *now*, Ralph. What kind of ambition is that? It's like saying you want to end up on a toilet."

"Sadie—"

"And do you know what else? She said her favourite restaurant was Frankie & Benny's."

His wife was oblivious to her own snobbery. Ralph blamed this on her parents, a lecturer and a mathematician who discussed current affairs, played the banjo and made home-made pesto, all at the same time. They were brilliant, quick, sarcastic. They lived in France and never visited. No child could ever emerge from their narcissism without hating herself, and Sadie had converted her self-loathing into something more tolerable: snobbery.

Ralph's mother had been a housewife. His father worked for an upholsterer. It was no worse than Sadie's background, it was just different, but try telling *her* that.

"Whatever," he said.

"You sound like Arthur. Is that his hoodie you're wearing?"

"Of course not. I don't go around wearing our sons' clothes. I bought this last year for running, don't you remember?"

"I don't think I've ever seen you run," she said, head down, fiddling with her phone.

Ralph went upstairs, leaving a bowl of washing-up water that was supposed to smell of lavender and lemon, but actually smelt like the passageway between Asda and the car park.

Sadie Swoon @SadieLPeterson
Off to MK's this pm for the works: colour, cut, massage.
Spirits need lifting!

Kristin Hart @craftyKH
@SadieLPeterson Coffee afterwards at Monkey Business?
We need to talk

Mark Williams @markwills249
@SadieLPeterson You're gorgeous as you are
#Ifonlyiwere10yearsolder

Sadie Swoon @SadieLPeterson
@craftyKH Coffee sounds great, meet you at 5pm?

Upstairs, Ralph was confused.

"Well blow me, I've forgotten why I came up here," he said to no one.

Blow me. He almost Googled this phrase once, to discover its origins, but decided against it when he imagined the kind of sites that might pop up. He tried not to utter these words, especially when working with female clients, but saying *blow me* was something he had inherited from his father, along with narrow shoulders and a pert little bottom. Frank Swoon had been famous for his buttocks. Women wolf-whistled as he walked down the street. "Oh you do make me swoon, Mr Swoon. Just look at those little cheeks." It was the kind of comment a man would have been slapped for.

Ralph's confusion ran deeper than trying to recall why he had come upstairs.

In fact, it was chronic.

He was perpetually bewildered. He knew less about his own desires these days than his clients knew about theirs. Compared to him they were models of sanity, able to sit in front of him once a week and articulate their emotions with astounding clarity. Sometimes he wanted to tell them. He wanted to say hey, do you know how *astounding* this is, the way you know what you want? You may have a catalogue of neuroses, you may be anxious and depressed, but *you actually know what you want.*

Sadie had her own theory about his confusion. She was convinced that he hadn't been the same since Easter, when he walked into a giant garden gnome in B&Q. Who puts an enormous gnome right at the end of an aisle? Ralph had complained to the manager, calling it a MAJOR SAFETY ISSUE. When the manager laughed, trying to hide his amusement inside an unconvincing coughing fit, Ralph threatened to call the police. Yes, he was overreacting. Yes, he should have been looking where he was going. But sometimes a gnome is not a gnome: it is a giant symbol of everything that's wrong with your life.

Seconds before he headbutted the gnome, he was pretending to admire a vase of plastic daffodils. Insisting that they buy six bunches, Sadie was tweeting about how authentic they looked, how satisfying it was to have flowers that never died, and why hadn't she thought of this before? Other people, miles away,

were responding to her tweet. She was reading out their comments. Ralph stormed off down the aisle, unable to tolerate the
peculiar hoo-ha evoked by the plastic daffodils, and he spotted
Julie Parsley. *Julie Parsley?* And *that* was when he collided with
the giant garden gnome.

Sadie held up her phone, took a picture of him rubbing his
head, sprinted into the customer toilets.

What was Julie doing here in his local B&Q? Hadn't she
moved away? He remembered her singing 'Move Over Darling'
on stage at the King's Head; remembered her singing Ralph
you're so lovely, you really are lovely, to a melody she made
up on the spot.

Her hair was short and wavy now, like that French actor—
what was her name? Audrey Tautou. Yes, that's the one. Ralph's
memory was still intact, despite the bump on his head, but Julie
Parsley was nowhere to be seen. Her absence made him furious,
even though she had been absent for much longer than the
past few minutes. It made him shout. It made him complain
about HEALTH and SAFETY and the BLOODY STUPIDITY
of making a gnome that was as SOLID as a FUCKING WALL.

Ralph's confusion had nothing to do with that day in B&Q.

It had nothing to do with Julie Parsley, his first love, aged
fifteen.

And it had nothing to do with garden gnomes.

3

W hen the headmaster set eyes on Frances Delaney, sweeping the floor of the school corridor wearing nothing but a pair of trainer socks, he stood perfectly still and watched. He had never seen anything as strange and beautiful. His face was usually grey but not today. She had coloured him in. All around her, children were being children: wild, callous and despicable. They were like beetles, creeping bugs with hard shells. They said what they liked with vile spontaneity. Apart from little Miriam Delaney, of course. She was quiet, well behaved, positively ghostly. And with a mother like this, who could expect anything less?

He walked towards her, flicked the children away, took off his jacket and wrapped it around her shoulders. She was warm, because her sweeping had been furious. When Frances cleaned, the bugs knew she was coming. Beside her feet the floor was shining.

"I think you should come with me," the headmaster said, leading Frances along the corridors to his office. Her eyes were glazed, there were no words in her mouth. He pulled his National Trust blanket from the cupboard, blue and white and scratchy, smelling of tobacco. "Here," he said, offering it to Frances. "We'll find your clothes and then I'll drive you home. Does that sound like a good plan, Mrs Delaney?" His palms were wet, his breathing was quick. "Were you actually wearing any clothes when you left the house?"

That afternoon, at the end of the school day, Miriam walked home by herself as usual. She worried about the safety of cats outside all day long, worried about what kind of concoction she would be given for tea, worried that other children would be meaner than ever and what that meanness might look like. Today had been the loudest day. *No wonder you're a fucking weirdo, Delaney. Your mother's a nutter. Get your kit off, show us what you got, you both fucking nudists, is that what you are?*

She opened the front door of 7 Beckford Gardens, walked along the hallway to the kitchen.

They were on the table.

On it.

Just like her boiled egg and soldiers this morning.

Just like her colouring books and felt-tip pens.

No amount of disinfectant would ever make this right.

She thought about that as she stood in the doorway.

Thought about cleaning products, wondered how many bottles there were in the world.

And eventually they stopped grunting.

He stumbled backwards and zipped up his trousers.

She was still wearing her trainer socks.

And her black bowler hat.

"Well hello, Miriam," the headmaster said. "Did you have a good day at school?"

*

Miriam has vacuumed the front room and the hallway and it's time for a celebratory cup of tea. She dashes past the glass panels in the kitchen door and catches sight of her own body. She pauses, her eyes widen. *Is that me?* A woman in knickers and novelty slippers, who has just sucked up dust using a hoover called Henry as though there is nothing in the world to be afraid of.

She remembers something Fenella once said: "The past is the past." Stating the obvious makes Fenella happy. "It is what it is," she often says.

Miriam tried stating the obvious for a while, to see if it improved her well-being, but it only made her feel crazier than usual:

"This is a packet of Weetabix."

"The future is the future."

"Death means never seeing someone again."

"This is a pint of milk."

"The present is the present."

"I've never spoken in more than a whisper."

"What I mean," Fenella explained, "is no one can set foot in this house without your permission. Your mother's gone. The past is the past. Catch my drift?"

None of those statements seemed connected, but Miriam caught her drift. It can take a long time to believe that something is over. *That's* what Fenella had been trying to say. But it is. What's done is done.

She sits at the kitchen table and sips her tea. For once, just for a few minutes, there is no history on her back. There is no history crawling over her skin and poking into her mouth. History will return as quickly as you can whisper *Frances Delaney*, but these small moments, these victories, have to be marked. They are the flags of progress. Signposts to normality.

The letterbox rattles.

Who gets post at eleven o'clock at night?

It's another postcard, the sixth one Miriam has received over the past few weeks. On the front, a photograph of an old-fashioned bike, leaning against the wall of a French cafe. On the back, written in green ink:

> YOU COULD SIT AND READ A BOOK IN A CAFE,
> MIRIAM. YOU COULD CYCLE THROUGH THE
> STREETS WITH THE WIND IN YOUR HAIR

Like the others, this postcard is anonymous. She sticks it on the noticeboard beside the rest and looks down at her slippers. These slippers are not sexy, she thinks. But have I ever been sexy? She flexes her toes, making the two West Highland terriers nod and say of course you have, Miriam, of course you have.

Sex. Now *that* should have appeared on the list of things she is afraid of. It's not sex itself that's the issue, it's the fact that it has to involve another *person*. She told Fenella this last week.

"What on earth do you mean?" Fenella said.

"Well, it's not the *act* of sex," Miriam said, wishing she hadn't phoned. Fenella had just got home from Zumba and was disarmingly energized.

"Right."

"It's having to *be with someone*."

"So you'd be fine with a blow-up doll, is that what you're saying?"

"That is certainly not what I'm saying."

Fenella laughed. She opened a packet of Quavers and settled into an armchair.

"What's that noise?"

"I'm eating crisps."

"Doesn't that defeat the object of Zumba?"

"How could it?"

"I don't know."

"Exactly. So back to sex. It's never too late to get started," Fenella said, but it was all right for her. She started when she was sixteen in a caravan in Newquay with a boy who liked to be called Lucy. It was the Price family's summer holiday. Her parents were playing bingo in the town hall. Her brother was in the pub with a girl who liked to be called Pattie. It was raining, they were playing cards and Lucy (otherwise known as Martin Henley) said let's do it and they did.

"Just like that?" Miriam said.

"Just like that," Fenella said. "It was bloody awful but I felt fantastic afterwards."

"You're not exactly selling it."

"I don't *need* to sell it. It's everywhere. It sells itself."

"Why did he like to be called Lucy?"

"Why not?"

It was a good question. Fenella was full of those—questions that probed your assumptions and required no answers.

"At least I could do the pillow talk," Miriam said, which made both of them quiet and sad.

"One day," Fenella said.

"What if it never happens?"

"Whispering's not a crime."

So why does she feel like a criminal?

Miriam runs upstairs and puts on her pyjamas. That's enough cleaning for one night—no need to overdo it. She sets a track playing on her CD player: 'Wicked Game' by Chris Isaak. It's a song about the wickedness of love and a woman who has made someone think about her all the time. Miriam understands *that* kind of wicked—the taking over of mind and body—but she knows nothing about love. She has never experienced the kind of thing Chris Isaak is singing about, never fallen in love or had anyone fall in love with her. In fact, she is not even sure that she has met someone who is in love. Do they look different to other people? Are they easy to spot? Her mother always said that love was for people with dirty houses.

She looks in the mirror and knows what she is. She is buttoned-up. Buttons and buttons, moon-high. Imagine a night sky studded with buttons. Imagine Miriam's buttoned-upness living in a jar—the jar would be full of navy-blue ink, the kind you might use to write a letter to your grandmother, a letter on Basildon Bond writing paper, watermarked blue, saying you were sorry, so sorry, for everything.

> Dear Granny,
> I am so sorry Mummy does not let me visit. She says you are too normal to be good for me. I have looked for normal in the dictionary at school and copied out what it means in case you cant remember.
> *conforming, usual, typical, expected, free from physical or mental disorders*
> I think normal is nice can we meet in secret to be normal soon? Please write back and tell me if you think this would be nice.
> Lots of love,
> Miss Miriam Delaney

Chris Isaak has a soul-stirring voice. Some people can do that—they can reach into your soul and stir things around. He is truly soulful. *My voice is full of your soul—the parts I took when I stirred you around.* His crooning makes Miriam wonder what it would be like to look at her bed and see someone lying under the duvet. *Someone else*. What a wicked song! It's the soundtrack to a future that feels terrifying, exciting, possible, impossible. Her toes tingle inside her fluffy slippers.

Dear Granny,

I have still not heard from you and it has been two long days. Please reply immediately thankyou. I need to know if you would like to be normal and have a secret life with me.

Love Miriam xxx

Dear Mrs Betty Hopkins,

It has now been three days and I hope you are not ill. You are my hero Granny. I will keep this letter short in case you are very very busy. I love you.

M xxxxXxxxx

Dearest Miriam,

How lovely to hear from you! I daren't call, because your mother isn't well and she says that my phone calls upset her. Don't fret about things, Miriam. Your mother is trying some new medication and all will be well soon. When she recovers I'll take you to the park, or into town, and we'll revel in normality. Look up "revel" in your school dictionary, Miriam—I think you'll like it. It means to have lively and noisy fun. Your mother doesn't like noise, and this must be hard for you, but please remember she is poorly and it isn't your fault. Keep in touch, and if anything nasty happens just run out of the house and get in a taxi and I will pay the bill when you get here, all right? In the meantime, I've enclosed some new buttons for your collection. I bought them while I was on holiday in Scarborough. There are lots of buttons up north.

With love, as always,
Granny

Miriam sighs. She still misses her grandmother. The sight of those envelopes, her own name and address in that small, neat handwriting, made her feel like a real girl in a real house—a person of fixed abode, properly and officially there. But just as important was what happened in the act of writing. When Miriam composed her sentences, the voice inside her head sounded like any other girl. There was an unbroken stranger inside Miriam Delaney—the same age but louder, the same height but taller.

That stranger is now a woman and she is still buried deep. She is a doll inside a doll. Pull a string on the outer doll and nothing happens. Pull a string on the inner doll and she speaks. Trouble is, no one can hear the inner doll. No one knows she's there.

How long is a piece of string?
People just string me along.
What's done is not done.

She blinks her thoughts away, walks across her bedroom to the window. What's happening out there in other people's houses? She imagines a parallel world, another Miriam, then another. The multiplication of a person. All the possible versions of Miriam Delaney. Longer hair, short hair, dressed all in black, multicoloured, tomboy, girlish, a woman with a powerful voice, a leader, a follower, an artist, a midwife, a waitress, a driver, a baker, a scientist, a policewoman. No, not a policewoman—then she would have to arrest herself for the thing that happened. A woman with a boyfriend, a girlfriend, a son, a daughter, a cat, a dog. A woman who receives invitations and says yes please, thank you so much for inviting me. A woman who receives compliments and says thank you, how kind of you to say so, instead of blushing and squirming and hating the person for taking the mickey.

Which version would she be now if Frances Delaney had handed her to her father and walked away? A brand-new baby, a brand-new life. He lived in this house for almost a year after she was born, then he went into the garden and never came back. Ruptured brain aneurysm. He was hanging out the washing—Miriam's Babygro. It was yellow, with a brown monkey on the front. It had to be washed again because it fell in the mud. So many details but none of them matter.

He was here and he was gone.

It was what it was.

It is what it is.

She closes her eyes, watches him smile as he jiggles her up and down, hears him sing a lullaby as he puts her to bed.

Made-up memories of a dad.

Stupid.

4

Ralph was in his consulting room in the centre of town, drinking coffee by the window. He watched a woman in the street below, clacking along in flip-flops, sipping cider from a can. Then a young man in a pinstriped suit, a woman and a child, three conspiratorial teenagers nudging each other.

It was Saturday morning. 9.30 a.m. His birthday.

Some people love birthdays. Not Ralph. He has always hated them, now more than ever. The spotlight, the *pretence*. That's why he was at work, standing by the window, watching a man selling the *Big Issue*, a woman jogging in Lycra.

He thought about his parents, remembered all the birthday parties they threw for him, the house full of balloons and children and pass-the-parcel. "Never waste an opportunity to celebrate," his mother said, her hands on his face. "We know you'd rather sit on your own, but relationships are everything, Ralph."

He turned around and looked at the room. A desk and a wooden chair. A white fireplace. Two leather armchairs facing each other. This was where it happened—the conversation that formed the centrepiece of his working life.

Before becoming a psychotherapist, Ralph worked as a gardener. He was happy doing odd jobs for odd people who hovered in the background while he worked, chatting about the flowers and the weather and then, charmed by his softness and discretion, about their innermost thoughts. Sadie didn't like being married to a gardener. She didn't like him working for odd people who hovered in their gardens. She said it was beneath him, his face would age quickly in the sun, and soil would remain lodged in his fingernails.

"Why can't you set up a proper business and work for bigger clients? You could get a decent van with a company logo on the side. A tree would be nice. A grey van with a big white tree. Oh yes, I can see you driving through town in one of those."

"What a waste of money. I'm fine as I am."

"You spend all day *talking*."

"Yes, but I get paid for it, don't I? And I get plenty of work from personal recommendations. I don't need a bloody logo."

After years of weeding, digging and planting, of discussing dreams and anxieties and the knottiness of self-awareness, Ralph realized that he was, in fact, doing more talking than gardening. Egged on by one of his clients, a psychoanalyst named John Potter, he picked up a leaflet about psychotherapy courses. The training sounded expensive and intrusive, but John Potter assured him that all the best things in life were expensive and intrusive. (This led John to recall an energetic weekend in Amsterdam, which cost him two thousand pounds and triggered an episode of angina, but it was worth it.) And besides, he could study one day a week and continue with his gardening. What did he have to lose, apart from his savings?

Sadie was keen. "I'd like to say my husband is a psycho-therapist," she said.

"What does that even mean?" he said.

Seven years later, he emerged from his training with a master's degree and a stomach ulcer. He rented a consulting room in town and gave up his gardening. He spent his weekdays in that room, listening to people's stories, searching for patterns in their thoughts, feelings and behaviour, until a few months ago, when he had a small epiphany with a client named Jilly Perkins.

"And so I've realized," said Jilly, flicking her highlighted hair, "that I like to be free. I just need it. I like to take on short commitments, because that way the end of the tunnel is always in sight. It's nothing to do with fear of commitment. I just need to be able to see the end of the tunnel." She leant forward and looked him in the eye. "It's who I am," she said. It sounded like a threat.

The end of the tunnel, he thought. That's where the light lives. *That's* where it's been hiding. Tunnel vision, darkness and darkness, tunnelling through pockets of time.

Jilly Perkins was a genius. Ralph wanted to tell her this, but she hated compliments. They filled her with wind and suspicion. This was the issue they planned to work on next, and in the meantime she had a handbag jammed full of Wind-eze capsules. "I love Wind-eze," she said. "I think of them as mints with benefits."

Ralph stifled his compliment by slapping his leg. Jilly laughed. She had never seen her therapist look so happy. In fact, had she ever seen him look happy? Does a person have to look happy to be happy? And what does happy mean anyway? She sighed. The questions had dispersed her happiness like small hammers hitting a row of pills. A wave of melancholy carried another insight: *Happiness is easily dispersed, Jilly Perkins. Just you remember that. Don't question everything. Don't forget the small hammers.*

That evening, inspired by Jilly's tunnels, Ralph wrote new text for his practice leaflet:

RALPH SWOON MA HIP, UKCP REGISTERED
Specializing in short-term psychotherapy
(No long-term work undertaken)

Moving to short-term work was a step down a tunnel towards a light. He was on his way out of a profession, edging backwards, coming undone. His clients weren't to blame. They were brave and open and he admired their attempts to make sense of themselves. He simply wished they were plants.

Ralph sat at his desk. The building was quiet. No one else was here. He looked at the photo above his desk: a bluebell wood in Guernsey.

His mobile rang. It was Sadie.

"Where are you?"

"I'm at work."

"Really?"

"I had some paperwork to do."

"Really?"

"Why do you keep saying *really*?"

"It's your birthday."

"I went for a run, so I thought I'd call in and finish a few things off."

"A run?"

"Yes."

"What things?"

"Admin."

"I woke up and you weren't here."

"Sorry. I should have left a note."

"No, you should have stayed. I bought croissants."

"I'll be home soon. An hour at the most."

"We need to get the house ready for the party."

"I know."

"People are arriving in ten hours."

Ralph laughed.

"What are you laughing at?"

"Ten hours is a long time."

"Only a man would say that."

"What?"

"A man who doesn't feel responsible for cleaning the house, preparing the food, sorting the drinks, hanging the decorations."

"Sadie, you paid a cleaner to come in. The place is immaculate. I'll be home later this morning and we'll sort the food then, okay?"

"Well make sure you are."

After ending the call, Sadie realized that she hadn't wished him a happy birthday. Never mind, she would do it later when she gave him his presents. She spread out her arms and legs, enjoying the coolness of the sheet as she rolled onto Ralph's side of the bed and pressed her face into his pillow. She stayed in that position for five minutes, thinking about the party, thinking about what had to be done, thinking about Kristin Hart.

Yesterday, during his final session with Jilly before her two-week holiday in Cornwall with Trevor the Great Dane, Ralph had discovered something disturbing about his wife.

"I like your jumper," said Jilly.

"Do you? It's a bit old."

"Did your mother knit it for you?"

"Sorry?"

Jilly blushed. What a leakage, what a spill. Clean it up quickly. Make it disappear. "Some people's mothers knit jumpers for them, don't they?" she said, wriggling in her chair.

"You seem a bit embarrassed, Jilly."

"It's not my fault."

"What isn't?"

"If your wife puts it all online, you can't expect us not to look."

Ralph squinted, frowned, put one hand on his chest.

"Your wife, Sadie."

"How do you know my wife?"

"When we started working together, I Googled you."

"Why did you do that?"

"It's what people do. I'm not weird."

Ralph glanced at the floor, then looked at Jilly. "And?"

"I found your wife's blog and Twitter page. I started following them. I follow your sons on Twitter too."

"What?"

"I'm not the only one."

Ralph's mouth fell open. Jilly wanted to get close and peer into it, preferably with a tiny torch. How many fillings did he have? Were his teeth really his own?

"You're stalking me?"

"Absolutely not. I'm not really interested in *you*. Well I am, but you know what I mean. I'm interested in your wife. Not in a dodgy way, if you know what I'm saying."

Ralph's stomach hurt. It was probably his ulcer. Sadie had a blog? He knew about the ceaseless tweeting but a blog as well? Where did she find the time? Were *all* his clients following his wife on Twitter? Were they following each other? For an intelligent woman, Sadie was being shockingly stupid. Didn't she realize the impact this would have? How unprofessional he would look? How he couldn't possibly work with clients who knew the intimate details of his private life?

Then he woke up. He woke from the sluggishness, the naivety. He opened his eyes and saw moments with clients who had seemed so perceptive, so smart—clients who guessed that he was *probably* married, *probably* had children, *probably* had no idea how it felt to be divorced. How dare they slip *probably* into their sentences when they knew for certain? He had never noticed his wife, perched in his consulting room, tweeting in the background of every fifty-minute hour.

Well blow me, he thought. Then his mind was full of Abba, knowing me and knowing you, and he closed his eyes and listened, really listened.

"Sadie hates that jumper," said Jilly. "But she's probably just jealous of your mother. Do you ever worry that Sadie's having an affair with her friend Kristin? I'm a little suspicious, to be honest."

"Jilly, you're always suspicious. That's why you came to therapy in the first place."

"Just because I'm always suspicious doesn't mean there isn't something shifty going on."

They sat in silence for a while, looking at the floor, looking at each other.

"Are you aware that sometimes you slip into a vacant state?" she said. "It's all right, though, I don't mind. It's your kindness that soothes me, not your interpretations."

"Are you trying to change the subject?" he said.

"Probably," she said.

She was right about the vacant states. They had been happening for a long time. How else would he have survived all those childhood parties? Not to mention all the singing and dancing and *embracing life*.

"Embrace it, Ralph," his mother said, while dancing and sipping a sherry. "You can't just read the *Beano*, life's too short, get up off that beanbag and dance."

Ralph looked at the clock. He had spent the entire morning staring out of the window and doodling. By now, Sadie would be fuming. The kitchen would be full of bumper-size packets of party food and bottles of champagne. She was probably balancing on a chair in the garden, hanging the old paper lanterns that she always dragged out for summer parties. He hadn't told her about his session with Jilly Perkins. He was carrying his anger around as though it was something delicate, something precious, something he had only just found after years of looking.

Sadie Swoon @SadieLPeterson
Just getting into bubble bath. Molton Brown pink pep-perpod. Heaven! How are you spending your Saturday?

Marcus Andrews @MAthebakerboy
@SadieLPeterson Now I can't concentrate!

Kristin Hart @craftyKH
@SadieLPeterson Getting ready for your party tonight. Magic knickers!

Jilly Perkins @JillyBPerks
@SadieLPeterson On Daymer Bay beach with Trevor, listening to All About Eve on iPod. Blast from past!

Chris Preston @ChrisAtMacks
Tomorrow 7pm: Ben Paige reading new poems at Mack's. Pls RT
Retweeted by Sadie Swoon

Lucinda Demick @LuciBDemick
Just me and a Borgen box set. Worth waiting for!
Retweeted by Sadie Swoon

Beverley Smart @bearwith72
@SadieLPeterson Just seen elderly lady fall over and smash
her glasses. Why am I crying when I don't even know her?

Before leaving his consulting room, Ralph looked down at the
doodles scattered on his desk. Some lyrics to 'Alexandra Leaving'
by Leonard Cohen. A rough sketch of Julie Parsley holding a
microphone. The words *happy birthday to me.*

5

THE MADNESS THAT LOOKS LIKE SANITY

S ix months into his affair with Frances Delaney, the head-master knocked on Miriam's bedroom door and walked straight in. He was holding a Walkman and a pair of head-phones. She was sitting on her bed, reading a letter from her grandmother. "This is for you," he said. He pulled something out of his pocket. "I also brought you this." It was a cassette. Cliff Richard. The corner of the box was chipped. "You're a lucky girl," he said. The room was full of old smoke. He was wearing a brown corduroy jacket with leather patches on the elbows and mustard fingerless gloves. There were no batteries inside the Walkman.

Miriam is watching the ten o'clock news and wondering why newsreaders never sniff, sneeze or blow their noses. Do they take special pills? Do they have special noses? It seems rather suspicious. Are they robots? Mechanical clones with accept-able accents and inactive noses? These newsreaders are calm, dispassionate, unruffled by the terrible events occurring all over the world. They have clean clothes, tidy hair, inexpressive eyes. They don't show emotion, they don't upset us, but Miriam doesn't buy it. The newsreaders disturb her. These people are the bearers of unspeakable news, so where is their shock and disgust? If they were really sane, they would look haunted and dishevelled as they spoke of murder, war and debt.

Beware the madness that looks like sanity, thinks Miriam. It is *everywhere*.

She switches off the television. Bye-bye newsreader. Bye-bye members of the public who have been asked to make a comment about something that has happened out in the world. (He was such a lovely boy he really was. Are they trying to make us homeless, is that what's going on? My husband shouldn't have to live like this—this isn't living, it's constant pain. When will this government realize that our teenagers are being bullied online and they are killing themselves, *they are actually killing themselves*.)

Trees rustle in the wind.

Water drips from a tap.

The house creaks.

Someone walks past the house, whistling a tune, then they are gone.

Miriam wonders if the tune was 'Careless Whisper' by George Michael.

There is no one to say this to.

She can hear her own breath.

(It sounds like sorrow.)

She frowns.

Blinks.

This used to be easier.

The passing of time.

The slowing down and the

slowing down.

Now it hits her in the stomach.

It makes her throat hurt.

Move Miriam.

Move.

(Listen to yourself.)

Move.

She gets up and walks through to the kitchen.

That's better.

Makes a hot chocolate, takes it up to bed.

She sits and stares at her bedroom curtains, pink and cream, made by her mother twenty years ago.

These curtains have never fully closed. The outside world leaks in. The inside world leaks out.

I am the whispering wind, she thinks. I am the small breaking wave. But human? I just don't know.

Imagine a woman abseiling down the side of a cliff. When she looks up at the person holding the rope, she sees that there is no one there. At that moment, halfway up and halfway down, she realizes that this has been the story of her life. She has never been alone and there has never been anyone there. This is Miriam's dream when she finally falls asleep after drinking her hot chocolate, after reading an old letter from her grandmother, after crying about nothing in particular.

6

Ralph arrived home to find his house full of Leonard Cohen. How unusual—someone was playing some of *his* music. He made his way from room to room, bumping into no one. Was this his birthday present? An empty house and 'A Thousand Kisses Deep'? If so, he liked it. It was the perfect gift.

He went to the bathroom and took a shower. With a towel wrapped around his waist, he walked into the bedroom to find that Sadie had emptied the entire contents of her wardrobe onto the bed. She was standing by the window, wearing a red bikini.

"Hello gorgeous," she said.

"Hello."

"Happy birthday."

"Thanks. What's going on in here?"

"I have one word for you darling, and it's *Turkey*."

"Turkey?"

"We should go to Turkey. What do you think? I'm just making sure I can still fit into my bikini."

Ralph imagined spending an entire week on a beach with Sadie. He sat on the bed. He felt exhausted. He wondered if he might be deficient in something, missing an essential vitamin, a vitamin that other people had plenty of. Vitamin D perhaps? He never used to feel this tired when he worked outside all day.

"I think Turkey would be fabulous," Sadie said, joining him on the bed. "And we could invite Kristin and Carol. What do you think?"

"Why would we invite them?"

"They're our friends."

"I'm sure they'd rather go away on their own. Carol's under huge pressure at work. She's—"

Sadie was belly dancing in front of him. "She's what, darling?"

"She's under a lot of pressure," he said, standing up.

Still dancing, she edged closer until her breasts were against his chest. "You like her, don't you?" she said, kissing his neck.

"You know I've always liked her."

"Yes, but I think you *like* her."

"I've never liked her in that way."

"Oh come on, Ralphy, I've seen the way you look at her."

Then she was pulling him down onto the bed, his towel was on the floor, she was running her fingers through his wet hair, he was untying her bikini.

Afterwards, Sadie sat up against the pillows and grabbed her iPhone from the bedside table.

"What are you doing?" Ralph said.

"Just checking my messages."

"Since when does checking them involve typing?"

"I'm tweeting."

"Let me see."

"Why?"

"I want to know what you're writing."

Sadie Swoon @SadieLPeterson
Turkey here I come!

"Why?"

"Why not?"

"It's none of your business."

"What you share with the world is none of my business?"

"Don't be silly, Ralph."

"I'm not being silly."

"It's only a quick tweet, you can read it later."

He tried to snatch the phone from her hand. "Give me that fucking thing."

"Get off me, will you? You're hurting my arm."

A tangle of damp limbs, writhing on the bed.

He pounced, pinning her down, reaching for the phone as it fell to the ground.

She wriggled free, hung off the bed, landed on the floor, crawled along the carpet.

He jumped to his feet as she clambered up, holding her phone, lifting it above her head, defiant. Then they were off again, lunging and wrestling.

"You've lost it," she said, holding the phone behind her back. "You've really fucking lost it."

"Give me that bloody phone."

"I'd rather die than give you this phone."

"Oh really?"

"You're an arsehole."

"I'm what?"

"I said you're an arsehole."

"Well you're a fucking joke, Sadie."

He grabbed her left wrist, reached around her for the phone, pushed himself against her. They landed against the wall, her right arm still behind her back. She screamed until he let go and stumbled backwards.

"You bastard," she said, covering her eye with her hand.

"I didn't hit you."

"You bloody well did."

His shoulder had slammed into her face, just below her right eye. He tried to touch her, to see what he had done.

"Get off me."

"Sadie, it was an accident."

"An accident? You attacked me to get my phone."

"For God's sake, I didn't attack you."

"You tried to mug me."

"You're being hysterical. Let me see."

"Just back off. I should call the police. I should tell them you raped me. How does that sound, darling? How's *that* for a joke? Happy fucking birthday."

His body recoiled. Internal damage. Invisible.

"Mum?" It was Arthur's voice.

Sadie grabbed her dressing gown. Ralph snatched his towel off the bed and wrapped it around his waist. Arthur stared. He was wearing shorts and a pale-blue T-shirt with Keep Calm and Carry On across the front. Ralph hated that T-shirt. He hated the tea towels, mugs, posters, aprons, cufflinks and bags. What did people derive from the mass reproduction of government posters, designed to boost morale during the Second World War if Britain was invaded? How could that notion be uplifting? He didn't get it. He had seen a baby in a pram wearing a Keep Calm and Carry On T-shirt last week. The baby was scream-ing. Last month, a client who had never been able to express his anger bought him a Keep Calm and Carry On postcard for his consulting room, and when Ralph refused to put it on the mantelpiece, explaining that it encouraged repression, the client shouted so loudly that the counsellor working in the next room had to thump on the wall and yell KEEP IT DOWN.

The rapid musings of a nanosecond, then Ralph's thoughts slumped back onto his wife. Could she feel them? Flabby indecipherable weights.

"I'm glad you're home," she said. "Can you go and mow the lawn?"

"What the hell's going on?" Arthur said, his hands deep in his pockets.

"Nothing's going on. The lawn really needs mowing before the party."

"Are you all right? What's wrong with your eye?"

"A little mishap."

"Mishap?"

In Ralph's mind, a swarm of broken sentences. The swarm split. It split again. He was ragged and torn, he was subdivided. Hate buzzed through him. Regret rose and fell in pathetic bursts. Not real regret—not the stuff that makes amends.

Sadie's words were still in the room.

We should go to Turkey.

I should tell them you raped me.

Happy fucking birthday.

If they gave out awards for denial, Sadie would win every year. She was an expert, a pro. This domestic song and dance—*look at my bikini, let's go to Turkey, I think you like Carol*—was a deflection.

Last week, Sadie and Kristin went to a reading at Mack's, their local bookshop. The author was Rosanna Arquette, a poet. Much to the audience's disappointment, this particular Rosanna Arquette was not the woman who played Roberta in *Desperately Seeking Susan*, but this was soon forgotten. The poetry was dark, graphic, erotic. It was full of love that felt like pain and pain that felt like love. Rosanna spoke of bedposts, bruises and handcuffs. Clearly something had happened to this poet since her previous three collections, which were about nature, global warming and the Lake District.

Rows of small wooden chairs were packed tightly into alcoves. The windows were steamed up. Every complimentary glass of wine was empty. Wood creaked as people shifted position in their chairs, trying not to make a sound. Chris Preston, who owned the shop, wished he hadn't sat beside Rosanna with every member of the audience facing him, looking him up and down for signs of arousal. Throughout the whole reading, he tried to think of nothing but his dead mother.

At the back of the crime section, Sadie resisted all attempts to stop breathing heavily. She closed her eyes and listened. She let the words take her. She gave in. Without thinking, she moved her leg so that it was touching Kristin's. With her eyes still closed, and while Rosanna spoke of surrender and submission, she felt Kristin's leg push back against hers. Then they were both pushing and something had changed, something had shot through them, and Sadie pushed so hard that Kristin's left leg jutted into a shelf of Ruth Rendell paperbacks, knocking over a display copy of *Tigerlily's Orchids*.

She opened her eyes.

It was over.

"Sadie Swoon, we are pleased to announce that you have won the annual Woman In Denial award for the sixteenth year running! How do you feel about that?"

"I have no idea what you're saying but have you ever been to Turkey? I hear it's lovely. Would you like to see me belly dance in my bikini?"

"**M**iriam Delaney don't you dare drop litter," the headmaster said.

"I didn't."

"Yes you did, I saw you." He dropped a sweet wrapper on the floor and winked.

They were standing in the playground. Children were running, screaming, shouting. Miriam had been leaning against the wall, reading *Charlotte's Web*. The sun was shining. The playground was a thicket of skinny shadows.

"You'd better come to my office," the headmaster said.

"I don't think so."

"I'll give you a Tango."

"I hate Tango."

He leant forward. "I just want to talk," he said. "Away from your mother."

For once he was telling the truth. No one noticed them walk through the playground and into the main building because the headmaster was grey and brown and Miriam was only visible when the children were bored. He told her to sit down. He had something important to say and she needed to listen.

"There have been rumours," he said. "About me and your mother."

She shrugged.

"Someone has seen me visiting your house. My line is this: I'm a friend of the family. I visit in a supportive capacity. Do you understand?"

She nodded.

"My wife is not to find out about this," he said. "Your ongoing silence is appreciated."

"Just leave me alone," she said.

"Well that's not very friendly."

"I want to be left alone."

He laughed and picked up a can of Tango from his desk. "Off you go," he said. "And no more littering."

She walked back to the playground, dropped the can in the bin, thought about the noise that came from her mother's bedroom in the evenings before the front door opened and closed and there were footsteps, close at first, then moving further away. She thought of the headmaster's wife, wondered what she looked like, wondered what she would think when Miriam found her and whispered the truth in her ear.

Miriam is watching series one of *The Bridge*. It is Swedish and Danish. Saga Norén, one of the two main characters, is Miriam's definition of charming—she tells the truth and never speaks in riddles. Miriam whispers this observation aloud and feels her neck stiffen. Then her whole body is stiff, just like that. It's a reflex. Historical.

She can't hear you, Miriam.

You're allowed to speak.

She's dead, Miriam. Remember?

Frances Delaney had possessed a special kind of hearing. If Miriam made a noise, her ears picked it up and she followed the sound. She was like an animal, attuned to the pitch of her only child.

"Do you think I want to hear you talking, Mim? Going on and on and on? Do you? Button your lip. Just button it."

"My name's not Mim."

"Everyone needs a nickname, Miriam. That's the long and short of it." Frances burst out laughing.

Mim, short for Miriam, and also the beginning of the words mimic and mime. It was fitting for a girl who was terrified of impersonating her mother and getting locked inside it—forever a copycat, a pale imitation.

"Imagine this," Frances said. "Imagine that we're not really people at all. We're tiny woodland creatures. Can you picture it? No need for that school uniform today, Mim. We're going to play in the woods. But just be quiet, you mustn't disturb the creatures."

Frances couldn't bear the din of her offspring. She couldn't bear the din of the world.

Washed lettuce must be washed.

Trimmed beans must be trimmed.

The world is full of liars and—

Miriam glances at the cuckoo clock and stands up. Her thoughts are turning strange again. This is what happens when she thinks for too long about her mother. She takes a deep breath and sits back down. She inhales though her nose, exhales through her mouth. Her eyes are closed, her breaths are long. She puts her hand on her stomach, feels it rising and falling and the memories stop. All she can hear now is what's coming from the TV: a man singing about an echo stuttering across a room. A new episode of *The Bridge* is starting. Its theme tune reminds her of Chris Isaak, wicked love, the possibility of something new.

She switches off the TV and jumps to her feet.

Move, Miriam.

She moves towards the radio, switches it on.

Yes, that's it.

What she hears isn't what she expects to hear. Who *is* that?

It's Stevie Nicks, Miriam. It's Fleetwood Mac.

A song about a woman who is a cat in the dark, darkness itself, a bell you can hear in the night.

Miriam wants to move again.

Her body is brave.

Her arms, branches in the wind.

She is dancing, swaying around the room in her black T-shirt and faded jeans, because today is a good day, closer to the end than the beginning. She is soon to emerge from the house like a missing person who no one has missed. The sun is shining. It is August and three years have passed. She has done her time and look at her dance and who cares if this is weird? Compared to the weird she has known, this dance in the middle of the living room is a demonstration of normality, sanity, logic. Frances had not allowed music. She had not allowed dancing. *Well look at this, mother. Look at this. I am dancing to a song called 'Rhiannon' and there's nothing you can do to make it stop.*

It's good that Frances is dead. When Miriam thinks this while waving her arms, wiggling her hips, she does so with a twitchy mix of compassion and relief. Frances would never have coped with how the world has changed. For a start, she hated the very notion of the Internet. People living, breathing, speaking out in the world *and* inside all manner of objects? It was too crazy to be true. An online community, a small world that never falls silent and never disappears, where every move you make can be seen by anyone?

Miriam stops dancing. She is being watched. It's Boo the herbalist, walking past her window, looking in. She expects him to shout *peekaboo!* but he doesn't, because Boo is a sensible man. A man with a habit of walking past Miriam's front window as he makes his way from door to door, delivering home-printed leaflets about natural medicine. As usual, Boo is wearing his red tracksuit. His moustache is a flourish of curl on a tentative face.

Realizing that she has spotted him, he waves and sprints off, vowing to use the proper footpath next time so as not to disturb the intriguing lady who lives next door.

Miriam is tired now. She has been awake since five o'clock this morning. She doesn't seem to need as much sleep as she used to. So far today she has made a lemon drizzle cake, cleaned the kitchen with a new range of eco products, emptied her mother's wardrobe, watched four episodes of *The Bridge* and danced around the living room, clapping her hands and kicking her legs. It is unusual for Miriam to be gleeful like this, because her default personality setting is melancholy infused with kindness, which sounds like a room spray for introverts. What might that smell of? Not grapefruit and ginger—too zingy, too energetic. Not patchouli or bergamot—too musky, too sweet. Not wild mint—too much like sticking your face straight into a pot of herbs.

She sprays the hallway with vanilla, goes into the kitchen and makes herself a cheese and pickle sandwich. Then it's time to return to the bin bags.

Over the past two days, Miriam has been throwing things away. The patio in the back garden is now hidden beneath a pile of black bags. The bags are spilling onto the grass and the rockery. Soon they will be in the pond with the goldfish and koi carp. The past is taking over and the fish can see it coming; they are deep down, hidden beneath the weeds.

Miriam picks up the phone. "Fenella, I have a question."

Fenella mumbles something. Her mouth is full of Wotsits.

"Are you eating crisps again?"

"I might be."

"I need to know how to get one of those metal boxes outside my house."

"Metal boxes?"

"For rubbish."

"Do you mean a skip?"

"That's it, a skip. How do you get one of those?"

"You call a company and order one. They'll drop it off and collect it for you. Just one problem, though."

"What?"

"You'll have to leave your house to put stuff in the skip."

"Can I hire a man?"

"One can *always* hire a man." Fenella bites a cheese puff in half and giggles. It is not an attractive sound. She accidentally snorts, which has been happening more and more lately. The snort silences her. What if it finds its way into every laugh from now until her dying day? And if she dies laughing, does this mean she will die snorting, like a common pig that finds death funny?

"Fenella?"

"Yes."

"My garden is full of black bin bags."

"Well that's easy to fix. You don't need a skip for that. Just dump them on your porch like you usually do and ask your neighbour to drag them onto the pavement. The bin men will take them away."

"Even if there are twenty bags?"

"I don't think there's a limit."

Unlimited history. A past with no boundaries. It is finished but it never ends.

"You're brilliant," Miriam says.

"I know," Fenella says. She finishes her crisps and opens a second bag. Life is for living, she thinks.

"Have you heard of Stevie Nicks?" Miriam says.

"The singer?"

"Yes."

"I have. Why?"

"You never told me about her."

"Sorry?"

"Well, I've only just discovered her."

Fenella laughs. "I can't tell you about every singer and every band," she says.

"I just wish I'd known about her before."

"Why?"

Miriam thinks for a moment. "I heard a song and it made me feel something," she says.

"Something?"

"I felt like me and not like me. It was surprising."

Fenella smiles. "You make me laugh," she says.

"Also, I've been watching *The Bridge.*"

"Have you? What do you think?"

"I love it."

"I thought you might. Do you like Saga?"

"She's very nice."

"I'll lend you *The Killing* next. I've got three series. It's Danish."

"Thanks."

"You'll love Sarah Lund."

There is a pause. Miriam has no idea who Sarah Lund is.

"You know my brown and cream jumper?"

"The one that cost three hundred pounds?"

"It was two hundred and sixty, but yes, that one. It's in *The Killing*."

"What, that actual jumper?"

"Well no, not *my* jumper."

Miriam doesn't know what Fenella is going on about, but this makes her a handy person to know. Fenella is always in the loop.

"It's organic and self-cleaning. Special oils in the wool, apparently. I never have to wash it."

"Doesn't it get smelly?"

"Not really."

The most expensive jumper Miriam ever bought cost fifty pounds from M&S. It was cashmere. Her mother shrank it on purpose. She said it was a symbol of corruption and greed. An hour later, it was small enough to fit one of the Queen's corgis.

"Actually, I probably won't have time to watch any more box sets."

"Really?"

"Yes."

"You're almost ready?"

"Any day now," Miriam says.

"Hello, is that Mr Boo?"

Boo knows that it's Miriam. She is the only person who calls him Mr Boo.

"This is Boo. How may I help you, Miriam?"

"I have a favour to ask in return for a lemon drizzle cake."

"I accept."

"I haven't told you what it is."

"I don't care. I love lemon drizzle cake, and I will never refuse you, Miriam."

"Goodness."

By the end of the day, the goldfish and koi carp have risen from the depths of the pond. The patio has been power-hosed by a man in a red tracksuit whose stomach is full of lemon cake. He has offered to pop round tomorrow to give the windows a deep clean with the new squeegee he bought from Lucetta the travelling saleswoman—another woman he can never refuse.

"Oh, and I will leave you this," Boo says, holding out a bottle.

"What is it?"

"A remedy for dancers with tired legs."

The bottle is full of luminous liquid, glow-in-the-dark green. It feels warm, which is comforting and disturbing.

"Thank you," Miriam says. "You've been a lovely neighbour over the past few years."

"I only moved in last June."

"That's right," she says, wondering if Boo's tracksuit is velour. It would only take a few accessories to make him Santa.

That night, before getting into bed, Miriam looks out of her bedroom window. In the half-light, Beckford Gardens looks like a rubbish tip. Frances Delaney's belongings are out in the street: her clothes, her cheap jewellery, her cookbooks, even her bedding. Tomorrow, men in thick gloves will take them away and Miriam will be watching. Should she peer through the window? Wear black and stand in silence in front of the house? Her mother is inside the bags: her fingerprints, her handwriting, the fabric that covered her body, the beads that hung from her neck. But what about the bowler hat, Miriam? The one she found in a charity shop, the one she wore non-stop until her dying day, her final act. Why is *that* still here in your bedroom, watching you from the top of a chest of drawers?

A desire to run outside and pull every bag back into the house rises into Miriam's throat. It tastes of bile. She closes the curtains as far as they will close, gets into bed, switches off the lamp. Beside her, something is glowing. She opens her eyes. It is Boo's luminous remedy, impossibly bright. She immediately falls asleep.

8

IT WAS FINE AND IT WAS NOT FINE

For his birthday, Arthur and Stanley had bought him a ticket to see Leonard Cohen. Ralph looked for a second ticket in the envelope but there was only one. Sadie had bought him a black shirt, a pair of trousers, three pairs of socks and a feng shui owl for his office.

"Thank you," he said, with the presents on his lap. "They're all lovely."

Sadie was pressing a bag of frozen peas against her face. "You're welcome."

"Why the owl?" he asked, holding it up to inspect it.

"It represents wisdom. Helps you acquire it, apparently." She tried to smile. Her sneer was another small failure.

"Right."

Putting aside the matter of the swollen eye and frozen peas, Sadie looked beautiful this afternoon. She was wearing old jeans and her I Love New York T-shirt. Ralph remembered her buying the T-shirt from a store near Central Park while they were on holiday three years ago—their first holiday alone since the twins were born. She put the T-shirt on there and then, in the middle of the store, pulling it down over her white long-sleeved top. He preferred her like this, natural and relaxed, but by the time their guests arrived this evening she would be dolled up and pretty in heavy make-up. What had happened to the woman he went to New York with? Yes, the cracks were beginning to show, but as they drank cocktails in their Tribeca hotel, called his parents to check on the boys, hunted for paperbacks in the Strand bookshop, walked through Central Park to the Guggenheim Museum, they were happy. Well, perhaps not happy, because happy is difficult to define, but they respected each other. She was in old jeans and old trainers, with a heart on her T-shirt and a hot dog in her hand. It was simple, it was easy. She took his photo in the park because she liked him.

"Anyway, I'd better get changed," said Sadie, leaving Ralph alone in the kitchen with Arthur, Stanley and the cocker spaniel.

"I know it's your birthday, Dad, but we have to ask," said Stanley.

"Ask what?"

"Did you hit Mum?"

"Of course not. I would never hit your mother."

"What the fuck happened then?" said Arthur.

"Why do you feel the need to swear all the time?"

"Just answer the question."

"We were messing about. I was tickling her."

"Tickling her?"

"Yes. Haven't you ever tickled anyone?"

Stanley wanted to say actually yes, I've been tickling Joe Schwartz and he's been tickling me. Instead, he found himself asking if anyone fancied a glass of Ribena. Telling his parents that he was gay wasn't the problem—he knew they wouldn't care. The problem was telling them something personal, revealing, sexual. Did they really need to know the intimate details of his private life?

"No thanks," said Ralph. "I'll have a lager, though."

"I'll have a lager too," said Arthur. "But no fucking Ribena. What are you, eight years old?"

"People of all ages drink Ribena. Stop trying to show everyone you're a grown-up, it's really boring."

Ralph smiled, which made Arthur want to pick him up and throw him across the kitchen.

Upstairs, Sadie applied all the usual make-up, apart from foundation. She had no intention of covering up her husband's mistakes, which were swelling on her cheek and around her eye. She set a Suzanne Vega album playing and turned up the volume. How had Suzanne Vega's music eluded her until now? She had been listening to this acoustic collection of old songs on repeat over the past few weeks. It was poetic, funny, clever, romantic. It belonged to Kristin.

Sadie Swoon @SadieLPeterson
Suzanne Vega: total goddess

Jilly Perkins @JillyBPerks
@SadieLPeterson Lost my virginity at a Suzanne Vega concert (Marlene on the wall)

Arthur stood beside his father, swigging Peroni from the bottle, appeasing his own toxicity. How did he know that he was toxic? His mother told him after his and Stanley's sixth birthday party. "How did I end up with such a toxic son?" she said, her hands gripping his shoulders. "What's wrong with you? You have everything a boy could ask for. Why are you always sulky or angry? Why can't you be more like your brother? Look at him, Arthur. I said look at him. He's smiling, see? That's what normal boys do. They smile every now and then."

TOXIC. The word had lit up inside his brain. He was hotheaded, headstrong. He was *poisonous*.

Years later, Arthur read about a psychological experiment in which one group of children (group A) were told that they were especially clever and another (group B) that they were less clever. In the tests that followed, every child in group A achieved better results than they used to, while the little Bs got lower results and seemed unmotivated. Over time, motivation levels in group A also began to fluctuate (if you've been labelled "clever", why bother to try and *appear* clever?). Arthur read about this experiment and shook his head. It reminded him of something—something uncomfortable—but he couldn't quite reach it. All this thinking made his head hurt, so he finished his chicken sandwich and went into the back garden to throw a chair across the lawn.

"Hormones," the doctor said. "He's brimming with hormones. And if you call him toxic, that's what he'll become. I should know. I'm toxic. I shoot pigeons for fun. Real ones. It's not illegal. It's pest control. But keep it to yourself. Is there anything else I can do for you, Mrs Swoon?"

"What did it feel like?" said Arthur.

"What?"

"Hitting Mum."

Ralph stood up and slammed his bottle on the table. "I'm going to say this one last time, all right? I did not, I repeat *not*, hit your mother. I've never hit a woman in my life. Have you got that?"

Arthur shrugged.

"What kind of question is that anyway? What a fucked-up thing to ask."

"Now who's swearing?"

Stanley was standing in the garden with a pint of Ribena. He looked around at the multicoloured lanterns hanging from trees, the citronella candles waiting to be lit, the chairs positioned in a semicircle to the left of his mother's gargantuan, top-of-the-range, six-burner gas barbecue. It arrived last summer after another of her trips to B&Q. She had called it a *symbol of independence*.

"I will not be a suburban cliché," she announced, releasing the shiny red beast from its cardboard cage while her family watched. "I'm not going to cook all week in the privacy of our home, then have my husband stand in the garden in front of our friends, tossing burgers like he's king of the cooking, king of the barbecue, king of everything while I run in and out of the house, in and out all the time, carrying bowls of lettuce. I refuse to become one of those women who stands by while her husband takes the glory. If I cook in private, I cook in public."

"Fine by me," said Ralph.

It was fine and it was not fine. He hated the pressure of barbecues, having to stand there in a silly apron and produce the perfect burger (chargrilled but not burnt, tender but well done) for everyone they knew. He was glad she wanted to take over, but his gladness was not the whole story. He felt as though something had been stolen that he couldn't describe. The longer they were married, the stronger this sense of unknowable loss.

Stanley sat on the wooden bench at the bottom of the garden and looked up at the house. He could see the shape of his mother upstairs in the bathroom, fiddling with her hair in front of the mirror. She wasn't like other mothers. She did all the driving when they went on holiday. She bought his father flowers and chocolates. "Norms thrive because they're invisible," she once said, holding a bunch of roses. "It's only when I overturn them that you're able to spot them. Do you get what I'm saying? Why are you looking so fed up?"

The kitchen door opened and closed, revealing Harvey, black and glossy, tumbling towards him, landing on his lap, making him laugh. Daft dog, running up and down the bench, licking his face, jumping off again, pulling a paper lantern from a low branch and ripping it to shreds.

Inside the house, Ralph was on the phone to his father.

"Happy birthday, son."

"Thanks, Dad."

"How old are you now?"

"Thirty-seven."

"Thirty-seven, deary me."

"Are you still coming tonight?"

"Of course. Your mother has prickly heat, but we're still coming. She thinks her sweat glands might be blocked."

"Are you sure it's prickly heat? It's not that hot out."

"I never argue with your mother's diagnoses. She's here now, she's grabbing the—"

"Hello?"

"Hi, Mum."

"Happy birthday, dear. Are you having a good day?"

"Lovely, thanks."

"What have you been doing?"

"I popped into work this morning, but other than that, just pottering really." He thought of Sadie, naked on the bedroom floor, crawling away from him. "What time are you coming over?"

"What time are we allowed to come?"

"You don't have to ask that."

"Oh I do."

She was referring to the secret contract. A few years ago, Frank and Brenda had decided to move closer to Ralph and their grandsons. Before they sold their bungalow, Sadie posted an agreement for them to sign and return as discreetly as possible. She was advised to do this by an agony aunt called Suzie who worked in the local farm shop. Suzie kept a cardboard box in the corner of the shop for customers' letters, which she promised to respond to within a week if the writer supplied their initials. She left her replies—short, blunt, alphabetized—in a basket beside the organic dog biscuits. Suzie made the biscuits too. She was multitalented, buxom, often warm, often sharp, depending on the day. Sadie found her trashy and intimidating and she longed for her approval.

FAMILY AGREEMENT, WRITTEN WITH LOVE AND GOOD INTENTIONS

1. We, Frank and Brenda Swoon, realize that this agreement is for the benefit of *all* parties.
2. We promise not to turn up unannounced at the home of Ralph and Sadie when we move to the same town, despite the fact that we are prone to bouts of spontaneous excitement and affection. We will always telephone first.
3. We acknowledge that everyone needs privacy and space.
4. By moving closer to Ralph and Sadie, we are not expecting them to meet our needs and care for us in old age.
5. We realize that Sadie is protecting us with this agreement, not herself. She is minimizing the chance

of conflict, thereby maintaining good relations all round.

6. We can confirm, before selling our property, that we definitely plan to buy another property. We have no intention of living with our son, daughter-in-law and grandsons, because we realize that this would be unhealthy.

7. This agreement is a private matter between Sadie Swoon, Frank Swoon and Brenda Swoon.

"Come over any time you like," said Ralph. "You're always welcome, you know that."

"What time are other people arriving?"

"About seven-thirty."

"So that's when we'll arrive."

Ralph sighed. Today was hard work. "Dad said you have prickly heat."

"Did he? Fancy telling you that. Well don't worry, I'll cover myself up. I've bought new trousers and a lovely yellow cardy from TK Maxx. They're women's golf clothes. Quite nice, I think. I've never tried golf. Have you tried golf? Did I mention that Auntie Madge has piles?"

Ralph knocked on the bathroom door.

"What?"

"We need to talk."

"No we don't."

"Of course we do. Before tonight."

"I don't see any point."

"Sadie, can you unlock the door?"

"Not right now."

"Why not?"

"I'm on the loo."

"No you're not."

"How do you know?"

"I can tell."

"How?"

"Just let me in."

"No."

"Why are you listening to Suzanne Vega? You hate Suzanne Vega."

"I do not hate Suzanne Vega, I've never said that."

"Are you smoking in there?"

"Of course not."

"What's that smell then? Are you tweeting and smoking?"

Ralph thought about kicking the door down. Was he even able to do such a thing? Was he strong enough? He'd seen it done a thousand times in films, but the doors were probably made of imitation wood with fake locks. Did he and Sadie have a fake marriage? They had sex today. Sex means hope, surely? He told himself that if Sadie unlocked the door within the next two minutes, everything would be all right. She would find him and he would find her. He looked at his watch. He waited. He listened to the music coming from the bedroom, a song about a soldier and a queen, and he followed its narrative, mesmerized by the words and the melody, wondering what it was called, walking into the bedroom to find out, not hearing the bathroom door open and close as Sadie made her way downstairs.

9

A SUPERHERO, A COW, A BISCUIT

To celebrate their one-year anniversary and the way they first met, Frances Delaney and the headmaster entered a nudist phase. (Why say it with flowers when you can say it with your whole body?) It was during this time that Miriam started to wear as many items of clothing as she could, all at once. While her mother sprinted around the house, naked apart from her bowler hat, talking about the end of the world and how they must prepare, Miriam sat in front of the TV in pyjamas, jeans, three T-shirts, five jumpers and a bobble hat. It was an act of rebellion, a corrective impulse: *I will wear the missing clothes so that the clothes are no longer missing.* And it was HOT. Miriam's super-smart unconscious hadn't thought of that when it spawned the corrective impulse. She wobbled from room to room, feverish and slow, wondering if five jumpers could kill a person. She pictured five jumpers hovering in front of her with machine guns. Death by excessive knitwear. She was delirious. By trying not to be her mother she had ended up just like her. Would this become the pattern of her life?

She ran upstairs, feeling like the Honey Monster, and took off all her clothes apart from her Batman underpants (Frances hadn't been able to find any Batman knickers, because only boys have superheroes on their underwear, according to the lady who owned the shop). She looked at herself in the mirror: a girl in boys' pants with no control over anything in the world. The headmaster popped his head around the door. "Dinner's ready, Miriam. Chop chop. Nice pants."

A ceramic cow. A Superman pyjama top. A pair of Batman underpants. A fisherman's jumper, bought for a girl who had never been fishing. Miriam found these things this morning in the cupboard on the landing. Why had her mother kept them? Frances had never been a hoarder—she preferred throwing things away to keeping them. When people bought her presents she said she felt burdened, saddled, loaded.

Miriam squeezes into the Superman pyjama top. I'm wearing the past, she thinks, or is the past wearing me?

She takes it off and wanders into the kitchen. From here she can see Boo's legs and feet. He is halfway up a ladder, cleaning her windows with his new squeegee, whistling the theme tune from *The Littlest Hobo*. Two cloths hang from his back pockets, one to remove the dirt, the other to polish the glass. Boo is taking this seriously because he takes Miriam seriously. She isn't used to it. It is peculiar.

"Can I get you a cup of tea, Mr Boo?" she asks, through the kitchen window.

"Miriam, that's most kind."

"Not really. What's kind is you cleaning my windows."

"Do you have any herbal tea?"

"No. Just normal tea."

"That'll be lovely, thank you."

While she is making tea, Miriam hears the letterbox open and close. It's another postcard. On the front, a photo of a black cat stretched out across a wooden floor. On the back, in handwriting that has now become familiar:

WHEN SOMEONE SPEAKS LOUDLY, IT DOESN'T
MEAN THEY HAVE FOUND THEIR OWN VOICE

Instead of putting this one on the noticeboard with the others, Miriam stands it beside the kettle so that she can look at it every time she makes a hot drink.

The ceramic cow. It's also there, near the kettle. She picks it up, runs her fingers along the cracks sealed with glue.

"Imagine that your buttons are your friends," said Frances.

"Why are we always imagining?" said Miriam. "What's wrong with ordinary things?"

"No one wants an ordinary life."

"I do."

"No you don't, you just think you do. Wouldn't you rather have buttons with voices and personalities than boring buttons with nothing to say?"

"Not really, I like my buttons as they are. I think they're beautiful."

Frances slapped her daughter's face. "Beautiful? Really?"

Miriam didn't cry. Not any more. She fastened herself up tight, held on to her tears. One day they would all come out in a great hysterical flood, a great *historical* flood, but not now, not in front of her mother. She gritted her teeth, curled her fists, focused on the ceramic cow on the mantelpiece. It was the only ornament in the house. *I don't care what you like and don't like, Mim, we will not be weighed down by dusty objects, do you hear me?*

Don't you look at me like that—I let you keep your buttons, don't I? Not to mention all the stamps for your precious little letters to my dreary mother. I don't know what you see in her, I really don't.

Stamps instead of pocket money. Letters instead of visits.

Miriam picked up the ceramic cow, carried it to the bottom of the garden and threw it on the ground as hard as she could. Fragments of a fake cow, reimagined in clay, scattered all over the patio. "You were never actually a cow," she whispered. "You were just dotty pottery." She giggled, then picked up one of the pieces. It was sharp. It made her finger bleed. The sight of her own blood surprised her. She was *alive*.

Dear Granny,

I cant remember what you look like. This is a postcard I bought from the corner shop. Do you like the dog on it? I like the dog.

love from Miriam
xxXXxx

Dear Miriam,

I have enclosed a photograph of myself, taken by my friend Doris on the pier at Weston-super-Mare, so you can't forget what I look like. I am wearing new glasses in this picture but am not at all sure I like them and Doris is not sure either. I have also enclosed a postcard of a dog. This one is a Westie. Shall we call him Bill?

I am always here, Miriam.
With fondest love,
Granny

Miriam shakes her head. The silence of the past three years has made things louder than ever. That's what silence does.

It amplifies the sound of what was here and what was never here. Hibernation has turned this house into a cinema and every room has its own screen. The snacks are poor, the intervals short.

She opens the kitchen window and passes Boo his tea.

"Oh lovely," he says.

"Would you like to drink it indoors?"

Boo looks surprised. Miriam has never invited him in before. "Are you quite sure?"

She nods. Two minutes later, Boo's trainers are positioned neatly by the back door and he is sitting at the dining table, drinking tea, while Miriam explains that it is almost time.

"Almost time for what, Miriam?"

"Time for me to leave the house."

Boo looks disappointed. "You're a mystery to me," he says.

"Am I?"

"Yes. There are many things I'd like to ask you."

"Really?"

He nods. "I often wonder about your voice. Perhaps you have a medical condition that makes you speak so quietly? I wonder about your agoraphobia too."

"I'm not agoraphobic."

"Oh."

Miriam takes a large mouthful of tea, too much to swallow at once. She looks like she is gargling. Thunderous gulps inside her head. *The storm is always close. Don't forget your umbrella.*

"I just assumed."

"I'm not scared of public spaces."

"That's good."

She remembers the last time she was outside. The rain and the darkness as she ran home. The rainbow she saw through the kitchen window.

Boo waits, hoping that this conversational tap is all it will take to make Miriam's psyche crack open like a nut. He thinks of macadamia nuts, of the plantation he worked at while travelling around Australia in his twenties, of losing his virginity (*finally! Such a relief to be rid of it, thank you Dougie thank you*) to a woman who worked for the Australian Macadamia Society. (Dougie's parents had been expecting a boy called Douglas, and when they looked at their new baby and said that's not our Dougie, the baby opened her eyes as if to say yes, it's me, I'm your Dougie, *it's me.*)

"Also, there's no medical condition," Miriam says.

Boo isn't listening. He is on the other side of the world with Dougie, drinking peppermint tea while she lists the health benefits of macadamia nuts. Funny the things you remember. Funny the things you forget. He wonders what Dougie is doing now, at this very second, and whether she still dresses like a cowgirl. She used to call him Boo-Boo. As in Boo-Boo Bear.

"Are you all right?" Miriam says. She holds up a plate of malted milk biscuits.

"I'm so sorry. What were we saying?" He takes a biscuit and bites it in half.

"Nothing really," she says, noticing the pinkness of Boo's cheeks.

"Life is short," he says.

"Yes."

"People come and go and then it's too late."

Miriam takes another malted milk biscuit.

"So what the hell," Boo says. He puts down his cup and brushes the crumbs from his tracksuit bottoms. "I'm just going to ask you, before it's too late," he says. "Before you leave the house and meet someone else."

Someone else?

Miriam looks at the cow on the biscuit, notices its head hanging low. She puts it back on the plate.

"May I take you out for dinner one evening?" Boo asks.

The solitary tear that runs down her face is not the response he was hoping for. Miriam begins to sob. She covers her face with her hands, but not completely, and one eye peeps at him through her fingers. Boo is terrified, guilty, not sure what's going on. He had never intended to upset her, but here she is with a dripping nose and red eyes, crying in the way that a child might cry after being left alone for too long.

"I'm so sorry," he says, leaning forward to touch her hand. "What did I do?"

She tries to speak through the sobbing but she can't breathe. Boo waits. He should never have been so impulsive—broken people don't respond well to impulsiveness. He wonders whether it would be insensitive to eat a biscuit.

Finally, the tears stop. They look at each other. Boo knows that Miriam is not going to say yes. She is not going to join him for dinner. He stands up, puts his arm around her shoulders and gives her a squeeze. She buries her wet face in his tracksuit top.

"You treated me like a normal person," she says, before filling the house with a low moan that frightens them both.

10

Joe Schwartz was the first guest to arrive. He was early, nervous, drenched in aftershave.

Stanley answered the door.

"You look amazing," said Joe.

"Thanks," said Stanley, his nose twitching. He hoped he wasn't allergic to Joe. It was too early in their relationship for hypersensitivity, aversion, turning into his parents. "Come in."

Joe began to take off his shoes.

"Oh no, you don't need to do that."

"Are you sure?"

"Absolutely. Can I get you a drink?"

"That'd be great."

"Lager?"

Joe grimaced. "I've tried to like lager, but I can't get into it. It tastes old to me, and not in a good way." He adjusted his black glasses, pushed his fringe away from his eyes. "I know it's lame. Everyone likes lager don't they?"

"So what *do* you like?" asked Stanley, trying not to smirk, trying not to make it sound like he knew exactly what Joe liked because he had done it to him eight times last week.

"Black tea, milky coffee, diet Coke, apple juice, Vimto."

Joe Schwartz was weird. He looked like a model and was always serious, even when he was joking. He remembered things, unusual things, like the name of every character in a film, like the local cafe's entire lunch menu, like everything Stanley told him. He spoke in lists. He was a walking archive. He was earnest, immaculate, Canadian.

"I think we have most of those things," said Stanley.

"Great," said Joe.

Two weeks ago, Sadie had written another letter to Suzie the agony aunt. She slipped it in the cardboard box while Suzie bent down to pick up a tray of rhubarb muffins.

Dear Suzie,

Thanks for reading this. I don't know why I feel the need to write to you. I'm an intelligent, self-aware woman, Suzie. But sometimes even the smartest of women need advice don't they?

I think I'm in love. In love with my best friend. I sound like a teenager. I feel like one too. "Do you love your husband?" I hear you ask. Well yes I do. But I also hate him and I don't know why. I'm flummoxed. He's done nothing to evoke this so where did it come from? I'm not a hateful person, Suzie. I'm not aggressive. But there I've said it. Sometimes I hate him.

One of my sons is so angry and I worry that it's all my fault. Can he be carrying my anger? And to be perfectly honest, I've stopped liking people. I'm a people person and I find people tedious. Where does that leave me? It's like saying you're an adrenaline junkie who doesn't want to leave your sofa, or a painter who loathes the smell of paint. Where does that leave me, Suzie?

My husband is a psychotherapist and I can't talk to him about anything. Ironic, hey? I blog, Suzie. You'll probably have read my blog. I have a high number of followers. I keep track of these things. You have to, don't you? It's the new kind of watching your figure. Companies send me products and I rave about how good they are. So what with the blog and Twitter, I rarely get much time off. I love it, I really do, but you should read some of the shitty comments people write. People are so mean when you can't see their faces. They suck up to you, make sure you direct your hard-earned traffic their way, then slap you in the face. So now I'm a people person who's starting to hate other people. My husband doesn't know about the blog—he thinks I win a lot of competitions and that's why all these products keep arriving in the post. I kind of like that. I like the fact that he sees me as lucky. Luck is contagious, isn't it? If I'm lucky then he's lucky. Why burst his bubble? It's nice to give him something.

Anyway, this wasn't supposed to be an essay. Let me get to the point. If I tell my friend how I feel and she happens to feel the same, my small corner of the world is about to go up in smoke. If you see smoke rising, Suzie, you know where it's coming from. She and her partner are like family to our sons. I love her partner, she's been good to me, to all of us really.

Suzie, tell me this: do you think I've been full of hate since I was born and it's only now erupted? Do you think I desire my friend because I don't hate her, and the only reason I don't hate her is because I haven't slept with her, and if I do sleep with her, will I hate her too? Do you think the person I actually hate is myself?

Thanks for your time, it means a lot. I know you're a busy lady.

Very best wishes,

SS

PS My puppy really loves your home-baked cheese and broccoli dog biscuits.

Sadie was shocked by Suzie's reply.

Dear SS,

Jesus Christ! I've never read such a load of drivel in my life. Get a proper job—something meaningful, something to occupy your time that doesn't involve sharing your own opinions. Throw your gadgets in the bin—you're clearly addicted to them. You've forgotten how to relate to your husband.

How the hell would I know why you fancy your friend and whether you'll hate her if you sleep with her? Maybe you're in love with her. I've had my fair share of women, SS, and my advice is just make a move. Get with the programme, basically.

Also, there's no such thing as luck. Hate is as much a part of being human as love. Yes, you probably hate yourself. We all hate ourselves. Talk to your husband instead of treating him like an idiot. Being a people person is about whether contact with others enlivens you or makes you feel tired—it has nothing to do with liking people. Most of us dislike other people, but we don't go around saying so because that can of worms doesn't need opening.

Instead of simply regurgitating your thoughts online, start reading more. You're probably making yourself sick.

Look out of your window, watch the rain, walk your dog.

Suzie

How dare she? thought Sadie. Who the hell does she think she is? She's no Frasier Crane, that's for sure. What are her credentials? Does she have any qualifications? That's the last time I buy dog biscuits from her. I reckon she's had a boob job. Nobody's boobs are that upright, it's *disgusting*.

Earlier, while Ralph waited outside the bathroom door, Sadie set fire to Suzie's letter and watched it burn in the sink. She was scared that someone would find it. It was embarrassing and full of lies. Now she took a bottle of Prosecco from the fridge and poured herself a glass.

"Mum?"

Sadie turned to see Stanley and the Canadian boy from Bennetts Lane. "Hi, Joe."

"Hi."

"How's your mum?"

"She's good thanks. She's a brunette now."

"Really? Since when?"

"Last Tuesday."

"Wow, big change. Does your dad like it?"

"Of course. What are you drinking, Mrs Swoon?"

"Please, call me Sadie. I'm drinking Prosecco."

"I've never tried Prosecco."

"Would you like a small glass?"

"That would be lovely, thank you."

"You're very quiet, Stanley. Do you want one too?"

"Go on then."

Joe squeezed Stanley's bottom, which made his voice rise at the end of the sentence. His mother didn't notice. She probably wouldn't notice if the high note turned into a whole song from *Annie*, with Stanley singing as loudly as he could about the sun coming out tomorrow. She wouldn't notice if Joe gave him a blow job right there in the middle of the kitchen. She was tweeting, pouring Prosecco, muttering about whether she had bought enough sausages. His mother the great multitasker, always in her own world, always oblivious.

"So where's your dad?" asked Joe. "I bought him a card."

"Did you? That's thoughtful." Stanley moved closer until their hands were touching. "I think he's upstairs. Shall we go and find him?"

"Sounds good."

Ten minutes later, Sadie was drinking alone in the garden, staring at her mobile phone. Arthur was in the bathroom, staring at a photo of Keeley Hawes in the *Radio Times*. Stanley and Joe were up against a locked bedroom door. Harvey was cocking his leg against the sofa. Ralph was nowhere to be seen.

Sadie Swoon @SadieLPeterson
Husband missing on his birthday. Party about to start!

Marcus Andrews @MAthebakerboy
@SadieLPeterson More champagne for us

Sadie Swoon @SadieLPeterson
Gone for sparkly silver vest and white trousers tonight. I have smokiest BBQ sauce!

Sadie looked around the garden. Soon she would be wearing her Keep Calm and Have a Cupcake apron while cooking sausages. Their friends would be standing in the usual groupings, together but divided. She would make small talk with Ralph's parents. She would look like she was enjoying herself. Arthur would drink too much and get aggressive. Stanley would be charming but distant. Her lips would be on Kristin's lips.

"Where've you been?" she said, as Ralph joined her, wearing the clothes she had bought him for his birthday.

"I've been up in the loft."

"The loft?"

"Yep."

"Why?"

"Looking for my old guitar."

"Oh no."

"What?"

"You're not going to play it tonight?" she said, wielding the strongest of marital superpowers: the ability to evoke shame in her husband, which dismantled his spontaneity. Stun-gun Sadie had just shot him between the eyes.

"Probably not," he said. "Actually, I'm just going to run upstairs and get changed. These clothes are great but I feel a bit uncomfortable." (There are two types of people: those who put on new clothes straight after buying them and those who like to save them for days, weeks or months, until the right time, which sometimes never comes. Ralph was the latter.)

Knocks at the door, one after another, the kind of knocking that goes on and on until you think you're going to scream. Who had invited all these people? Arthur answered it every time, expecting to find his girlfriend. She was late. The garden was full of conversation and music and the sizzle of burning meat. Sadie was sweating. The barbecue was overpowering.

Ralph's parents were watching. Marcus and Luci were gossiping on wooden chairs beneath the apple tree. A group of psychotherapists were sitting around the old camping table, laughing wildly, topping up one another's glasses with red wine. Ralph was unwrapping a birthday present from their friend Beverley—"Just a little something, thought you might like it, no worries if you don't, I'll keep it myself." Numerous teenagers, friends of Arthur or Stanley, were dotted about in brightly coloured clothes (a new trend? Sadie didn't know. How could she not know? She followed the dots, her eyes hopping from red to blue to pink to yellow, not knowing who most of them were). Beverley was flirting with one of the neighbours, the one whose wife was in hospital (Sadie had only invited him out of pity).

No one asked why Sadie's face was swollen around her eye, they just helped themselves to salad, rolls, garlic bread, burgers, sausages, chicken, griddled vegetables, halloumi kebabs.

Marcus put the cooked food onto large plates and lined them up on the table.

Arthur's girlfriend finally arrived—her sentences were polite, her face tight with venom.

Stanley fiddled with the playlist on his laptop, sending music around the house and garden.

Sadie cursed herself for forgetting to marinate the chicken as she noticed Carol and Kristin holding hands.

Ralph's mother tugged a weed out of the garden and held it up to her husband as if he should know where to put it.

Yesterday afternoon, after a massage, haircut and highlights, Sadie met Kristin at Monkey Business for coffee. Kristin said they *needed to talk*, which made Sadie feel nervous. What did she want to say? Had she realized how Sadie felt?

Over two flat whites and a slice of chocolate cake, they discussed the benefits of getting a regular massage, the golden stripes in Sadie's hair, how Kristin was getting on with her prints, how Carol was still working long hours, how Sadie hoped it wouldn't rain tomorrow night, whether the album playing was *Buena Vista Social Club*. Then Kristin paused. She looked down at her coffee. Sadie waited.

"The other night," said Kristin, looking up. "At Mack's."

She was referring to what happened in the bookshop when Rosanna Arquette read about bedposts, bruises and handcuffs—love that felt like pain and pain that felt like love.

"What about it?" said Sadie.

"Something happened between us."

"Did it?"

"Didn't it?"

Sadie wavered. She could deny everything, put it all down to the highly charged atmosphere of the bookshop that night, or she could tell the truth. She glanced at the window. It was raining outside. She remembered Suzie's letter: *watch the rain*.

"There was a moment," said Kristin.

Yes, there was a moment, thought Sadie, seeing it once more in vivid detail. And I want there to be another. Let's do it right now, in the park, in the rain. *Let's go.*

"What do you mean?" she said.

Kristin sighed. She was supposed to be meeting Carol outside Pizza Express in half an hour. "We've been friends for a long time," she said.

"Almost thirty years."

"Really?"

"Yes."

"That makes me feel old."

"I know."

"Anyway, we've never crossed a line, have we?"

"Crossed a line?"

"We've never flirted with each other."

"No."

"Until last week."

Flirted with each other. Sadie replayed it in her mind. That was reciprocal, wasn't it? They both flirted. She looked at Kristin's mouth.

"And I think we should talk about it."

Kristin had always been direct. It was in her nature. You knew where you were with Kristin, even if it wasn't where you wanted to be, which right now, for Sadie, was in the band-stand in the park. She remembered the two of them walking Harvey, how they were drenched by the storm, how the water ran through Kristin's long dark hair, how she turned up the collar of her mac and stood there in front of Sadie, laughing. She should have kissed her then, while they were out in the fields. It would have been memorable and dramatic. Carol can do that whenever she likes. She can kiss her in the park, in the fields, in town, at home. Carol the GP, who somehow finds the time to run marathons for charity, who always buys Arthur and Stanley the perfect gifts, who seems so stable and content. Can anyone really be that happy? Perhaps that's what happens when you're married to Kristin.

"Look, you don't need to panic," said Kristin, finishing her coffee. "That's all I wanted to say. It's no big deal. I think maybe the wine had gone to our heads and the poetry was crazy and everyone wanted to fuck everyone else that evening."

Kristin flinched at her own words. Sadie raised her eyebrows.

"We don't need to read anything into it. That's all I wanted to say."

"Okay," said Sadie.

Kristin moved on to talking about her new screen prints and how Picador had commissioned another book jacket design. Sadie paid for their coffees and cake and walked with Kristin through town, but not all the way to Pizza Express. She wasn't in the mood for Carol.

"That was an excellent barbecue," said Marcus, watching Sadie untie her apron and lift it over her head. "You should set up your own business. You could have your own burger van in the middle of town."

"Why thank you," she said, exhausted. "That's what I've always wanted for myself—to work in a burger van."

"I meant it as a compliment."

A quick half-smile. She had nothing else to offer.

"I think you need to sit down," said Marcus. "You look knackered. Did you get time to eat?"

"Not yet."

Sadie took a hot dog from the table, covered it in ketchup and went inside the house. She poured herself a glass of champagne and sat on the stairs. Two teenagers squeezed past, giggling. She had no idea who they were, but the giggling was too loud, she wanted silence and darkness, just for a few minutes, then she would be all right. She wandered from room to room, not wanting to speak to anyone she bumped into, and found herself upstairs, outside the cupboard on the landing. No one would disturb her in there—she could sit on the wooden box full of old photographs, eat her hot dog and drink her champagne in peace.

A woman's voice. "Sadie, are you up there?"

The only voice she wanted to hear, but still she remained hidden in the cupboard.

"Sadie?"

Footsteps up the stairs and along the landing. Sadie carried on eating in the dark. She was starving. She wished she'd brought herself a plate of salad and some garlic bread.

"Hello?"

Come in, go away. I want you, I don't want you. She drank her champagne.

"Sadie, is that you in the bathroom?"

Bloody hell. No, it's not me in the bathroom, because I'm actually in the cupboard. Yes, that's right, the cupboard. Don't ask me why, I have no idea. Do you have any food?

Sadie listened to the music coming from the kitchen and garden—'Hit' by the Sugarcubes. She used to love this song. She remembered dancing to it years ago in the student union bar with Alison Grabowski. This memory had the same effect on her body as Rosanna Arquette's poetry. She saw Alison Grabowski, there in the cupboard, dancing in her black jeans and suede jacket, dancing so close. At university, Sadie and Alison were inseparable. They walked through the park holding hands, smoked their roll-ups in the bandstand, laughed dismissively when people called them a couple. She remembered watching Alison getting dressed, and how Alison just smiled when she noticed her watching. Then she recalled something else—how could she have forgotten this? Alison lying beside her on the bed, suggesting that they have sex just to see how it felt. Sadie wanted to say yes, that's a very good idea, and really we should do it twice, just to make sure we got it right, but she wasn't sure whether Alison was being serious or sarcastic and she couldn't take the risk. "Yeah right, as if," she said.

The moment was gone.

(Because I couldn't take a risk.)

In the days that passed, everything felt hollow. Then she met Ralph Swoon, who distracted her from the hollowness.

She knew what he meant when careful words came out of his mouth. He was sensitive, serious-minded.

Among the old clothes and shoes, Sadie wanted to cry but she couldn't. Missed opportunities flew at her in the dark, one after the other, the chances she never took. What had her mind done with these moments? Was it a kind of sexual amnesia? Would she forget Kristin too? Forget that she ever felt anything at all? That process had already begun—just days after it happened, she had forgotten the incident in the bookshop until Kristin brought it up.

There was a moment.

She heard a faint tapping and ignored it. The outside world could wait. She groaned, hoping it would release her tears, but it didn't.

The tapping sound again, louder this time. Someone knocking on the door. Sadie reached out to open it, but there was no handle on the inside. She was stuck.

"Who's in there?" said Kristin.

"It's me."

"Sadie?"

"Yes."

"Why are you in a cupboard?"

"I'm stuck. Can you open the door?"

And then there was light. Sadie didn't move.

"Are you okay?" said Kristin, stepping inside. "What's happened?"

An opportunity. A chance. Kristin sat beside her on the wooden box. Sadie leant forward and closed the door. *No running away now, Sadie Swoon, Sadie Peterson, whoever you are, whoever you were.*

"What's going on?"

"I've realized something," said Sadie, not wanting to waste another second. She put her hand on Kristin's leg.

"What are you doing?"

"Isn't it obvious?" She moved her hand higher.

"Sadie, I—"

She touched Kristin's face, pulled her closer. Then she kissed her.

A first kiss. Every kiss that should have happened. A hundred kisses rolled into one.

It grew darker. Sadie felt the darkness all over her. "I want you to fuck me," she said.

Kristin pulled away.

"Please."

"No."

"No?"

Kristin stood up. "What on earth's got into you?" She started banging on the door. "Hello? Anyone out there?"

"Kristin, don't. Don't go."

"Hello? We're stuck in here. *Hello?*"

Footsteps. The creak of floorboards. Then light from the hallway, cold and intrusive. Sadie's chance had escaped. It was gone. She felt hollow again.

Ralph looked confused. "Why?" he said, holding the door open. "Why are you two in here?"

Kristin stepped out and stood beside him. Now they were both on the outside, looking in at Sadie in the half-light, her head buried in her hands.

How quickly things change, thought Sadie. It's nauseating.

Ralph looked at Kristin. "What's going on?"

"Nothing's going on. I found her crying."

"I have a name. And I *wasn't* crying."

"Why were you crying in a cupboard? You were fine a moment ago, I saw you talking to Marcus. Did he upset you? Did he say something?"

Keep talking, thought Ralph. Keep talking to your wife and we can all ignore the fact that she stepped into a cupboard and closed the door and—

He remembered Jilly Perkins: "Do you ever worry that Sadie's having an affair with her friend Kristin? I'm a little suspicious."

"This house has so much storage space," said Kristin. "It's the ideal place to have a breakdown, when you think about it."

"A breakdown?" said Sadie, standing up. "Is that what you normally say to women you've been flirting with? Do you accuse them of being mentally unstable?"

"What the hell?" said Kristin.

"How dare you," said Sadie.

"How dare I what?"

"Blame it all on me."

"Blame what on you? Nothing happened."

"That kiss was nothing was it? Well that's charming."

"Ralph, this isn't how it seems," said Kristin, shocked by what was occurring on Ralph's face. Had he taken something? He was laughing. No, not just laughing, he was hysterical, he was bright red, tears were running down his cheeks.

Sadie and Kristin looked at each other.

The laughter stopped.

They were surrounded by a wild silence.

A wilderness.

Dear Granny,

Days pass in gales. I listen to the wind outside my window at night and it sounds like me. Might pick me up one day, fancy that. I tap my feet to music that isn't here. Yesterday I left school in the middle of the morning and went to the cathedral. Rope across a gap, no entry sign, I snuck under the rope, went up a winding staircase. (Wish the staircase would go up and up and up.) Room full of candles with Jesus on a cross. I sat on a gold cushion and prayed. This room is for grieving families the man said. You shouldn't be in here you're not bereaved. He said he wasn't joking but I wasn't laughing so I don't understand why he said that. I won't be posting this note. You are in Spain and I bore you. I'm fourteen now. I turned fourteen today. No birthday card from you. Funny how I still expect you to turn up and say it's time to get you out of here. Mum says you two fell out, people do that, they get sick of their children and their grandchildren, they lose contact, that's just the way it is. Look at EastEnders she said—people shout and scream and decide not to know each other any more. The world is gigantic and small and people get lost in it. End of. Sometimes it's like I imagined us. I hope you're happy and wearing sun cream.

Kind regards,

Miss Miriam Delaney

"You're not still cleaning are you?" Fenella says. She is on Miriam's doorstep, jogging on the spot, going nowhere.

"I'm not really cleaning any more. I'm *clearing*," Miriam says.

"Decluttering?"

"Something like that."

Fenella takes a bag of chocolate-covered raisins from her pocket, offers them to Miriam, throws one up in the air and catches it in her mouth. "Still planning to leave the house?" she says, chewing.

"Yes."

"When?"

"Tomorrow."

"Really?"

"Yep."

"Crikey. Will you recognize the outside world? Will it recognize you?"

"I've never been able to do that thing you just did," Miriam says.

"What thing?"

"Catching food in your mouth."

They stand there for five minutes, with Fenella throwing and Miriam bobbing up and down with an open mouth, until the bag is empty and the floor is covered with raisins. Boo's cat appears. It sniffs the raisins and walks away. Miriam notices that the cat's movements are like a performance of disappointment, feline theatre, a slinky enactment of her own feelings. She wants to reach out and touch the cat but it's always too far away.

"Oh well, you can't be good at everything," Fenella says.

"What am I good at?"

Fenella smiles. "Talk later," she says. She kisses Miriam on the cheek and jogs off across the lawn and the question disappears as if it never existed.

You cannot predict how long a question will live. Some questions are bigger than others. If you weigh them on special scales, you'll find that the small ones are usually the heaviest.

That night, Miriam makes herself a cheese and sweetcorn omelette and eats it fast. She pours herself a glass of white wine, holds it up, toasts the house. "To this house, for not growing sick and tired of me over the past three years, for not collapsing around me in exhaustion, for not going up in smoke. I'm leaving you tomorrow, maybe for a few hours, maybe for longer. I'm sorry you are so full of ghosts. It must feel like you have rats running through your walls and your pipes. I'm sorry I haunt you with my whispers."

She drinks her wine and listens to the reply. The humming, creaking and clicking. The humdrum. Her glass is empty now. She fills it up.

As it approaches midnight, she stumbles into the back garden.

Will you recognize the outside world? Will it recognize you?

The world has changed since Miriam was last out there. It has become faster and busier and chattier than ever. She knows this because she heard it on the radio last week. You have to be bionic, supersonic, virtually histrionic, in ten places at once and forever full of comment: *I am here, are you listening? I am sharing the minutia of my everyday life. Please reply with a comment, whoever you are.* The air is thick with opinion. Audible smog. But what if you have nothing to say?

She looks up at the night sky, the bluish star-studded darkness. Fenella is working tomorrow and she could never ask Boo to accompany her. This will be a solo mission, but where to go? What do people actually *do* out there?

There is a voice. It says: "They stroll around parks. They go to the cinema. They buy sandwiches and eat them while walking along."

The voice came from inside her. It was the unbroken one again, doll inside a doll, getting fidgety and excited under the skin.

12

Ralph was no longer laughing. He walked away from Sadie and Kristin, two statues on the landing. He went into the bedroom, sat on the bed, took off his trainers. He pulled his walking shoes out of the wardrobe, the ones Sadie hated, and put them on. Through the bedroom window he could see his friends and his parents in the garden below. Some of Stanley's friends were dancing, or maybe they were Arthur's friends. Beverley was in the middle, swaying about with her eyes closed. She looked strange and desperate, twenty years too old for the circle around her. If she had been a man, and the teenagers girls instead of boys, someone would have asked her to stop. They would have used words like predatory and sad. But Beverley wasn't a man and the teenagers weren't girls and she was dancing in the middle, eyes closed.

Ralph spotted Carol, walking through the garden by herself. He picked up his wallet and phone and went downstairs to find her, ignoring Sadie and Kristin as he passed.

"Carol," he said, out of breath. "Can we talk?"

On two wooden chairs beneath the apple tree, they drank whisky and ate peanuts.

"I've been confused," Ralph said. "I've felt sedated, like I can't get hold of my thoughts. I wondered if Sadie was drugging me."

"Why on earth would you think that?"

He shrugged, catching sight of Kristin stepping out onto the decking. "I walked into a garden gnome once," he said.

Carol pictured him knocking over a tiny gnome. Inconsequential. Odd.

"And I'm leaving."

"Are you?"

"In five minutes."

"Where are you going?"

"I don't know, but don't tell Sadie, she can't be trusted."

"Why not?"

Kristin arrived at the apple tree. "You two look cosy," she said, her face flushed.

Ralph finished the last of his whisky and stood up. "There's no need to worry," he said.

"He's drunk," Carol said.

"I'm the sharpest I've been for years. Sharp as a stranger."

Carol and Kristin glanced at each other.

"I'm a fucking stranger. That should feel awful shouldn't it? Bloody awful. But it doesn't. It's a relief."

Ralph spotted his guitar leaning against the wall. He walked past his friends, his mother and father, Beverley and the teenagers and the nondescript neighbour whose name he could never remember. He picked up the guitar, walked along the garden path, opened the wooden gate, marched down his driveway into the street. He could hear laughter and conversation and 'Papa Don't Preach' by Madonna, all coming from a party that was for him and never for him.

Sadie Swoon @SadieLPeterson
Sometimes all you can do is listen to the Smiths and hope
it all ends soon

Jilly Perkins @JillyBPerks
@SadieLPeterson What's up babe?

Sadie Swoon @SadieLPeterson
@JillyBPerks Do I know you? Have we met?

Jilly Perkins @JillyBPerks
@SadieLPeterson I'm sharing a black russian with my dog

Ralph kept walking. He walked through streets half lit and streets in darkness. He walked past empty shops, a queue outside a nightclub, people smoking outside pubs, urinating on walls, waiting for buses. He looked away from kisses fast and deep. He remembered standing at a bus stop with Julie Parsley, back when they were teenagers. She was leaning against a wall, her face lit by a street lamp as she offered to sing him a song, any song, all he had to do was name it. He pictured her standing on stage in the local pub singing 'The Look of Love'. That performance made everyone wonder what on earth Julie had been getting up to. She laced the song with violence, sang it so slowly, so mysteriously, as if the words had her crawling along a filthy floor in a torn nightdress. She revealed everything and nothing, it was eerie and irresistible. Julie Parsley was not like other girls—everyone understood this but no one knew why.

"You be careful around that Julie," his mother said. "I find her a little unnerving."

"What do you mean?" Ralph said.

"Well, she's not like you. She's *different*."

Ralph stared. He took a cola cube from a paper bag and put it in his mouth.

"She's stony."

"What?"

"There's something sordid about her. *Dirty*."

Ralph laughed. This was not the way to put a teenage boy off a girl.

And yet it did.

His friend had already told him that Julie was out of his league. Maybe it was true. He was inexperienced, shy. He ate cola cubes and read comics.

"You'll find a good woman when you're older," his mother said. "Don't you worry. And when you do, everything else will take care of itself."

Ralph walked across a meadow and along a footpath until he came to the woods. He looked at his watch. It was coming up to half-past eleven, the time of his birth, thirty-seven years ago in a hospital in Norfolk, right in the middle of his parents' holiday by the sea, right in the middle of Brenda's annual treat—highlights and a supercurl at Tiffany's Salon. He had emerged from a woman whose hair was curly on one side and straight on the other. Welcome to your mother. Welcome to your father. Welcome to the world, which is curly on one side, straight on the other.

He resisted the urge to cry as he entered the woods.

13

I t took a great deal of effort to locate Mrs Jennings. Miriam had to obtain information from other people, which meant asking questions and hoping for straight answers. Whisperers don't get straight answers. They get blank looks, rolling eyes, cold jokes, crookedness.

No one would tell her where the headmaster lived. In the end, she found out from her mother.

"Does he prefer our house to his house?"

"Of course he does."

"Does he prefer our road to his road?"

"His road is full of old people."

"Does he live in an old people's home?"

"Don't be ridiculous, he's not old. He lives in a row of bungalows."

"Oh I know the one, it's near the church."

"No it's not."

"It's near the town hall."

"No."

"It is."

"It isn't."

"It is."

"It's near the fancy-dress shop. What's got into you today? You're even more annoying than usual."

Knock knock. Who's there? Not Mrs Jennings, that's for sure. A man covered in tattoos. He said you've got the wrong house girly girl. The headmaster lives at number nine, yeah? Over there girly girl.

She had never been called a girly girl before and would never be called one again.

Knock knock. Who's there? A woman with long brown hair and a pretty face. Tight jeans, a pink jumper. She couldn't understand what Miriam was saying, asked her to speak up, asked if she was collecting for charity and if that was the case did she realize she was working illegally, charities shouldn't use children, why wasn't she at school?

"Are you Polish?" the woman said.

"No," Miriam whispered.

"What are you saying?"

"Is your husband the headmaster?"

"Speak up."

"Is your husband the headmaster?" Same words, same volume; obstinate.

"My husband is Mr Jennings."

"He's having an affair with my mother."

"I beg your pardon?"

"He's screwing my mother."

A barbaric pause, a deeper voice: "How dare you."

"It's the truth," Miriam said. She could smell the woman's violence, pressed into the stiffness of her lips.

"What's wrong with you?"

Isn't it obvious?

"I'm calling the police. This is a scam, isn't it? You're Polish and clearly unwell. Is your father breaking into the back of my house while we're out here? Is that what's going on? If he's looking for cash he won't find any."

Miriam knew a Polish boy once. His name was Sebastian and she liked him. He played ball by himself, bouncing through lonely hours, bounce bounce bounce—stop that noise, Sebastian, you're driving us mad.

"He comes to our house in the evenings. I can give you exact dates and times. I have them written down in a book." Miriam put her rucksack on the floor and delved about for the notebook. "Here," she said, handing it to Mrs Jennings. "I've listed every visit and how long it lasted."

There was a moment of inspection. Flicking through pages. Then: "I think you'd better come in."

"No thank you. I'm sorry for your loss."

Miriam has done it. She has actually done it. Stepped over the threshold of 7 Beckford Gardens. Walked through four streets. *Four* whole streets! She is standing in the sun. She feels like an alien that has just landed, even though it has only been three years. *Only?* Years the size of planets. Impossible trajectories. Inner space, outer space. Orbiting. Waiting. Orbiting. Waiting.

She steps into a small park. A woman walks past with a poodle and stares at her. The woman looks bemused (this is okay, because bemused is not frightened). The poodle has a strange haircut. The poodle itself isn't strange, only what a human has turned this poodle into; it has been poodlified, and underneath it's just an ordinary dog with ordinary needs. Miriam feels sorry for the poodle. She sees herself in it, but not literally, because the dog is not a mirror. She bends down and lets her fingers hang limp in front of its nose. This is human for *I'm no threat—sniff me and see.* The dog sniffs. It licks Miriam's fingers. The woman tugs its lead, much harder than necessary, and says something about the poodle having to dash off for a play date. "We're so late, we're literally going to get throttled," the woman says.

Miriam wants to say: That's not literally true. She wants to say: I know, because I've been chasing the truth, the facts, the exact and precise meaning of things for thirty-five years. So let's tell it like it is, not like it isn't. Let's choose our words carefully and only use the ones we really need. But she doesn't say any of this. Instead she whispers: "A play date?"

The woman looks curious. "With Billy the Jack Russell," she says, and follows this up with an observation: "You poor thing."

Miriam quizzes the woman with her face. She is good at doing this. That's what happens when the people around you have never made sense, your quizzical muscles flex at the drop of a—

Don't think it, Miriam. Don't think about the hat.

"It's going round," the woman says.

"Sorry?"

"Laryngitis."

Then she and the poodle are gone gone gone and Miriam is left alone in the small park with the heavy instruments of her own thoughts.

Bowler hat.

The memory detonates a bomb and her mind is under attack.

Blast from the past.

If we can't stop the bombs, the historical time bombs, how are we to live?

A memory is a minefield. The mind is a war zone. So many of us at war with ourselves.

Oh no.

Not again.

Breathe long, breathe deep.

It's all right.

This was bound to happen.

Take one step at a time.

She sits on a bench and tries to gather herself. She has heard this phrase a lot, *gather yourself,* but what does it mean? Is the self a collection of visible parts that can be pulled together in preparation for something or reassembled after a breakage? Miriam spends half an hour thinking about what it might be like to accidentally on purpose mix up the components of herself with those of another person—a woman, perhaps, who is also in the middle of gathering herself, a woman who has left the pieces of her character scattered on the grass in this small park where poodles come to sniff the hands of strangers.

This thinking is good. It is soothing. It clears up the aftermath of memory: Frances Delaney in her bowler hat saying you're tedious, Miriam—you have nothing to say to anyone.

Dear Miriam,

I have just made a spam sandwich and a flask of tea, because tomorrow I am going on a long walk (one whole hour) with a friend and I will need refreshments. I will think of you while I walk. I have asked your mother for a photo of you for my bedside table but she hasn't sent one yet. Anyway, this is just a brief note to slip inside a book I am sending you. The book is called Mrs Dalloway and I found it on the bus. I thought it might occupy your mind for a while and give you something to think about. If you find it difficult, don't be upset. I don't think it was written for nine-year-olds.

Sending you all my love,

Granny

The woman with the poodle reappears. "Still here?" she says.

Miriam smiles apologetically, even though she has nothing to be sorry for. She nods. Yes I am still here but why did you ask when you already know? Laryngitis isn't what's going round—there's a disease called Confirm What Is Obvious and everybody's got it.

The poodle is off the lead and it runs over to Miriam. "We got the wrong day," the woman says, as though the dog is jointly responsible for the mismanagement of their social calendar. "I think we'd literally forget our heads if they weren't screwed on."

Miriam ruffles the pom-pom on top of the dog's head. Fancy having a pom-pom for a head, a pom-pom at the end of your tail and pom-poms around your ankles. Why doesn't that make people sad?

She sets off again, walking through familiar streets and streets she has never been to before. She has nowhere to go and nowhere to be. This thought is a stone in her shoe, pushing into the soft flesh of her foot. She walks faster. The pain in her foot makes her feel alive and it makes her feel like crying, because surely feeling alive is about more than this?

There is a voice: "Spend some money. Buy something. Eat something."

When she died, Frances Delaney left a lot of money to Miriam and no one knew where it came from. Miriam saw it as dirty money, loaded with germs, highly infectious. She bundled it into a savings account and has lived on it ever since. Now she opens her purse. It is full of notes and coins and she has no idea how to spend them. Then she has an idea. She could see a film. She hasn't been to the cinema since 1987 (*Dirty Dancing*). Do people still eat popcorn or is that old hat? Imagine being given a tub of salty old hats. How much would that cost? If hats were advertised as the latest and greatest snack, would people actually eat them?

STOP IT.

"Your thoughts don't all have to end in hats, Miriam."

The unbroken one is on form today. She leads Miriam through town to the cinema—a quaint affair with two screens, a small kiosk and old-fashioned decor. But eight pounds for a ticket? Goodness me. How long have I been gone? She looks at the poster on the door—they are showing a series of ghost films, one of which starts in twenty minutes. She would have preferred a dark comedy or a feature-length episode of *The Bridge*. She buys a ticket, wanders over to the kiosk, buys a tub of salted popcorn, a hot chocolate and some Rolos, then settles into a seat at the end of an aisle and waits. She is good at waiting. Waiting is her middle name (not literally).

Other people start to come in. *Other people.* They join her in the darkness. Together they watch adverts and trailers and Miriam can't believe the noise of it all, coming from every direction. The screen widens—she hadn't seen *that* coming—and now it's time for the main event: *The Awakening.*

Miriam eats her popcorn and slides down low in her seat. She likes this film. It's slightly creepy, but she likes it. The main character, Florence Cathcart, is a no-nonsense truth-teller. She is scientific, rational, methodical. Using a mesmerizing set of equipment, she exposes charlatans and fakes and proves that there is no such thing as a ghost. The dead are not with us. The deceased do not haunt us. In our living, breathing bodies we are alone. That idea is as sweet as the hot chocolate in Miriam's mouth. She touches her face—her cheeks are hot. It is warm in here, she is watching a film by herself with other people, she is not at home and she is not outside.

Hold on a minute.

Miriam frowns at the screen, shocked by what is unfolding, shocked by the fact that no-nonsense Florence is *afraid*. She is running through hallways, peering through cracks, kneeling in front of a doll's house. The doll inside the house is a mini Florence with Florence hair and Florence clothes. What happened to her logic, her steeliness, her belief in the power of the living?

She has seen a ghost, that's what's happened. A boy who looks like any other boy, but not everyone can see him. *She* can see him, because he's her brother, Tom.

Miriam opens her Rolos and leans forward in her seat.

Tom was killed when he and Florence were children. He has missed her ever since and now he wants her back.

No!

Afterwards, Miriam stumbles out into the light. She is all churned up. The film has done it. Big fat churning machine. It's the idea of someone watching, lingering in the afterlife, about to reappear. It's the idea of a child, suspended in a life that is no life at all.

She sees a sign: Society Cafe. She goes inside, orders a cup of tea and sits in the corner. There is an old bicycle hanging on the wall. The walls themselves are stripped and worn. It looks as though a painter and decorator prepared the area and wandered off without finishing the job. Apparently this look is fashionable right now, it says so in the magazine on the table—*shabby chic*. It's all about salvaging, reusing, recycling. Miriam likes the look of it but not the philosophy. She is too immersed in letting go and throwing away to stomach this cafe full of old things that probably attract dead people who used to own them years ago.

"Thank you for the tea," Miriam says, on her way out of the door.

"You're welcome, honey," says the man behind the counter.

Miriam smiles. It's weird being called honey by a man. Fenella uses that word all the time but it feels different when she says it. She turns around and buys a flapjack from the man. The flapjack is made by a company in Devon called Honeybuns. The man tells her this as he smiles and chats so easily, so lightly, and Miriam wants to say isn't that a coincidence, you called me honey and this is a Honeybuns flapjack, and the way you talk so easily and so lightly is awesome.

Now she is eating and walking in the sun. She thinks of Florence, who is actually the actor Rebecca Hall, two women rolled into one, separate but never distinct. Thoughts of Florence lead to thoughts of the path. The one you take if you want to cross the fields and go to the pub; the one you take if you want to walk straight into the woods.

She remembers his eyes: brown, hard, confused, scared.

She remembers the words: "What the fuck? Are you crazy?"

She remembers running. Slamming the front door. Locking it with key and bolt and chain.

Is he still there? How ridiculous, Miriam—of course he's not. It's perfectly safe to go there again. So is that what I need to do? Is it like throwing away my mother's things? *Is that what I need to do?*

And so she walks.

Walks until she can see the woods.

Stops and stares.

The path is five minutes away—all she has to do is cross the meadow and she's on it.

Go, Miriam. You can do this.

She crosses the meadow.

Walks faster and faster.
Breaks into a run.
Passes the spot where it happened.
Runs straight into the woods.

14

"Do you know what you've done?" she said. "You've ruined my life. And do you know why? You've taken away the one person I love."

Miriam just stood there in a stripy polo neck and grey cords.

"Shall I tell you what happens now?"

She shuddered.

"You're going to run upstairs and fetch your writing paper."

What?

"Then we're going to write a lovely letter to your grandmother. We're going to tell her all about the fun things we've been doing and how happy we are. From now on, you're going to write what I tell you to write. Your words will be my words. What goes in your mouth and what comes out of it are up to me. Understand?"

That's the punishment for telling Mrs Jennings? Miriam expected her mother's fist or feet. She expected to have to eat a jar of mustard or a piece of stale fish. She expected a mouthful of cotton wool (*you're lucky I'm here to stop you choking*) or a pillow dipped in petrol (*be careful missy or I'll throw a match*). But writing letters?

Easy.

"What's a lovely thing like you doing out here, eh?" Ralph says, tickling Treacle's stomach. "You don't look like a wild cat. No collar, though."

Today is Ralph's third day with Treacle. He has made trips in and out of the woods to buy supplies and telephoned Kathy the receptionist ("Can you cancel my appointments this week? I need to start my summer break early, family crisis, if anyone needs urgent help refer them to Karl, yes that's fine, he's my emergency contact, it's absolutely fine, can you explain things to Karl, tell him he might get a call?"), but apart from shop assistants and Kathy he has spoken to no one. His mobile phone is loaded with texts from people he knows, people who claim to know him, people who don't know him at all because every one of us is fundamentally unknowable. The more we talk the less unknowable we feel, but speech is just a circus act, words thrown from frantic lips, dialogical hocus-pocus.

At 11.30 p.m. on his birthday, Ralph walked through these woods under a full moon with an unfathomable sense of purpose. On any other night he would have been terrified of being out here, but tonight he kept on going. His feet followed an unlit path until the path stopped. No street lamps, twenty-four-hour shops, headlights and neon signs. Just night and night and the cracking of twigs. Dried leaves, unbroken curls. Nocturnal rustling. Creaking branches. Minuscule legs, invisible. He went deeper and deeper, looking up at the moon. He tripped, fell, got back up. He reached out and touched soft bark. Was he approaching the middle or the edge now? He couldn't tell.

Was anyone else out here? Highly unlikely, but you never know what is looming, what is waiting, ready to jump out.

The ground turned level and easy. The trees seemed to disappear. Ralph was on another path now, which began nowhere near the entrance or the exit. He kept going until he saw something solid. Up close, a kind of hut or shed. Now came the fear. Who was in there? What was it used for? He felt around for a door, trying not to think about the episodes of *Wallander* he had watched on TV, especially the one about the man who lived in the woods, the man who killed swans and set people on fire.

It was even darker inside the shed.

"Hello?"

Nothing.

"Anyone in here?"

Nothing.

He put down his guitar. With his arms stretched out in front of him, he wandered in. He ran his fingers over the back of a wooden chair. On the floor, what felt like a bundle of sheets. He shook a box of matches. Stepped on a plate, cracking it.

On this August night, as his birthday ended and a new day began, Ralph sat on the floor and pulled the sheets over his legs. He didn't expect to fall asleep, not out here, but he did. He slept until morning.

When he opened his eyes, he didn't know where he was. He stood up with a sore back and a sore head and opened the door. The sun was already fierce, the birds were singing. He stepped out and looked around. He was in a small clearing in the woods, encircled by a thin path, and he had spent the night in an old shed that looked like it would collapse if someone kicked it. Inside, there was a chair, some old sheets, a box of matches, three metal tins, a cracked blue plate and a teaspoon.

He sat in the sun, leaning against the front of the shed. Yesterday felt like a week ago.

His phone vibrated inside his jacket pocket; he switched it off without reading the messages from Sadie, Kristin and Carol. He rubbed his eyes. No traffic, no passers-by. A stillness that was not still, a silence that was not silent. It was all going on out here: birth, death, eating, mating, idleness, murder, calling, calling back. It was all going on, wordlessly.

He watched. He listened. He fell asleep.

When he awoke, he saw a ginger cat. She was sitting and looking and he was sitting and looking. This went on for some time. Who would make the first move? She was a handsome cat with a white chest and white paws, but she was patchy and thin and one of her ears was torn. Ralph waited. The cat waited. Time passed. Was this a test, an initiation, or just laziness?

Slowly, he stood up. The cat remained in the same position. Ralph edged closer, bending, rubbing his thumb against his forefinger. He made a kissing sound with his lips. He didn't know why humans tended to approach cats in this way. The gesture was an imitation of something he had seen a hundred times before, but did that make it right? He stopped what he was doing. The cat was clearly unimpressed. He stood up straight.

"Hello, I'm Ralph. I'm new. Are you new, or do you live out here? I don't know much about cats. Might as well come clean about that one. All I know is you purr when you're happy and you like eating fish. I'm going to touch your head now. Don't scratch me, okay?"

He stepped forward and stroked the cat's head, which lifted and pressed against his fingers. He stroked her chin and behind her ears. The cat seemed to like it, she was definitely respond-ing, but she wasn't making a sound. She rubbed the side of her body against his legs, turned around and did it again. Weren't cats supposed to purr at times like this?

"I'm starving. Will you wait here if I go and get us some food?"

He didn't want to go. The thought of leaving the woods and seeing another person made him feel anxious, but what choice did he have? Hopefully he could buy some supplies without bumping into anyone he knew. He needed fish for the cat, a sleeping bag, food and a takeaway coffee. No, that wasn't going to be enough. He needed bottled water and lots of it, toilet paper, maybe a kettle and some teabags and dried milk. A cup for the tea. Some kind of gas burner. A tin-opener, a fork. A rucksack for carrying things back and forth, on a daily basis, for as long as he was here.

Ralph took the first of many trips out of the woods and returned with a rucksack, pilchards, a tin-opener, plastic cutlery, water, a latte with caramel, three sandwiches, some fruit, four toilet rolls, a paperback and a sleeping bag. It would do until tomorrow.

The cat was still there. She followed him into the shed and watched him empty a can of pilchards onto the cracked plate. It only took a few seconds for the pilchards to disappear. How long had it been since the cat ate a decent meal? Perhaps he should have given her half at a time in case it made her sick. "I think we'll call you Treacle," Ralph said. He drank his coffee, ate a bacon and egg sandwich, rolled the sleeping bag out onto the floor, took off his shoes and got inside. The cat climbed on top, fishy and slow. She curled into a smaller version of herself and fell asleep with his hand on her stomach.

That was Sunday. Today is Tuesday, and Ralph has taken the chair he found in the shed over to the trees, where he is sitting with his guitar. His phone is still switched off. He has not called Sadie. He is playing 'Footsteps' by Pearl Jam. It has been a long time since he sat like this, strumming and singing about scratches and falling apart, not worrying about who might be listening or about to interrupt with a sarcastic quip. In the middle of the woods, with no idea what time of day it is, he sings at the top of his voice and no one comments. No text is sent, ending with ha ha. No remark pops up on Twitter. No observation is committed to mind for blogging purposes. He is safe in his aloneness. (Safety can't always be found in numbers.) The stillness that is not still, the silence that is not silent, goes on and on.

He sings three more songs by Pearl Jam. Two by the Beatles. Then he stands in the afternoon sun, a wooden chair behind him, singing about a showgirl called Lola who has feathers in her hair. Treacle is stretched out beside the old shed, watching and listening.

Then Ralph stops singing.

He and the cat stare, but not at each other.

They stare at a woman.

She has run into the clearing and stopped. She is bent double, gasping for breath. She is coughing.

Ralph looks at Treacle, Treacle looks at Ralph.

Facts about the woman: she has light-brown hair and is wearing a white shirt, faded jeans, red shoes. A leather bag was across her chest, now it is on the floor. She is standing in a bubble of gasps and wheezes and is obviously not used to running. She is pale and curvy. Her eyes are big and brown with flickers of amber and orange. Actually, they are enormous. Now she is no longer coughing and wheezing. She is standing upright with her hands on her hips, staring at Ralph. She is crying.

"Are you all right?" Ralph says.

Facts about the man: he too has brown hair, but his is dark and tidy and short. He is wearing a checked shirt, black jeans and walking shoes. His eyes are bluish green, greenish blue. He looks rumpled and unshaven, but you know just from looking that no degree of unkemptness will ever destroy his neatness, because it burns inside him, relentless.

"Sorry," Miriam says.

"Pardon?"

"I said I'm sorry."

New fact about the woman: she has some kind of throat infection, possibly laryngitis. Fancy going jogging with laryngitis. She should be tucked up in bed, drinking plenty of fluids, gargling with warm salty water, sucking lozenges. Ralph knows this from when Stanley had laryngitis last year. He was told to avoid speaking until he was better, and that included whispering, which can damage the larynx. He will tell her this once they have calmed down and introduced themselves. He will tell her this and she will look at him like he's peculiar.

"What are you sorry for?"

"Startling you."

"No problem. I was just playing my guitar."

Miriam nods. Ralph nods back. His nod is fleeting, automatic.

"Were you jogging?" he asks. (Surely not in those shoes?)

"No."

He nods again, firmly this time, like he means it. (That's a relief. You'd have blisters the size of plums if you were jogging in those shoes.)

"Do you live out here?" she asks. (Please say no. I could really do without a scary man who lives in the woods. Will I make it out of here alive? Is yours the last face I will ever see? Is this how the story ends? If so, how fitting. Karma karma karma karma karma chameleon.)

"No, I don't live here. I'm just, well, I'm not sure what I'm doing." He shrugs, making light of what is heavy. "But it's nice," he says.

"Right," Miriam says. "I was running."

"Not jogging."

"No."

"Running away from something?"

"Yes and no. Sort of."

"I get that."

"Oh."

Treacle sits up and licks a paw. These humans have started speaking in the language of befuddlement. A curious lingo, short and woolly, full of *yes* and *no* and *sort of*.

"Well," Miriam says.

"Well," Ralph says.

"I'm sorry to interrupt your playing."

"It's okay."

Miriam looks at the cat. "Your friend?"

"I've named her Treacle."

"Have you been here all day?"

"I've been here for three days now—I've been sleeping in there." He turns to look at the shed. "I'm not homeless, though."

Miriam wonders if he is a criminal. He might have escaped from prison. He might have killed someone and now be hiding in the woods, hiding from the police, hiding from everyone. But she has found him. Or maybe he has found her. They haven't found each other, not yet.

"Sorry, I'm Ralph by the way," he says, walking over, holding out his hand.

"Miriam Delaney," she says, shaking his hand, hoping it's not dirty, half expecting him to tighten his grip and fling her over his shoulder. He doesn't look strong enough to do that, but people are savage and unpredictable.

"Ralph Swoon."

"Swoon?"

"Yes."

She smiles. He notices that it makes her look kind.

"That's an unusual name. Is it a kind of superpower?"

"Sorry?"

"Do you go around making people swoon?"

"Unfortunately not."

"Oh." He smiles. She notices that it makes him look sad. "That would be a good superpower," she says.

"I suppose it would." Nostalgia curves his lips. The puppetry of the past, it keeps us dancing, keeps us smiling these melancholy smiles. "My dad used to make people swoon, back in his heyday. Women used to stare at his bottom."

"His bottom?"

"He had a nice one, apparently."

"And did he?"

"What?"

"Have a nice bottom?"

"I couldn't say."

"Why?"

"Well, I'm his son. It would be really weird if I went around saying that my dad had a nice bottom."

"Technically speaking you do go around saying that, otherwise we wouldn't be having this conversation." Miriam grins and sniffs.

Ralph laughs by exhaling through his nose in short puffs. Miriam isn't sure what he is laughing at and she hopes it isn't her. She has had a lifetime of people puffing for all the wrong reasons.

"Is he dead?"

"Who?"

"Your dad?"

"No. Why?"

"You made it sound like he was dead."

"He and my mum are very much alive."

"Right."

"Would you like a cup of tea? I only have UHT milk."

"You have tea-making facilities?"

"I'll show you." He leads the way to the other side of the shed, where they both stare at his tiny camping stove and kettle. "I bought these yesterday. I only have one mug at the moment, so we'll have to have one cup at a time. Ladies first."

He makes her a cup of tea in a mug he bought from Starbucks and fetches the wooden chair for her to sit on. She looks even paler than when she arrived, probably due to her laryngitis. "You sit here," he says, glancing at Treacle, who is busy watching a blackbird.

"Oh no, that's your chair."

"It's not mine, I just found it in the shed. I have no idea who it belongs to. Have a seat."

"Thank you."

She sips the tea and he sits on the floor, stroking Treacle's head.

"This tea is nice," Miriam says, holding the mug with both hands.

"Is it okay?"

"It's lovely."

"That's good."

A man, a woman, a cat. Three hearts, eight legs, three noses, one tail. Seventy-five years of accumulated life. Put it all together and what do you get? You get this:

A man rinsing out a mug and making a second cup of tea for a woman he has just met. A woman who has braved the outside world after three years of self-imposed imprisonment. A man whose rational thoughts have been suspended like freshly washed sheets, blowing in the wind, just blowing in the wind.

"I suppose I should be going soon," Miriam says.

"Somewhere to be?"

"Not really."

"Don't rush off on my account."

"You probably want to get back to your guitar."

Ralph opens a packet of Maltesers. "Would you like one?"

"No thank you. I've eaten so much rubbish today. I went to the cinema."

"I haven't been to the cinema for ages. Actually, the last film I saw was *Beautiful Lies*. I've got a bit of a thing for Audrey Tautou."

"I liked her in *Amélie*. She was good."

"Very."

Miriam sips her tea. Ralph watches her. "Are you taking anything for your throat?" he says.

"Sorry?"

"You've lost your voice."

"No."

"No?"

"I always speak like this."

"Oh God, I'm really sorry. I just assumed you had laryngitis or something."

Second person today.

"Nope."

"Right."

"I'm so used to talking like this, it's just what I do. I think that's what happens when you do something for a long time. It becomes who you are."

He puffs through his nose again. A laugh of recognition.

How right you are, says the puffing, which is followed by real words: "You're absolutely right," he says.

Miriam looks up. She is not used to being absolutely right. "What have you been doing for a long time?" she asks, because she thinks she ought to. The laugh of recognition invites a question. It says ask me, go on, ask me why I'm puffing, *go on*.

Ralph tries to find words to describe the things he has been doing for a long time, but there are no words. He closes his eyes and sees sheets blowing in the wind, a dark cafe, a plate full of croissants.

"I've finished my tea," Miriam says. "Shall I wash this out?"

"I'll do it."

"Oh, okay."

As he rinses the cup with mineral water, he pictures more of the dark cafe, its walls lined with black-and-white photos. He knows he has been there before, this image isn't from a film or a TV programme, but he can't recall when. He would normally be frustrated by this, by not being able to remember, but he lets it go. He is tired of trying to work things out. All that effort for what?

Ralph was in that cafe with Julie Parsley. They ordered two coffees, two croissants. It was the day they said goodbye. He will not remember this moment until a week from now, when he will stroll into a different cafe, looking for Julie. When he does remember he will try not to cry, despite the shocking impulse, the *overwhelming* desire. He will straighten his back and walk across the room. She will see him, stand up, place her lips on his cheek.

"It's quite nice out here," Miriam says.

"Peaceful."

"Mmnn." She crosses her legs. "Do you mind if I tell you something?"

Don't do it, Miriam. He's not interested in your boring stories.

"Not at all," he says, pouring hot water into the mug.

She checks his face for sincerity but it's a pointless move; her gauge has always been faulty. "I hadn't left my house for three years," she says. "Until today."

"Really?"

She nods.

"Three years?"

"Yes."

"Have you been ill?"

"No, not ill." Oh dear. Now he is inspecting *her* face. Why is everyone so convinced that she is ill?

He notices her shiver. "Are you cold?" he says, walking into the shed. He comes back out with his cardigan. "Here, have this."

"Oh no, it's all right," she says, but it's too late. His cardigan is around her shoulders, thick and heavy and smelling of aftershave, and he is sitting on the floor, dipping a teabag into a mug of hot water.

A man's cardigan. *On her.* She wants to shake it off.

"Shall I tell you something strange too?" he says.

"Okay."

"I've just walked away from my life."

She frowns. What on earth does he mean by this? If his life is elsewhere then what is keeping him alive? What is pushing blood around his body? She thinks of little Tom in *The Awakening*, dead and alive, only visible to Florence and his mother. We can't walk away from our lives. We simply can't. How did we all end up like this, constantly saying things that are completely untrue? To walk away from life would be to die and this man is clearly not dead. Or is he?

"Have you?" Miriam says. Her whispers are tiny stones, only capable of making ripples. She wants to make a splash.

She wants to make waves. If only her words could trigger a rogue wave, the kind that appears out of nowhere, random and gigantic. She watched a documentary about rogue waves a few months ago. They are not caused by underwater earthquakes, like tsunamis. They are freakish and wild and—

"I just walked away," Ralph says.

"Was it a rogue wave?" she says, expecting to have to explain this and liking how that feels. Usually there is no one there and her questions hang loose like the headmaster's skinny arms.

"A what?"

"A rogue wave."

"Sorry, you've lost me."

"They're enormous waves that can appear on a calm sea with no warning or obvious cause. They're very real, but I'm talking about them *metaphorically*, obviously."

"I'm with you," he says, lying and telling the truth. He is here with Miriam in a literal sense, but he is not following what she is saying. In an attempt to understand this woman with light-brown hair and enormous eyes, he thinks it over. Has his life been a calm sea until now? Has a rogue wave carried him here? Is there a clear explanation? Could this moment have been predicted? He glances at Miriam, who is leaning forward, drawing circles in the dirt with a stick. He feels maternal. Yes, definitely maternal, rather than paternal. The M is all-important and today it stands for Miriam, who sounds like she has laryngitis, who speaks ever so earnestly, who looks like a cross between a ten-year-old girl and a woman in her forties.

"How old are you?" he says. "If you don't mind me asking."

"I am thirty-five," she says, beside the circles and circles.

"Are you from around here?"

"I've never been anywhere else."

"What do you mean?"

"I've never been anywhere else."

"Repeating something doesn't explain it."

"Sometimes it does. Sometimes you hear a sentence for the second time and it just makes sense."

"So what you're saying is you've never lived anywhere else?"

"Yes, and I've never *been* anywhere else."

"Not on holiday?"

"I've never been on holiday."

"Seriously?"

She draws a hard line through the circles.

"Well that's unusual," he says.

A squirrel runs past. It stops, looks at them and runs off towards the trees. Miriam wonders what squirrels see when they look at a human being. Do they have strong or weak eyesight? She wonders if there is someone in the world who can answer that question, and what that person might be like, the one with all the answers about squirrels and their eyesight. She pictures a man in a tank top, watching nature from behind cupped hands held close to his mouth. She likes him. Then she remembers Google and Wikipedia, which can answer any question you throw at them, and the man in the tank top disappears. His absence leaves an effervescent pocket in her stomach. The pocket is called Jeffrey, who was murdered by Google and Wikipedia. What a way to go. What a ridiculous death. Poor Jeffrey.

"Are you all right?" Ralph asks.

She looks at his face again. The pointer on her faulty sincerity gauge has crept over to the right, to the orange area, which means seven out of ten.

Don't be stupid, Miriam.

"I never know how to answer that question," she says.

THE LULL, THE PAUSE, BEFORE THE COMMOTION

S adie is asleep. Ever since the kiss with Kristin, she has
found herself dozing off every time she sits down.

Ralph has left her. Her life has been a lie. All she wants to
do is sleep and eat.

"You're comfort eating," says Stanley, watching his mother
wake from her nap and resume a bowl of pasta.

"I'm not."

"I think you are, Mum."

"I'm hungry all the time. You don't get that if you're comfort
eating. You just think of food without actually being hungry."

Her hunger feels simple, unlike other kinds of appetite,
especially the one she discovered three days ago in the cupboard on the landing.

Yesterday, Sadie visited a twenty-four-hour Tesco at three o'clock
in the morning wearing flip-flops, shorts, a sweatshirt and no
make-up. As she wandered around the aisles, she wondered
why she had never done this before. Talk about liberation. Talk
about the *ideal* time to shop—no traffic, no queues, just an

intriguing subsection of the general public, moving around in slow motion. She felt a sense of intimacy, as if the customers were members of a special night-time club, going about their business during the lull, the pause, before the commotion of daylight.

She looked at magazines, birthday cards, Lego.

She looked at Post-its, canned fish, frozen peppers. The idea of buying frozen sliced peppers had never occurred to her before. She threw six bags into her trolley.

"They're incredibly handy aren't they?"

Who was that? Wrong question, Sadie. *What* was that?

A giant panda.

I beg your pardon?

Holding a bag of frozen sprouts in one paw and a basket in the other.

"Sprouts in summer," was all Sadie could think of to say.

"I like sprouts all year round," the panda said.

"Have you come from a fancy-dress party?"

"No."

"Are you collecting for charity?"

"No."

"I see."

"Do you?"

"What?"

"Do you see?"

"Sorry."

"Don't be."

(Things have taken a cryptic turn among the frozen vegetables.)

"I watched a documentary the other day about the conservation of giant pandas," Sadie said. "They're actually quite stupid aren't they?"

No answer.

"The conservationists were all wearing panda costumes to prepare baby pandas for the wild. You'd think they'd know wouldn't you?"

The panda dropped the frozen sprouts into her shopping basket. Sadie wondered how often the costume got washed and whether it had to be taken to a launderette. She noticed a tear in the leg.

"A little shih-tzu," the panda said, lifting her leg. "It was frightened."

"Right."

"I used to go on lots of foreign holidays, now I just do this. You've got to find your thing. No point throwing money down the drain."

"What do you mean by *this*?"

The panda placed her basket on the floor and waved her front legs in the air: jazz paws. "I'm part of a group called EYI—Embrace Your Insomnia."

All Sadie could think of was EIEIO. Old MacDonald had a—

"How interesting," she said.

"Let me give you my card," the panda said. She reached into a furry pocket, extracted a business card, handed it to Sadie. "Like I said, you just have to find your thing."

"Lovely, thanks."

"No problem. It was nice to meet you."

"You too."

The giant panda shuffled down the aisle.

I forgot to take a photo, thought Sadie. A Twitter reflex came and went and she continued her slow-motion shopping.

Forty minutes later, she was piling items onto a conveyor belt. She looked at the woman working the till, whose badge said "Hi I'm Belinda".

"Quiet in here," Belinda said.

"Isn't it normally quiet at four-thirty in the morning?"

"It gets lonely," Belinda said, hoping her manager wasn't listening on some kind of hi-tech surveillance device. She was convinced that her uniform was bugged.

The two women stared at each other. For a few seconds they were united by an inexplicable sadness, as close as two people could be. Then came an announcement from a dislocated voice about two for the price of one on all Pantene shampoos.

"I'm sorry," Sadie said.

"Ah well," Belinda said. "Would you like cashback?"

"Where've you been?" asked Stanley, walking into the kitchen in his boxer shorts and slippers. "Have you been to the police?"

Sadie put her shopping on the breakfast bar. "The police?"

"About Dad."

"Your father's fine."

"How do you know?"

"He's just angry."

"Mum, it's been three days."

"Three days is nothing. He's at your grandparents' house, sulking. Trust me."

"Why?"

"Why what?"

"Why should I trust you?"

Sadie put the kettle on and opened the fridge. "Because I'm your mother."

"Why is he angry with you?"

"Not this again."

"We deserve to know."

She sighed. "This fridge is disgusting. Why am I the only one who'd ever notice? Why don't you see it?"

"If Dad's been murdered, you're going to feel like crap."

"Stanley," she said, spinning around, "will you just drop it? You're being melodramatic."

"Why have you been to the supermarket in the middle of the night?"

"There was nothing to eat."

"It's because you're sleeping in the daytime. You won't feel tired at night if you sleep all day."

Back in bed with a mug of tea, Stanley texted Joe.

—Hey gorgeous. Do you think I should report Dad missing?
—It's 5.40am
—Sorry, thought your phone would be off xxx
—Shall we talk later? Try not to worry. He's probably with a woman
—What woman?
—Get some sleep. I'll call in after breakfast
—Okay xx

Stanley loved the way that Joe never shortened words or used abbreviations in his messages. When they first started texting, he quickly discovered Joe's penchant for correctness:

—Had you done that before?
—Not B4 U!
—Me neither. You were my first x

Could a relationship survive its infancy when one person wrote their texts as if they were formal letters and the other wrote B4 and U? The answer was no and Stanley knew it, so he modified his behaviour to impress. That's what you do when you're in love, he thought. You make small alterations.

You change your shape. But what if he couldn't remember what shape he was in before? What if he ended up twisted like his parents?

After the party on Ralph's birthday, when all the guests had gone home, Sadie sat in the back garden beside a flickering citronella candle and smoked a cigarette from a packet someone had left behind. Having a cigarette in her hand reminded her of being a student.

Sadie Swoon @SadieLPeterson
Can't believe I'm smoking! Disgusting but true

She smoked and wondered where Ralph had gone. She smoked and wished she had kissed Kristin Hart years ago, before her civil partnership to Carol, their honeymoon in Mauritius, their semi-detached Victorian house with three bedrooms and two bathrooms, its walls lined with Kristin's artwork, with photos of the two of them in Mauritius, San Francisco, Cornwall, Paris, Berlin, New Zealand. She wished she had realized how much she loved Alison Grabowski when she was still in her life. She could be dead by now. Or living in New York. She always went on about Manhattan, and how she wanted to live in a Greenwich Village apartment and walk a small dog in Central Park and fall in love with someone who liked street art, Japanese food, James Joyce. But she hadn't kissed Kristin years ago or told Alison that she loved her. She was a wife and a mother with no real job or career. It was an insult to her intelligence, but who had delivered the insult? Funny how you can be shocked and sickened by your own life, when yesterday you were simply living it.

Sadie Swoon @SadieLPeterson
I can highly recommend spending whole night in back
garden

She closed her eyes and listened. A couple shouting, a bottle
breaking. High heels on concrete. A bark, a whistle, a lorry
rattling through green lights.

In the bathroom upstairs, she looked at herself in the mirror.
She looked at the bruise on her face, the new spot on her chin,
the lines and the smudged mascara. "For fuck's sake," she said,
pulling a cleansing wipe from a packet. She sat cross-legged
on the floor, wiping her face, as Harvey squeezed through the
crack in the door and jumped on top of her. "Not now, Harv,"
she said, throwing her arms around him. "Not now," she whispered, pulling him close.

16

PSYCHOANALYTIC ANARCHY

Jilly Perkins @JillyBPerks
Had message from Swoon's receptionist saying he's
taken break early, even though I'm on holiday! So
disorganized

Jilly Perkins @JillyBPerks
Anyone know why he's gone off early? V unlike him

Finn Chapman @thatchapfinn
@JillyBPerks Trouble at home or so they say...

Jilly Perkins @JillyBPerks
@thatchapfinn No surprise there. Should we set up group
therapy? Think of the savings!

Bryony Stamp @BryStamp
@JillyBPerks @thatchapfinn poor Ralph hope he's OK. I
was supposed to see him at 4pm

Ruth Gray @ruthandpaul68
@BryStamp @JillyBPerks @thatchapfinn Me at 5! Do feel free to say no but fancy meeting for coffee instead?

Jilly Perkins @JillyBPerks
@ruthandpaul68 @BryStamp @thatchapfinn OMG psychoanalytic anarchy! Think of the transference implications!

Finn Chapman @thatchapfinn
@JillyBPerks @ruthandpaul68 @BryStamp Could result in us all being stuck in therapy for years. May I come for coffee?

Jilly Perkins @JillyBPerks
@thatchapfinn @ruthandpaul68 @BryStamp This is the worst time ever to be away in Cornwall (feel a little excluded)

Finn Chapman @thatchapfinn
@JillyBPerks @ruthandpaul68 @BryStamp Oh poor you, off work and by the sea. Childhood issues?

Bryony Stamp @BryStamp
@thatchapfinn @JillyBPerks @ruthandpaul68 we all have issues Finn, and a little kindness goes a long way, don't you think?

17

YOU CAN CALL THE POLICE OR JUST STAB ME

They sat together on the sofa like any other mother and daughter, but one was the voice and one was the pen. Frances dictated the letters—*Mum is so much happier, we've been on lots of day trips, school is going really well, Mum helps me do my homework*—and Miriam wrote the words on sheets of pale-blue paper. This went on for several weeks and the response was mysterious. Granny never replied. She clearly disliked these letters, which made Miriam panic.

"Can we ask why she hasn't written back?" she said.

"Definitely not, that's rude."

Then, on Christmas Eve, Frances made her daughter a hot chocolate and asked her to sit down. "There's something I need to tell you," she said. "About your grandmother."

"Is she all right?"

"Very much so. I spoke to her this morning."

"I thought you didn't speak to each other?"

"She phoned with important news."

Miriam imagined a removal van, pulling up outside the house and depositing Granny and her things.

"Old people are unpredictable," Frances said.

"Pardon?"

"What you need to understand about old people is their personalities are unpredictable. Their brains can alter considerably."

Miriam held on tight to the removal van.

"Their tastes change—not just for food, but for people and climates."

Climates?

"She used to be chatty and kind, but now she's something else, all right, Mim?"

No, it was not all right.

"She doesn't find you interesting any more."

Miriam's lower lip quivered. She turned away from her mother, focused on the Christmas tree and its three decorations: a plastic pineapple, a plastic bunch of grapes and a plastic pear. Nothing says Christmas like artificial fruit.

"It breaks my heart to say this, darling, but I think she was humouring you before. She never told you her house has been on the market, did she? She's been wanting to move to Spain, darling."

Darling this and darling that.

"The house has sold."

Removal van removal van.

"So she's free to go. I'm so sorry, darling, but she doesn't want us to bother her." Frances put her arm around Miriam. "To be honest, this is a good opportunity. You need to learn that people are insincere. They humour each other, lead each other on, and my mother has always been very good at that. Her unpredictability damaged me. It makes me cross sometimes, but it's just you and me now so we need to stick together."

Just you and me.

"I've always tried to protect you, Mim. That's why I taught you to whisper. I've had a lifetime of people mocking me for the things I say. It's better that people can't hear you. It's *safer*."

"So I can't write to her any more?"

"I'm afraid not."

Miriam stood up. "I've had an accident."

"What?"

Wet pyjamas. Wet sofa. Wet floor.

"I'm sorry, Mum."

Frances wanted to slap her. She wanted to grab her curls and press her face into the dark patch on the sofa. But she didn't. She didn't need to. Her work was done.

There is a tumbledown shed, neither upright nor fallen, in the middle of the woods. It has been standing by itself through years of wild and mundane weather—battered by sleet, fattened by snow, cracked by sun. Its days are numbered, but so are all of our days. If we could see the numbers, we would know how long we had left to make things right.

There is a woman, sitting on a wooden chair beside the shed, drawing circles in the dirt. The circles tell the story of what went round and round, day after day, making her dizzy and sick.

There is a man, rinsing out a Starbucks mug and filling it with water for the woman to drink. He is worried about her throat, even though she has told him that her throat is fine. He doesn't know her well enough to decide whether she is telling the truth about this or anything else.

There is a cat, lying on its side, enjoying the feel of the man's fingers running up and down its stomach.

"Can I ask you something?" Ralph says.

"Okay."

"Have you really not left your house for three years until today?"

"Well, I suppose I told a bit of a lie there."

"Did you?"

"I went into my back garden to feed the fish."

"Probably good to get some fresh air."

Miriam nods.

"What time is it?" he asks.

She looks at her watch. "Just after six."

"Time flies when you leave the house."

"It does."

Ralph stands up and brushes the dirt from the back of his trousers. "Have you had a proper meal today?"

"Depends what you mean by *proper*."

"I'll take that as a no. Do you fancy a barbecue?"

"Here?"

"Yes."

"Now?"

"Unless you have to be going."

Miriam stands up. She looks into Ralph's eyes and finds nothing to distress or console her. What is his agenda? Where is this leading? "I need to keep my life simple," she says, which makes things feel more complicated than before she said it.

"Okay," Ralph says.

She squints, flicks her hair away from her face, rubs the thumb of her left hand around the palm of her right hand like she's soothing some kind of pain, but there is no pain. She is trying to decide what to do, but how do you make a decision when you don't even know what the options are?

"You look a little stressed," Ralph says.

"Yes."

"Why?"

"Well, I don't want to offend you."

"Go on."

"You seem very nice, but there's no one else around. Anything could happen and there's no one to help."

"I understand," he says.

"Do you?"

"Of course. You don't know me. I could be a serial killer. It's perfectly sensible to be stressed."

Miriam scratches her knee. Something has bitten her. "It's not that I don't want to stay and talk," she says. "And a barbecue sounds interesting."

Ralph half closes his eyes and clasps the corner of his bottom lip between his teeth. "I have an idea," he says. "Do you have your phone on you?"

"I don't own a mobile phone."

"Really? Well how about I give you mine? I also have a knife in the shed."

Is that supposed to make her feel less stressed?

"It came with the fork I bought for eating my tea."

"Oh."

"You take the knife and phone, then you can call the police or just stab me if I try anything stupid. Not that I would," he says, smiling.

Miriam isn't smiling.

Does he know what he's saying?

Does he know what she's capable of?

"I'm just trying to give you all the power," he says. It was enjoyable at first, meeting someone new, but now he feels a flicker of resentment. Of course a woman might feel scared out here with a man she doesn't know, but how does that make the man feel? *The personal is political*—that's what Sadie's always saying. All he wants to do is buy one of those cheap throwaway barbecues and cook her some chicken, and yet he feels like a lowlife. "Nothing's easy," he says.

"No," she says, looking like she might cry.

"Okay," he says. "Here's the plan. I'm going into town to buy some food, and if you'd like to you can walk with me. Then you can head home if that feels best."

"All right."

Ralph grabs his wallet and rucksack and Miriam picks up her bag. They set off through the woods, talking about the names of trees and birds and how neither of them knows as much about these things as they should. Ralph is better with trees than birds. Miriam owns a book called *Remarkable Trees of the World*, but she can't remember many names, apart from all the usual ones like oak and cedar and fir. It's pathetic really, when you think about it, which she rarely does, because she is usually thinking about less ordinary matters, like her father and whether he loved her, like madness and whether it's catching. She doesn't tell Ralph this part, because they are about to say goodbye and he is talking about how a person can snap.

"So in a nutshell," he says, "something snapped. That's what people say, isn't it? But to be honest, now I hear myself saying it, I don't think that's right. I wonder if something *mended*. Maybe something joined up." He looks pleased with himself.

Make your mind up, Ralph. Did you snap or did you mend?

"Maybe your tolerance snapped."

"Tolerance?"

"Yes."

"Maybe."

Now Ralph is saying what a long story it is, the story of what he can no longer tolerate, and Miriam isn't listening. They have walked through the woods and come to the path, the one that passes a gate and a field, the one that leads through a meadow

and into town. She can hear Ralph's voice, it is warm and pleas-
ant but she can't really hear what he is saying. She wonders
how she would reply if he asked what was going on inside her.
MY HEART IS IN MY MOUTH. Those are the words. An easy
cliché. She thinks of her heart moving up her body towards
her throat. She imagines it sitting on her tongue, beating by
itself, just sitting there with its own branches, pathways and
tracks, bloody and plump. She imagines coughing it up onto
the floor and no longer having a heart. What a stupid phrase.
Sickening. Nonsensical.

"Miriam?"

She is walking the tangent tightrope, skirting around the
outskirts, circling the outer circles, looping the loop. Welcome
to the fringes of reality, but who says that the fringes are even
the fringes? Maybe they're the crux of it. Maybe they're the
real deal. Miriam has thought about this a hundred times but
she doesn't think about it now. She and a man she has only
just met are about to hit the spot. The spot where it happened.
Where push came to shove. Her arms, a shocking necklace.
Her body, a trailing pendant. "What the fuck? Are you crazy?"
he said, trying to shake her off. That was more than three
years ago. Miriam tells herself this as she walks over the spot.

"I'm going to Asda," Ralph says.

Miriam looks at him. He has no idea. He seems sweet. She
hasn't noticed the sweetness until now.

"I'm going to get one of those throwaway barbecues. I'm
rubbish at barbecues, but how hard can it be? You just drop a
bit of chicken on it and wait, don't you?"

"I haven't had a barbecue since I was six," Miriam says, walking into the meadow. In the distance she can see the children's
play area, a woman with a toddler and a pram, a man in a red
coat walking three dogs.

"You've got a good memory."

"Yes."

Ralph has the sense that he might know things about this woman that he doesn't yet know. The known unknown is full of sorrow. "I'm sorry," he says.

"What for?"

"I don't know."

Miriam likes this. She asks if she can come to Asda. He says yes, of course, and he wants to hold out his hand but he keeps it in his pocket.

"I don't really want to go home," she says, as he throws a pack of chicken breasts into his shopping basket.

"Don't go then."

"I have to."

"Why?"

"Nowhere else to go."

"Stay in the shed with me."

"I beg your pardon?"

"Not like that."

"For how long?"

"Just for tonight."

"With you?"

"Why not?"

"I'm not sure."

"You're safe with me."

"Am I?"

"Yes."

"Why?"

"Why?"

"Yes."

"You just are. Think of it as a camping trip. A one-night mini-break."

She has never had a mini-break before. Fenella had one last month—she went to Berlin and met Leon, who bought her a spicy sausage and kissed away her tiredness.

"I don't want any funny business," Miriam says.

"I know," he says.

She is glad that he knows, but also disappointed. It means that she wears her reticence like a high-visibility jacket, which makes her a lollipop lady or a child on a school trip. Her buttons are fluorescent. Her innocence glows in the dark.

18

REGRET

S adie is wearing tracksuit bottoms and one of Stanley's T-shirts. She is smoking on the sofa, eating popcorn, drinking Coke. Why? Because fruit smoothies are overrated, low-calorie snacks are disappointing and resisting temptation is dangerous. Look where it gets you. Just look.

On the floor in front of her, all the photos she could find from university. Alison Grabowski outside their student house, holding the neighbour's kitten. Alison Grabowski in their kitchen, wearing a Smiths T-shirt, laughing, a glass of wine in her hand, a cigarette in her mouth. Alison Grabowski here and Alison Grabowski there and you get the picture but what else do you get? Nothing at all, because the moment passed, it just disappeared, so you may as well eat popcorn and smoke. (This is what's known as hitting a brick wall while sitting on your sofa.)

Ralph wasn't the one who kissed another woman, but earlier today, Sadie cut some of his clothes into shreds with scissors. It felt good and necessary. She feels better now the shreds are visible, scattered all over the bedroom floor—outside herself, instead of inside.

"Sorting out your photos?" Arthur says, walking into the room and eyeing his mother's oversized T-shirt and tracksuit bottoms with apprehension, disgust, anxiety.

"Kind of."

"Looking back at your past?"

"Something like that."

He picks up a photo. Alison Grabowski wearing nothing but a long checked shirt, making a pasta salad. "Who's this?"

"Just someone I went to college with."

"She looks like Kristin."

They stare at the picture. Sadie's cheeks flush. "No, I don't see any resemblance," she says, tossing the photo onto the floor. She puts her glass on the coffee table, placing it in the middle of the square coaster so that she no longer has to look at a moose dressed as a waiter. She doesn't understand why she spent money on coasters with drawings of animals wearing random outfits—just totally *revolting*.

"Did you find any old pics of Dad?"

"Haven't come across any yet."

"Right. What's with the smoking?"

"It's just temporary."

"It's gross. Makes the house stink."

"Am I supposed to believe you've never smoked?"

"Not that shit."

"My son the connoisseur of cigarettes?"

He shrugs. "I want to watch TV."

"So watch TV."

"Can you go and smoke somewhere else? Like in the garden?"

"Will you and your brother stop bossing me about? I'm taking some time out."

"Time out from *what*?"

She looks at her son, the one who resembles her the most, and sees contempt on his face. She looks at the tulips, the ones you plug in so they light up, the ones you can set to flash on and off, which turns your sitting room into a disco, a bloody fucking disco. She jumps to her feet, opens the window, picks up the tulip lamp, throws it outside.

"What the fuck?"

First the lamp, then two vases of plastic daffodils smashing into pieces on concrete outside the window. The wedding photo is next, then the photo of Arthur and Stanley in the silver frame, the little Buddha, the carriage clock, the pot full of pens and pencils and rubber bands, the plate on the wall from a holiday in France, the DVD box sets, the tiny jug from a Spanish market, the one that just sits there, empty, through all days and all the nights, gathering dust while everything changes and stays exactly the same.

Arthur just stands there.

Cushions, a blanket, the telephone, an address book, a carriage clock, four batteries, the TV remote, cufflinks. Better out than in. Better than murdering someone. Better than killing yourself. Possibly. Marginally. She picks things up, throws them out of the window, relishes the sound they make, a symphony of regret.

"Doesn't that look better?" she says.

"Mum, for God's sake."

"Give me your glass."

"No."

"No?"

"No."

"It's *my* glass. I bought it."

"You're having a breakdown. I'm ringing Gran."

"Don't you dare."

*

"Hello, is that Brenda?"

"Sadie?"

"Yes. How are you?"

"Oh not too bad. Is everything all right?" Brenda had seen Ralph's home number appear on her phone's display and expected it to be him. She hasn't had a call from Sadie for years. Actually, has Sadie ever called? She tries to remember, but she can't think of a reason why her daughter-in-law would ever have bothered. Which can only mean one of two things: she wants something, or someone is *dead*.

"Is Ralph there?" Sadie asks.

"Here?"

"Yes."

"No, he's not here. Is he supposed to be?"

"I thought he might be."

"What's happened?"

"We had a fight, nothing major. It'll blow over."

"But you don't know where he is?" Brenda covers the phone with her hand and whispers to her husband: "Ralph's left her." Frank, who is not usually prone to childish gestures, claps his hands together and squeaks. The squeak takes him by surprise, it was supposed to be a kind of mmmmm sound, rising at the end like a question, like a sound that says oh really, *how interesting*. His glee descends into self-disgust and he looks down at the carpet.

"He's probably staying with a friend," Sadie says, wishing she hadn't phoned.

"How long has he been gone?" Brenda's panic has infused her voice with headmistressy strictness, sharpening her casual round vowels, making her sound like Hyacinth Bucket from *Keeping Up Appearances*.

"Only a few days," Sadie says.

"A few days? Oh I don't like this, Sadie, I don't like it at all. Ralph would never go off for a few days without letting *someone* know where he was."

Sadie listens to the rustle and crackle of Brenda's hand over the receiver. She listens to the muffled voices of her in-laws: he's missing, surely not, no it's true, *gone for a few days*, no idea where he is, good grief, *I know*. She pictures a pigeon in a golfing jumper, standing in the middle of a puddle, flapping. She thinks of Catrina, a woman she used to go to school with, who now makes a surprisingly good living from drawing things like birds in jumpers, dogs in pyjamas, monkeys dressed as tennis players. She had a stall at last year's Christmas market and Sadie bought coasters, a tea towel, four mugs and three cards, her pity dusted with fake excitability, her disdain sprinkled with festiveness.

There is a discussion about what to do next and Brenda says she's feeling nauseous, she has a *very bad feeling*, and Frank pulls the phone from her clammy hand, says it's time to call the police.

"There's no need for that," Sadie says. "Actually, I think I might know where he is."

"Really?"

"I've just thought of it. Can't believe I didn't think of it before really, but sometimes you don't, do you? The blatantly obvious is right there and you just don't see it."

"Just spit it out, for God's sake."

"He might be with Catrina."

Sadie can hear Brenda saying what, what's happening, Frank what's going on?

"He's having an affair?"

"Well, they've been spending a lot of time together."

"That's such a relief."

"Oh that's charming."

"Well he's probably with this Catrina, isn't he? That's all I meant."

"You're relieved to think he's betraying me?"

"Of course not." Frank rolls his eyes. High maintenance, that's what she is.

Brenda is beside herself now, she's yelling about a speakerphone button, saying push the bloody speakerphone button, and Frank, who is technologically challenged, has no idea what she means.

"I don't wish to be rude, but I'd much rather he was with another woman than under a bus, and I'm sure you feel the same," he says.

"I'm not sure I do."

"Well that's indecent."

"Indecent?"

"Not indecent. What's the word? Dishonourable, that's what it is."

"I'm going to ring off now, Frank."

"Will you ring Catrina? We'd like to know for sure."

"Fine."

Sadie goes upstairs and collapses onto the bed. She lies still for a few minutes, thinking about Catrina and her husband Rupert, smirking at the preposterous notion of Ralph and Catrina together. Then she sends Brenda a text: I've spoken to Catrina and Ralph is there. She says they're not having an affair. He's sleeping in the guest room. All is well. He just needs a little space x

Brenda replies straight away: Oh thank GOD for that!

Sadie sends another text, this time to her husband: Where the hell are you? Text me immediately

And another: Do you think this is acceptable?

Followed by: Just give me a call so we can sort things out

And: Are you all right?

And: I'm furious now!

And: If you don't call within the hour I'm going to leave you & take the boys & Harvey

And: I AM NOT FUCKING JOKING

Sadie Swoon @SadieLPeterson
Does anyone fancy going out tomorrow night? Husband away on business. Bored!

Chris Preston @ChrisAtMacks
Visit shop tomorrow between 9 and 9.30 wearing a tea cosy for a free copy of Pride and Prejudice!
Retweeted by Sadie Swoon

Beverley Smart @bearwith72
@SadieLPeterson Pizza and pub quiz at the Dog?

Twenty-four tweets. Nineteen texts. Three Jaffa Cakes. Then a phone call from Beverley Smart, who is halfway through her third banana daiquiri.

"Hi, Sadie."

"Where are you? I can hardly hear you."

"Bar 246."

"God, I haven't been there for ages. Who are you with?"

"If I tell you, don't think badly of me."

"Now you *have* to tell me."

"I'm with your neighbour."

"Sorry?"

"The one from the party."

"Bev, why are you with *him*?"

"I like him."

"Nobody likes him."

"You must, surely?"

"Why must I?"

"You invited him to Ralph's party."

"I felt sorry for him. His wife's seriously ill. You know he has a wife, do you?"

"Sadie, I haven't called to talk about this. I've only got a sec. Is Ralph really away on business?"

"He's at a trauma conference."

"Right."

"Why?"

"Well, I don't know how to say this really."

"What?"

"Sadie, I'm so sorry, but I saw him."

"What do you mean?"

"I saw him earlier, coming out of Asda with a *woman*."

Since he left, Sadie has been picturing Ralph in a mid-priced hotel, somewhere clean and comfortable rather than luxurious, revelling in obstinacy and US sitcoms on Sky TV. She hasn't entertained the idea of a *woman*.

"Sadie, are you still there?"

She is sitting on the edge of her bed, thinking that she would like to slap the woman who has stolen her husband, the husband she doesn't really want, but that's not the point, not the point at all.

"What did she look like?"

"Who?"

"The woman with Ralph."

"Nothing special."

"Young?"

"Our age, probably. I didn't get a close look. Brown curly hair, jeans. Let's talk about it tomorrow night, yeah?"

"Tomorrow night?"

"At the pub quiz."

"Actually, can we go somewhere else?"

"Fine. You choose. I'll pick you up at seven."

Sadie walks through to Arthur's bedroom and looks out of the window. He is on the front lawn, picking things up and throwing them into a holdall. It's the first time she has ever seen him tidying up. Stanley appears, their faces turn serious, then Stanley starts picking things up too and they look like they're doing community service in their own garden.

She watches Stanley answer his phone. Some girl probably. Pretty and thin.

She takes Arthur's iPad from the desk, opens Safari and types five words into Google: *Jackson Townhouse Crossley Street gay*. She heard about this bar years ago, back when it had a rainbow flag in the window—is it still a gay bar? Do gay bars actually exist in this day and age or have they been phased out, integrated, assimilated into the postmodern homogeneous world, local and global, all of us in touch all the time on a shifting spectrum? She would like to ask Kristin but it's too soon for that. So she types *Jackson Townhouse Crossley Street gay* into Google and reads the description on screen: *Drink and be merry with people not labels*. What on earth is *that* supposed to mean? Oh fuck it, she thinks. I'll go anyway. I'll take Beverley with me. Tomorrow night.

She types two more words into Google: *Alison Grabowski*.

In a few days from now, Sadie will watch Alison through a window, observing the changes in her appearance, wondering if she would recognize her if they collided in the street. But this evening she puts Arthur's iPad on his bed, leaving Alison's website to disappear as the device goes to sleep, and walks across the room, down the stairs, into the kitchen to see her sons.

"Your father's fine," she says, trying to look neutral and calm while glancing at the holdall on the floor, the one containing a little Buddha, a carriage clock, DVD box sets and a tiny jug from a Spanish market. "He's staying with a friend. He just needs some space, then he'll be back. All right? So you can stop worrying about everything."

Stanley puts his arm around her shoulder. "We know," he says.

"Sorry?"

"Gran just rang me. She wanted to know what Catrina was like."

"Oh for God's sake."

"Come on, Mum," Arthur says, his mouth full of ham and white bread. "Dish the dirt. Who the hell is Catrina?"

19

A STRANGE KIND OF MINI-BREAK

A camping trip. A mini-break. It begins like this.

Chicken and halloumi, cooking on a disposable barbecue as the daylight fades. Two gas lamps. Torches. Cautious laughter between two strangers. Wine that tastes of apples and sherbet.

She tells him about *The Awakening*, about Florence Cathcart and a little boy who was dead and alive, visible and hidden. He says sometimes I feel like that at home, like I'm there but not there, like no one really sees me. She says I've felt like that my whole life, like I'm hidden when I want to be seen, like I'm visible when I need to hide. He says that's sad, she says it's normal, he says that's sad, she says maybe. He gives the cat some leftover chicken. They unwrap two individual slices of cheesecake and eat them with plastic forks. Then the conversation stops.

"What was that?" Miriam says.

"What?"

"That sound?"

"I didn't hear anything."

"A twig cracking."

"Really?"

"Someone's out there."

"You hear all kinds of noises out here, don't worry."

"Don't worry?"

"Really, it's okay. I would've heard it too, wouldn't I?"

"You were talking."

"Do you want me to go and look?"

"I'm not sure."

"I'll go and look."

"No, don't go. We should probably stay together."

"Are you ever afraid in your house?" Ralph asks, which seems like a strange question. It feels like he is saying she is always afraid.

"Not since my mother died."

"Did she used to visit a lot?"

"We lived in the same house."

"Oh. And you were more afraid when she was alive?"

Too much too soon, Ralph. Stop being a shrink.

She nods. He says something to change the subject, something about his own mother, Brenda Swoon, who wears golfing trousers and spends ten minutes a day counting her blessings. They talk about Brenda, and Miriam drinks more wine, and she forgets about the sound of a twig cracking. They don't hear the footsteps, careful and slow, backing away through the darkness, backing away through the woods.

"Can you sing?" Ralph asks.

"I'm afraid not."

"Not even a little bit?"

"Listen to me," she whispers, which makes him blush.

"Sorry."

"It's all right."

"Can I say something that might sound a bit rude?"

"No."

"No?"

"If you like."

"I find it hard to understand, the whispering thing, because for me whispering's a real effort, it's hard to whisper for a long time, so wouldn't it be easier to speak normally?"

Easier? How little he knows. There is a gap between them, a knowledge gap. It makes her feel lonely. Words could bridge the gap but she doesn't know if her words would stick.

"Try, Miriam," says the unbroken one. Doll inside a doll. She is here, she is sober, she is pushing from within. "Tell him something else."

Like what?

"Tell him why you whisper."

Is she out of her mind?

I whisper therefore I am not told off.

I whisper therefore I am not an irritation.

I whisper therefore I am.

"Imagine you're a little boy," Miriam says.

He closes his eyes, which surprises her—she doesn't know that psychotherapists take visualization seriously.

"How old am I?" he says.

"Eight."

"Okay."

"If you speak, if you speak *normally*, you'll get hit with a cricket bat."

He opens his eyes, looks at her, closes them again.

"You'll get yelled at."

He exhales loudly for a long time.

"You'll get locked in your room without food and water. Or you'll have to drink your own urine."

His eyes are wide open, his forehead creased. "What?"

"At school they say cat got your tongue cat got your tongue, and still you don't speak because you're sure that she'll hear you. She always manages to hear you."

"I'm so sorry, Miriam."

Why do people say that when it wasn't their fault?

Holy moly.

Did those words just come out of her mouth?

She has never told anyone, not even Fenella.

"Holy moly," she whispers.

Ralph stands up and opens his arms. Without thinking about whether it's right or wrong, without worrying about the consequences, Miriam steps into them, he is a cave in the woods and he holds her in the dark, just holds her in the dark.

"This is a strange kind of mini-break," she says, pulling away, embarrassed.

"Why?"

"I don't know really. I've never had a mini-break, so I have nothing to compare it to."

"If I were a real man, I'd light a fire and play you a song. That's what you're supposed to do when you're camping, isn't it?"

"Go on then."

"I'm not sure how."

"I am."

"Are you?"

"Yep."

"Really?"

Miriam gathers wood, she asks if he has a penknife, some matches, a newspaper, and then she makes a stack, a crisscross-ing stack, it takes a long time, it's carefully built, and when she is finished she sets it alight and they watch it go up in flames.

"Well," Ralph says. "I'm impressed."

Miriam smiles. "And now I'd like my song," she says. "If that's all right."

He starts strumming 'Pills' by the Perishers, then realizes that it's probably too dark, too solemn, so he switches to 'Hello, Goodbye' instead. She mouths the words without making a sound, singing in the only way she knows how, and there's a lot of you say yes and I say no, and this is probably the most fun she has ever had with another person.

A twig cracks again, then another, but they are too busy singing as quietly and as loudly as they can to hear the cracking. Two sets of footsteps this time, meandering through the trees, coming closer.

"You're quite a good singer," Miriam says, holding her hands close to the fire.

"Thanks."

"Who taught you to play the guitar?"

"My dad taught me a bit, then I got lessons."

She nods, because she has seen other people do this—*nod nod nod, I'm listening, please go on.*

"So what do you do, Miriam?"

"What do I do?"

"For a living."

"For a living?"

"For money."

"I don't have to work at the moment. I inherited some money."

"Have you ever worked?"

"I worked in Morrisons for a bit," she says, "at the deli counter, you know, with all the cheeses and cold meats."

"Did you enjoy it?"

"I enjoyed the cheese."

"Did you eat it?"

"Absolutely not, but I spent a long time looking at it. Stilton's the best, mainly for its strength and blue veins. I like the way it's shaped like a cylinder, it reminds me of a felled tree."

Ralph refills her glass with wine and she sips it quickly.

"There was a lovely man behind the fish counter at Morrisons, people called him Crackhead but his name was Philippe."

"Crackhead?"

"There was a party one night after closing, and he headbutted a packet of Jacob's cream crackers."

"Why?"

"He was angry. He didn't know why. I liked him a lot. They made him pay for the crackers."

Was that an anecdote, Miriam? Are you telling stories like a *normal person?*

Miriam and Philippe. Philippe and Miriam. It was never going to happen, she knew it all along, but she couldn't stop watching his hands as he slapped the cod loins down onto ice, one loin after another, boneless and yellow. How can I help you madam, how can I help you sir, always with a smile, bright eyes, fishy fingers. He had worked at this branch of Morrisons for nine years, but really, underneath the white hat and coat, underneath the blue plastic gloves, Philippe was a world-famous wrestler. Or he would have been, if not for his father, a pacifist from Luton who hated his son's passion for wrestling and boxing and all things physical. You can't call it sport, his father said—it doesn't even come *close* to sport. So Philippe wrestled in secret at the back of Morrisons with David Flint, the assistant manager, and the staff gathered around to watch, putting bets on who would win, and it was always David, always David Flint. Flinty was a right-wing homosexual with a left-wing wife, and Philippe didn't have a snowball's chance in hell of beating him, not ever. Flinty's frustration could power an army, a tank, a submarine.

"You know the phrase *snowball's chance in hell*?" Miriam says.

"Yeah."

"I like the idea of a snowball in hell, thriving in the heat."

Her thoughts begin to drift.

I am the snowball. The snowball is me. It's a funny kind of reflection, but it's mine.

She drifts further back.

"None of us is what we think we are," said Frances to her daughter. "I know it, Mim, but no one will admit it. We are nothing but sights, sounds and sensations. There's no Mummy in my head and no Miriam in yours. You don't exist, I don't exist." She picked up a copy of *Charlotte's Web* and waved it in the air. "What's this?" she said.

"A book."

"A book of what?"

"It's about a girl and a spider and a pig."

"Is the girl real or fictional?"

"She's made up."

Frances whacked Miriam on the head with *Charlotte's Web*. For a small paperback it packed quite a punch. Miriam thought this was probably because the paperback had lived for a very long time. It cost 50p from Mr Garbon's second-hand bookshop and was previously owned by a woman who sold all her books to help pay for her wedding dress, which made this battered paperback very special indeed. According to Mr Garbon, it was a book that made love possible—a book to have and to hold from this day forward, for better for worse, for richer for poorer, in sickness and in health, to love and to cherish till death us do part. "I do," Miriam said, giggling, as she handed Mr Garbon 50p.

"Charlotte is as real as we are, you silly girl," said Frances. "The very *idea* of fact and fiction is preposterous. We make it up as we go along, *we are all made up*, do you understand, are you listening, can you hear me?"

The book came down hard a second time, then a third. Miriam imagined a spider and a pig inside it, jumping up and down in protest. They were on her side. Someone had to be.

Now Ralph is saying that one of his sons, the one called Arthur, should have taken up a sport like wrestling to channel his aggression. He is saying that maybe Arthur has some kind of food allergy, maybe that's what's causing his fatigue and hostility. Miriam is saying that she always feels a little anxious after eating pumpkin, but this could be something to do with Halloween and ghoulish associations. The wine that tastes of apples and sherbet keeps flowing. Miriam has never drunk this much so quickly. Ralph is topping up her glass and she is emptying it and he is topping it up and—

A suspicion comes and goes. If you were a man who wanted to take advantage of a woman in the woods, you *would* top up her glass, wouldn't you? No, of course not, you stupid woman. You'd just punch her, kick her, push her to the floor. You wouldn't go to the trouble of buying wine and cheesecake and cooking chicken out here, where no one is watching or listening, no one at all.

Apart from two men.

Two men who have been watching and listening but not hearing very much.

Two men who have been whispering to each other, using words like *you* and *when* and *maybe* and *dunno*.

20

B everley Smart opens her eyes. It takes a few seconds for her to realize that she is not in her own bed. So whose bed is this? She turns over. What? *HOW?* She looks under the duvet to confirm her suspicions—yes, she is naked. She is completely naked. And so is Sadie Swoon, who is lying beside her, snoring. She looks at Sadie's body—her breasts, her flat stomach, her narrow hips. *Bloody hell!*

She had arranged to pick Sadie up at seven o'clock. That was Plan A. But when you make plans with Sadie Swoon, you don't expect Plan A to be the whole story. Why? Because Sadie is flighty, changeable, some might call it *undependable*. So here comes Plan A, made verbally or on text, and just when you've started to make other plans around it, the telephone rings. "Actually, I was thinking that 7 p.m. isn't good for me. Can we make it 7.30? Fab. That's fab." So now we have Plan B. But hold on, what's this? Another phone call? Who can it be? "So sorry, I'm a complete idiot. Don't bother picking me up, I'll meet you instead. Is that *okay*? Let's say 8 p.m.

Do you know a place called Jackson Townhouse? I'll text you the address."

Plan C is good going. Once it went as far as Plan G. But where the hell is Jackson Townhouse? Is it a cocktail bar? Beverley hopes so, because she's dying for another banana daiquiri. Those things are addictive. Life feels better with a banana daiquiri in her hand. No, not just better—it feels *bearable*.

So here she is, sitting on a leather sofa, drinking a glass of white wine in the Jackson Townhouse, where they only sell cocktails on a Thursday.

"Why do you only sell cocktails on a Thursday?" she asks.

"Because Thursday is cocktail night," the barman says. His manner is acerbic, his hair is a mighty quiff. "Three pounds each and they're all you can buy."

"No other drinks at all?"

He shakes his head. "Best cocktails in town. Things taste better when you've had to wait for them."

Do they? Beverley isn't so sure. What about the anticlimax? What about delayed gratification that's been completely mistimed, the delay lasting too long, resulting in a loss of appetite? He is talking to an expert here. Beverley's *Mastermind* specialist subject would be Waiting For Things That Do Not Come.

As the barman turns to use the till, Beverley notices that he has no hair at all apart from the quiff. It springs up out of nowhere, a white wave, unexpected.

Sadie is late. No surprise there. She hates tardiness in others, yet she is always late. Beverley heads towards an unoccupied sofa in the corner and watches two men kissing beside a pool table. How lovely, she thinks. The men spot her watching and she looks away.

"Oh my God, I'm so sorry I'm late. I got a taxi. The traffic was dreadful. What on earth's going on with the weather? Did you hear the rain last night? The streets in town are just waterlogged. *Totally* waterlogged. I had to borrow Ralph's umbrella. Look at this thing, it's hideous. Who would buy a *brown* umbrella? What are you drinking? Shall I get you another drink?"

Whirlwind. Tornado. Dressed in the skinniest jeans Beverley has ever seen. How did she even get inside them? *Mutton* springs to mind, and Beverley's hand instinctively rushes to her mouth as if the word might otherwise burst out. She isn't proud of her bitchy streak; it used to amuse her, but now it mainly feels cruel and shameful, like a habit she can't quite break. She had some counselling once, to deal with this problem, an issue that can only be described as *mushrooming anger*—the kind that springs from the most concealed of beginnings, pops up from life's undergrowth, spreads and spreads like fungi—and it emerged during this counselling (yes, just like that, no one saw it coming, it was *amazing*) that her bitchiness was a kind of inflation, a rancorous *puffing up* when she felt insecure or diminished. *So how do I stop this happening, counsellor?* Well, Beverley, this mushrooming anger is just a smokescreen. *Really?* Yes. What you need to do is address the diminishment, otherwise you'll keep puffing up.

ADDRESS THE DIMINISHMENT. DO NOT PUFF UP!

While Sadie is at the bar, Beverley's forehead tightens, creating an unforeseen world of wrinkles as she tries to restrain her bitchiness. She draws two equations on a blackboard in her mind. Bev sees friend in skinniest jeans ever + Bev feels fat and frumpy in comparison = diminishment. Mutton dressed as lamb = bitchy thought = a way to turn friend into an idiot = also a way to turn Bev into smug person who dresses appropriately for her age = puffing. If only the counsellor could see her now! But she can't, because she moved to Nashville, which made Beverley gulp and cry and say *you are a disgrace to your profession.*

Sadie is on her way back now, holding two large glasses of wine. She stops to speak to a group of young women, then slides onto the sofa beside Beverley. "Those girls," she says, "gave me this." She puts a leaflet on Beverley's lap.

"No, I don't think so."

"Why not?"

"I'm not going to a pole-dancing night."

"Too late," Sadie says, pointing at the leaflet. "It's tonight."

"What?"

"Downstairs, apparently."

"Absolutely not. What's going on with you?"

"What do you mean?"

"Is this because I saw Ralph with a woman?"

Sadie is about to answer when she hears squeals from the other side of the bar. Muffled voices.

"Dear God!"

The lights have gone out. The music has stopped.

"It's all right everyone, just stay where you are," says the man with the mighty quiff. He is waving his arms around but no one can see him waving. "It's a power cut. Looks like the whole street is out. We lost power last night too, but only for an hour. Don't panic!"

Darkness. Giggling. Voices louder now, even though the music has stopped and it's easier to be heard. A frisson of excitement. Contagious childishness. Everyone feels less alone.

A light comes on in Sadie's hand as she begins to tap on her phone.

Sadie Swoon @SadieLPeterson
Lights have gone out in Jackson Townhouse! Bev and I are in the dark

There are other lights too. Hands illuminated by smartphones.

"It's all right everyone, just sit tight," says Mr Mighty Quiff. He dashes from table to table with a tray of lit candles, saying "time to get romantic" over and over like a creepy pre-programmed robot.

"It's the weather," Beverley says.

"Yes," Sadie says, without looking up. She is summoning the attention of followers with her fingers.

Then there are drinks. Free drinks. To say thank you for sticking it out, thank you for not leaving. Such community spirit! We don't have music or a working till, but we have atmospheric lighting and free drinks and just listen to the rain, have you ever heard rain like this?

Sadie is laughing. She is enjoying this small drama about weather and electricity, revelling in the melodrama on Twitter, the #freaksummerstorm flurry of activity. What did people do during blackouts in the time before smartphones (BS)?

Beverley has other matters on her mind: cocktails. She is sauntering through the darkness, destination Mr Mighty Quiff, and when she reaches him she puts on her best flirty voice: "You're doing a marvellous job."

"Why thank you, dear. I've always been good in a crisis."

"Shall I give you a hand?"

"Really?"

"I'd be happy to."

"Have you ever worked behind a bar?"

"Of course. Who hasn't?" (She hasn't, actually, but this is an emergency. Time to *pull together*.)

"I'm Dylan," he says, holding out his hand. "Fancy a rum and Coke?"

"Don't mind if I do."

Mark Williams @markwills249
@SadieLPeterson need me to come and save you Mrs S?

Kristin Hart @craftyKH
@SadieLPeterson Jackson Townhouse? Seriously?

Marcus Andrews @MAthebakerboy
@SadieLPeterson *waves* we're not far from you—Fungs
noodle bar #tryusingchopsticksinthedark

Jilly Perkins @JillyBPerks
@SadieLPeterson Where is your husband?

Lucinda Demick @LuciBDemick
@SadieLPeterson cellar is flooding. We're consoling
ourselves with Courvoisier #freaksummerstorm

Beverley and Dylan have come up with an idea, and this idea is called Prosecco. Glasses and glasses of it, being passed around on a tray. "Can I interest you in something fizzy?" he says. "A lovely glass of Prosecco on the house?" she says. Sadie is so busy typing that she doesn't even recognize Beverley's voice. She nods and mutters and takes a glass. Beverley doesn't care. She is buzzing with camaraderie, revelling in the joy of an evening interrupted. Normal service will be resumed soon, but how wonderful, just for a while, to be snapped out of the daze, the stupor of consciousness, the trance of breakfast lunch and dinner (breakfast lunch and supper if you're Sadie Swoon). The on and on. Every working day spent driving around in a black Mini with the words GEORGE MICHAEL ESTATE AGENTS on the side. Beverley hadn't planned to be an estate agent. She always wanted to be a cartoonist like Chris Ware,

Alison Bechdel or Simone Lia, and write a graphic novel about love and aloneness and the futile nature of existence. But her mother got ill. Her father moved to LA with a thirty-year-old. Forget art college, life said. You need to get a job, otherwise your mother will die alone and you will spend your entire life choosing the wrong kind of lovers to assuage your guilt. *And if I get a job and look after Mum, what kind of lovers will I choose then?* Still the wrong kind, but at least your mother will be able to meet them.

Tonight, however, Beverley Smart is not an estate agent. She is a barmaid, swigging Prosecco from the bottle while Dylan's back is turned. An hour later, she sways across the bar and puts her arm around Sadie Swoon. "What's wrong? Why are you crying?"

"I'm not crying."

"Are you sure? Did those girls upset you?"

By *girls* she means the women who are two years younger than they are, who shop in Superdry and have messy haircuts. They were just talking to Sadie, asking about the nearest Indian restaurant and whether she might like to join them.

"What girls?"

"The ones you were sitting with."

"My phone's gone off."

Silence. Is *that* why she's upset?

"It's never happened to me before."

"What hasn't?"

"The battery just died."

Beverley looks into Sadie's eyes. She sees fear. Distress. Over a dead battery? "Come downstairs," she slurs, holding out her hand.

"What for?"

"Pole dancing."

"In the dark?"

"They have candles."

"Isn't that dangerous?"

"Come on. You wanted to go, didn't you?"

"You can't dance without music."

"They have a ghetto blaster. Now *come on*."

Sadie's face brightens. She takes hold of Beverley's hand. Beverley Smart, the straightest woman she knows, inviting her to pole dance. The room is spinning as she gets pulled through it, and now they are downstairs, where everyone is doing it with everyone else.

"What?" Beverley shouts.

"I said this is brilliant."

"Fuckingwell is."

"It's my first time." Sadie laughs. It's a dirty laugh. Sid James.

Thankfully, there are no professional pole dancers here to witness this. A room full of inelegant legs twisting around poles, bodies swinging round and around, rubbing up and down, mouths opening to release the words *look at me—sexy!* Mock erotic. Urban abandonment. A spoof. Liberation. Free alcohol. Dance music from a 1997 ghetto blaster. *We have no electricity! Look at us—we're fucking pole dancers, that's what we are.*

Dylan can't remember a better night than this. A night when people were so uninhibited, so open. This bar doesn't usually know what it is. It caters for everyone and no one. It gets it wrong. But not tonight. The front door is locked, nobody can get in or out, the roof is leaking and he's dancing topless with a woman called Bernadette who is fully clothed, looks like Penélope Cruz and calls him Deelaan. *I like your little quiff, Deelaan. I like the way you dance, Deelaan.*

Sadie wants to take a photo of all this and post it to Instagram. She wants to text and tweet. What's the point of an experience if you can't share it? If you can't tell other people what's going on?

"Just let it go," Beverley shouts, grabbing Sadie's hands.

Let it go? Is Beverley some kind of mind reader? What else does she know?

They break away from the crowd and dance by themselves. Sadie closes her eyes. She thinks of Alison Grabowski, eighteen years ago, Friday nights in the student-union bar, indie night, dancing in each other's arms, the snakebite and black giving them permission to act like lovers, and when they left the bar they would no longer act like lovers. The oscillation between gain and loss: intoxicating, wonderful, unbearable.

What is this, some kind of mid-life crisis?

No, it's not a mid-life crisis. It's the feverish prelude to divorce. The undoing of what was too quickly sewn up. The unmaking of a promise. Deconstruct and demolish. Wrestle your way out of one life and into another.

Beverley is smiling inanely and swaying from side to side. She sees Sadie open her eyes. Now Sadie is smiling too, there is hunger in her smile, it's a smile Beverley hasn't seen before, not on her friend anyway, not on Sadie Swoon, who leans in close, touches her face, kisses her. Now they have both closed their eyes, they are kissing and kissing and when Sadie breaks the kiss she says the word *taxi*. Now they are kissing in the back of a car, the driver is watching them in his rear-view mirror and he wants to laugh, he wants to say blimey but he sits in silence and drives. Now they are kissing in a hallway, on a staircase, on a landing, in a bedroom, in a king-size bed. Sadie kisses Alison, she moves up and over her and then back down, taking it all in. No, not Alison. Beverley Smart. She hears Alison gasp, Alison Grabowski, here in her bed, doing what should have been done, making it all right, those losses and gains, the excruciating oscillation, the things they missed out on.

Beverley wonders what time it is. Have they slept through half the morning? And what's *that* on her arm? One word, written in black pen: ACQUIESCENCE. She tries to rub it off but the letters stay in place. Did she write it herself with some kind of permanent marker? Did Sadie write it? She can't remember this or anything else from the night before. Maybe they got drunk and collapsed. They must have undressed first, probably squealing like teenagers, laughing at their nakedness.

Sadie stirs beside her. Beverley pulls the duvet up to her chin, waits for Sadie's eyes to open, says well fancy waking up here of all places, how much did we drink, do you think it's finally stopped raining?

21

T wo men, watching and listening, whispering words like *you* and *when* and *maybe* and *dunno*. The men are in their twenties. Their hairstyles are heavily worked, excessively gelled affairs, swishing this way and that way like hair sculptures, super-thin matches leaning left and right, glued to impress, intended to remain in place until head hits pillow and the sculpture flattens into a dusty chaos. One man is wearing white Adidas trainers with three blue stripes, skinny red chinos, a royal-blue jumper. The other is in black jeans, a white long-sleeved T-shirt, an olive-green gilet. They are young and tense and impatient. They are *livid*.

"Do you think they've nicked them?"

"Bloody hope not."

"How do we play this?"

"Depends what they're like. Can't pre-plan it."

"Bloody hell."

"I know."

"This is your fault."

"Bollocks is it. You left them here."

"Not on purpose."

"Do you reckon they're having an affair or what?"

Miriam's fire is dwindling. Ralph is too busy talking to notice. Dying light, tiredness setting in, it can only mean one thing— time for bed. But *which* bed? Miriam's thoughts turn to practicalities and bodies and terrifying awkwardness. A man, a woman, a wooden floor. Oh dear God!

Ralph is still talking about his son, Arthur, who takes after Sadie in so many ways, what with his temper and discontentment. Miriam is saying right, oh right, he sounds a bit *difficult*. She thinks about running, but heading through the woods in the dark is not an inviting prospect. Who knows what's out there? Once again there is nowhere to turn. It feels horribly familiar but it also feels different—a tiny bit exciting. Miriam can't contain excitement, she isn't used to it, it races all over her, makes her arms and feet itch.

"Stan's more like me, I think," he says, rubbing his hands together. "He's easier to please."

Seriously, Ralph? You think you're easy to please? All you and Stan have in common is tidiness and excellent personal hygiene. Try harder, Ralph. Keep looking for yourself.

He glances at the sky. When he was a boy, his mother told him that every star made a different sound and when the moon was full, if you listened carefully, you could hear a big band, a raucous symphony, a love song. Brenda was drunk when she said this, drunk on Babycham (the happiest drink in the world, it says so on the label), and Frank had listened with amusement after six pints of Guinness and two packets of pork scratchings. They were celebrating again. It was their anniversary. They were checking on their son after an evening in the Bell. The stars were playing cellos and violins, piccolos and harps, an oboe and a double bass—all for the moon, *the swooning moon.*

"Swooning moon?" Frank said later, as he snuggled up to his wife beneath their new feather duvet, bought from Tilly's bedding stall at the market. ("This new duvet's my pride and joy," Brenda had said, feeling like she'd made it to the top of a small mountain from which everything looked brighter and less daunting. "Tilly says it contains the feathers of more than five hundred ducks. Can you feel how heavy it is? Feel it, Frank. *Feel it.*")

"I came over all fanciful," she slurred, stroking his stubbly cheek.

"You're a poet."

"Don't I know it."

"You always show it."

Brenda tried to think of another line, but it's hard to come up with poetry when your husband has lifted up your nightie, your brand-new nightie, Cadbury purple, made of silk, bought in the BHS sale especially for your anniversary.

"Well *Mr Swoon*," she said.

"Swoon by name, Swoon by nature," he said, kissing her neck.

Ralph could hear them in the night, talking and laughing and making other kinds of noises. He looked out of his bedroom window and pictured a star playing the drums like Animal from *The Muppets.* It sounded good. He picked up two pencils and played along with Animal on the windowsill until his mother burst in, rosy and dishevelled, and took the pencils away. When she had gone, he got back into bed and pulled the duvet over his head. He could still hear them laughing. Their great romance, always on show. He found it embarrassing. It made him blush. His friends' parents were irritable and tired, which was easier to be around—he could do his own thing, he didn't have to be happy.

(The hefty shadows of other people.)

(A boy who just wanted to plant seeds.)

Tonight, in the woods, Ralph leans back and props himself up on his elbows. He looks at the silhouette of branches against the night sky.

Then he sees two figures.

Two figures coming through the trees.

Walking towards them.

Throwing torchlight all over his face and body.

Throwing torchlight all over Miriam.

Bastards.

How dare they?

Ralph and Miriam are torchlit.

Trapped.

Fuck.

Miriam gasps.

"It's all right," Ralph says, standing up. "It's all right."

Is it?

Careless words. Automatic. Placatory.

The figures are men. This much is obvious in the light of the gas lamps and the full moon. Ralph's own torch is a few metres away. He can see it on the floor (small, silver, out of reach). *The Road* by Cormac McCarthy, Ralph's favourite book, flashes through his mind. He thinks of the father and the boy, listening out for strangers in the night, strangers who want to steal their food and cut the stringy meat from their bones.

"Hey there," says one of the men, the one in red trousers (let's call him Red).

"How are you doing?" says the other, the one in the green gilet (let's call him Green).

"All right," Ralph says, trying to sound confident.

Miriam just stands there, stiff as an exclamation mark.

"Don't worry, we're not staying," Red says.

"We think you might have some stuff that belongs to us," Green says.

"What stuff?"

"Three little tins."

"We left them in the cabin."

The cabin? Ralph hasn't been thinking of it as a *cabin*. It's more of a hut really. A flimsy old shed. A cabin sounds too purposeful, too inhabitable.

The men walk over to it and open the door. They disappear inside, bouncing torchlight around the walls and the floor. Ralph and Miriam wait. They listen to the mumbling and the restlessness, a two-man chorus of disgruntlement. Red and Green (*should never be seen*) are not happy.

"Do you have the tins?" Miriam whispers.

Ralph shakes his head. "I remember seeing them."

"Where are they?"

"I don't know."

"Did you put them somewhere?"

He tries to think. Yes, there were three tins. They were on the floor when he arrived. Small, faded, probably quite old, the kind of thing Sadie would buy online from a website specializing in "retro & vintage"—modern reproductions of household objects from the Fifties and Sixties, expensive tat. Come on, Ralph, what did you do with the tins? *I picked them up while tidying the place—that's what I did. Just before feeding Treacle for the first time. Are you sure? Yes, I'm sure, I can remember doing it.* So they must still be in there, right?

Wrong.

Oh Ralph!

Red and Green emerge from the shed, swinging their big-man torches (shock-proof, rain-resistant—truncheons with bulbs, basically, and much *manlier* than their old torches, which were palm-sized, wind-up, shaped like penguins). They stole the torches from their local camping shop last week, because why spend money when you can get it for free? This is their motto, their mantra, and sometimes Green turns it into a little ditty, sings it like it's a slogan in an advert about small crime (harmless) and real crime (capitalism).

"We have a problem," Red says, shining his torch into Ralph's eyes.

"No tins," Green says.

"So where are they?"

After all the wine this evening, Miriam's bladder feels like it's about to burst. But this is not the time to go, and it's not the time to cry either, she knows it's not, so she stands up straight and looks into the light.

"I'm not too sure," Ralph says.

"You're *not too sure?*" Red says, mocking Ralph's voice. He looks at Green, who knows what the look means. They've been friends long enough to read the signal for *let's do this, let's have some fun.*

"You two an item or what?" Green says.

"I don't think that's any of your business," Ralph says.

"Oh really? You don't feel inclined to answer a polite question, is that what you're saying?"

"Well, I—"

Red looks Ralph up and down. "I don't like you very much," he says, taking a step closer, then another.

"Stop," Miriam whispers.

"What?"

"He hasn't taken your tins."

Green looks bemused. "What's wrong with *her*?" he says. "Why's she speaking funny?"

"She said I haven't taken them."

Red belches. They all look at him. Miriam looks at the floor. She feels Green's words climbing into her ears, tiny word-worms—*what's wrong with her what's wrong with her*—slithering along, oily. She forgets about her bladder. She forgets that she is afraid. A wild fury rises against Green's words, washing them out of her ears. She clenches her fists.

"I'm crazy," she whispers.

Ralph catches her eye.

"You're fucking creepy," Green says.

"Do you know what we're doing out here?" Miriam whispers. "We're hiding. Because of what we did."

Red and Green exchange glances. Maybe these freaks are more trouble than they're worth. They just want their tins. Or, to be precise, what's *inside* the tins: six bags of pills and an engagement ring.

"Just give us the tins," Red says, staring at Miriam.

"I'll need to look for them," Ralph says.

"So you *have* seen them?"

"I remember seeing them, but I had a bit of a tidy-up."

Red grimaces. What kind of man has a tidy-up in the woods? This guy needs messing up, would probably do him good. Better be quick though, there's a party to get to, goods to deliver, a woman to propose to with a stolen ring. The woman's name is Janie. She is Welsh. She earns good honest money from squeez-ing women's breasts into a machine that takes a photograph of their internal worlds. *What's the bloody word for it?* Red grits his teeth. *Come on, you've said it a thousand times.* The effort of thinking makes him belch again, which seems to release the word from its hiding place. (Imagine what would happen if neuroscientists discovered a connection between semantic memory and burping. The sales of carbonated drinks would rocket. People with murky minds would rub one another's backs until every trapped word burst up and out.) "Mammogram," Red announces. Why can he never retain that word? It drives Janie mad. She slapped him once when he couldn't remember. She slapped his face and called him stunted.

"You got Tourette's?" Green says to his friend.

"I'll just grab my torch," Ralph says, edging forwards. He picks up the torch and switches it on. It's not a big-man torch. It's not a truncheon with a bulb.

Red rolls his eyes. "Here, use this." He holds out his torch.

"This one's fine," Ralph says, with a supercilious smirk. (Why choose a 4x4 when you have a perfectly sufficient Volkswagen Polo?)

Red didn't like that. He didn't like the smirk. If Janie stuffed it into the mammography machine (*woohoo! How's that for a memory, eh, Janie? No link between cannabis and memory loss at all, see? I hate to say I told you so*) and took a photograph of its internal world, she would find it jam-packed with condescension, and if she squeezed it, really tightened the machine's grip, it would all come oozing out—lashings of condescension jam.

Snooty fucker, turning down my supertastic torch.

"I'll help," Miriam says, picking up the gas lamp.

"No, you can stay here."

"She's got better eyesight than me," Ralph says.

"It's not like you're looking for a needle in a haystack."

"How quickly do you want to find these tins?"

Green sighs. "Fine."

Inside the shed, Miriam whispers her plan into Ralph's ear. "If we don't find the tins, I'll freak out, okay? I'll howl like a banshee. I'll turn feral. They won't stick around. No man wants his eyes scratched out."

He isn't sure how to respond to this.

They pick things up and look underneath them. Nothing under the sleeping bag. Nothing on the floor or buried in the pile of sheets. Ralph checks the pockets of his rucksack, which feels completely pointless, because he would never have put the tins in his bag, especially without opening them to see what was inside.

"Oh, hold on," he says, flinching as he straightens his back. Sleeping on a hard floor for three nights has taken its toll. "The bucket."

"The toilet bucket?" (Miriam has already familiarized herself with the blue plastic toilet.)

"No, there's another one. I tidied some stuff into it, mainly bits and bobs. I like things to be in one place," he says, as though she has demanded an explanation.

Now he is outside again, with Miriam close behind, with Red and Green watching as he picks up a bucket and emp-ties its contents onto the floor: matches, travel tissues, food wrappers, disposable coffee cups, plastic cutlery, a guitar pick, a pair of headphones, four screwed-up carrier bags, a biro, three metal tins.

"Hallefuckinlujah," Red says.

"Check inside them before you say that," Green says.

"Good point."

"All present and correct?" Green asks, as Red opens the tins one by one.

"All good."

"Well, I'd like to say it's been a pleasure," Green says, pushing his hands deep inside the pockets of his jeans, "but it's been a royal pain in the arse." He turns to go. "Come on," he says.

But Red isn't moving. He is glaring at Ralph. "Hold on," he says.

Ralph knows what's coming. It's obvious, isn't it? Here we go—a man's fist, or feet, God knows what else.

"Goodbye," Miriam whispers.

Red looks at her. *Weirdo.* He looks at Green, can't read his face. What is his friend trying to say? Closed mouth, tight lips, something like a sneer but it's not a sneer. He looks a bit ill, is that what he's trying to say?

Red has never seen apprehension on Green before, only on other people. He is lost. He needs to find Janie. *Enough.*

"Goodbye freaks," he says.

Ralph cups his hands over his mouth. "Well blow me," he says, as the men disappear into the darkness.

Miriam grabs the bucket and toilet roll and hides behind the shed.

And that's when it hits him. How fragile they are out here in the woods. How *exposed.* The violence and indignities they could suffer. But is anywhere really safe? Ralph thinks of his house, how simple it would be to break in. The only difference between the woods and the house is timing. He thinks of Julie Parsley: right woman, wrong time? He pictures Sadie, Arthur and Stanley, sleeping in their beds. Hopes they are all right. Switches on his phone.

Jesus Christ, how many texts? The phone beeps and vibrates as Sadie's vitriol floods into it. This level of toxicity could make a device explode. She has threatened to leave him if he doesn't text back—how arrogant, when he has already left *her.* He doesn't want to respond. He wants to leave her to poach in her own vitriolic juices, stew in her own bitterness, text and tweet and blog herself stupid. NO COMMENT, SADIE. His sons, however, are another matter.

—Hi Stan. Just a quick text to say I'm staying with a col-
league. Mum & I not getting on too well. No need to worry
will see you soon. Text if you need me. Poor reception so
best not call. Love Dad xx

—About time dad! Are you leaving mum for Catrina?

—Who is Catrina?

—Oh come on. Mum says you're with Catrina

—I don't know anyone called Catrina. Are you & Arthur OK?

—We're fine but mum being weird

—In what way?

—Drunk, smoking, threw dvds out of window

—Tell her to grow up x

—When are you coming home?

—Soon x

He pours water into a paper cup and brushes his teeth. He
hums 'Good Feeling' by the Violent Femmes, not because he
is cheerful and feels like humming, but because he is nervous,
jittery, full of adrenalin. He is thinking about Miriam and her
plan to freak out and go feral. *No man wants his eyes scratched
out.* Was she speaking from experience? Is this something she
does on a regular basis? Was he safer when Red and Green
were still here? *Please God don't let her take my eyes.*

Treacle brushes against Ralph's legs. He picks her up and
holds her against his chest. Miriam appears, carrying an empty
bucket. She places it on the floor and stands there, fiddling
with her hands. The feral woman has been replaced by a girl,
her eyes sad and dull.

"Are you tired?" he asks.

"Exhausted."

"Shall we try and get some sleep?"

"Okay."

Old sheets on a cold floor. A single sleeping bag, unzipped and open to cover them up. Her pillow, a squashed rucksack. His pillow, a leather bag and folded cardigan. In the corner, on a chair, propped against four cans of pilchards, a torch points at the roof.

A chattering bat launches itself into the air from a wood-pecker hole in a beech tree. It shrieks, flaps its webbed wings, emits an ultrasonic sound, inaudible to the human ear. *Echolocation.* The sound travels, ricochets off the environment and bounces back, a message in an echo, informing the bat about its position and prey. A second bat peers out from the woodpecker hole before soaring into the darkness, closely followed by another.

The chattering, the shrieking, the silence that is not silent.

A helicopter circles overhead. Louder, closer; fading, almost gone; closer again. The circles tell us that something is missing, it is still out here, undiscovered.

A tawny owl bickers over boundaries with another tawny owl. Round face, feather and bristle, a symbol of wisdom with acute hearing and binocular vision. It strains to pick up the rustle of a mouse on the woodland floor and two seconds later, swallows it whole.

"Everything sounds louder from in here," Miriam whispers, not mentioning her rapid heartbeat or the whooshing in her ears. She has never done this before. Never been *in bed* with a man. Not that you can call this a proper bed—it's makeshift, pretend, and they are both fully dressed—but proper or not they are side by side, planning to sleep, and she can feel his arm against hers. When they speak, it will be pillow talk. It's improperly real, really improper.

"Miriam?" Ralph says.

"Yes?"

"I probably don't have any right to ask you this."

Oh God, this doesn't sound good.

"But, well, I'm just curious really I suppose."

"What about?"

"The feral thing."

"Feral thing?"

He pauses. How to say it? "When we were looking for the tins, you said you would freak out."

Yes I did, she thinks. I did say that. That's quite right. It was that feeling again, that *insidious* feeling. It happened again.

"It was quite an unusual thing to say," Ralph says, trying to lower his voice, wondering if she is finding it too abrasive. "The thing about scratching a man's eyes out."

There is an opening to another world. His words have carved the opening. Miriam can hear it in the distance, this other world: the buzz, the aliveness. There is a passage, a walkway, a crossing from one world to another. This is the intersectional moment. Take it or leave it, Miriam? Walk the same old path or do something different?

Why couldn't I just let it go? Ralph thinks. What's wrong with me? She was only trying to be helpful, to get us out of something—she tried to protect me, for goodness' sake. Maybe *I* should have said what she said. Me, turn feral? What a joke. I'm a weed. Too polite. Lying in a filthy old shed with a stranger, prying like a shrink. I'm not her shrink, though, am I? Maybe we could become friends. Why don't I have many friends? Would she care if she never saw me again?

Miriam loiters at the intersection. Ralph sits in his own world and turns himself into old rubbish. He advises his clients about this kind of thing, encourages them to notice the narratives they carry around, the way they diminish and judge themselves. The trick is to make the narrative conscious and explicit, that way you're observing it, you've bought yourself some distance. But Ralph can't master the trick. It's like juggling with three balls—some people can do it, some people can't. Ralph is no juggler. He has never been good with balls.

A passage, a walkway, a crossing. Hanging above its entrance, written in neon lights: WELCOME TO YOUR FUTURE (I'VE BEEN HERE ALL THE TIME). It looks like one of Tracey Emin's neon signs. Miriam *loves* Tracey Emin. She loves the bed, the tent, the monoprints, the needlework and neon. She loves how everything is autobiography, everything is a message. Tracey Emin is not buttoned up. Like Fenella, she is a beacon in Miriam's world, but a different kind of beacon. Tracey is a flare. A signal. And tonight that signal says GO, DO IT, TAKE THE RISK, GO ON, MAKE YOURSELF VULNERABLE.

"Ralph?"

"Yes?"

"I did turn feral once."

Ralph lies perfectly still.

"That's why I stayed in my house for three years."

"You don't have to tell me," he says, more for his sake than hers.

"I think I want to. You're easy to talk to."

"That's my downfall," he says.

"Oh," she says.

"Shall we have a cup of tea?"

"All right."

A kettle whistles on a tiny camping stove. Miriam is wearing a sleeping bag as a cloak. Ralph is wearing a cardigan as a scarf.

"People think I'm cuckoo," she says.

"I don't," he says.

"Don't you?"

"No."

"I bet I can change that."

"Go on then."

"Are you sitting comfortably?"

"Not really," he says, from a carrier bag on the floor. He crosses his legs. "But tell me anyway."

When Miriam's mother died, all that was found was a bowler hat, floating in the sea. Mad hatter. Jumped and didn't swim. Sank deep, dead weight.

A bystander spoke to the police: "I saw a woman in a tweed jacket and a black bowler hat. It looked like a long jump, it really did, quite peculiar to say the least. You can imagine someone standing at the edge and stepping off, but you don't expect to see a *long jump*."

Take a running jump.

Don't mind if I do.

Go on then.

Here I go. (Bye Miriam.)

Miriam lost many mothers that day. The mad one. The one who was sometimes nice. The one she loved, despite herself, and the one she hated. The one who provided a roof, water, food. The one who made her feel unsafe. And most devastating of all, the mother she never had—all hope of her, gone. The mothers had drowned, they were all underwater.

There was no body to cremate or bury. It was typical Frances Delaney, refusing to let anything be simple and clear. Her death is something Miriam has to believe in—an act of faith. Her absence requires as much effort as her presence. A sunken woman, mauled by sea creatures, her bones on the ocean floor. This woman couldn't tolerate her own company or the company of others. In its rare moments, her happiness was inconsolable. Joy was wretched. Only sadness and repulsion made her feel secure—they stood by her when she hit out at them, came back when she pushed them away.

There was a poorly attended memorial service. Later, a plaque—FRANCES DELANEY, LOST AT SEA—attached to a bench in the botanical gardens.

After the service, Miriam slept for nineteen hours. She was woken by Fenella, banging on the front door.

"Are you all right? I've been calling you," Fenella said.

"Sorry, I was asleep."

"I was worried."

"Why?"

"You looked terrible yesterday."

Fenella made tea while Miriam took a shower. She waited in the kitchen, expecting Frances to walk in at any moment. She opened the kitchen window, walked through to the front room and opened the windows in there too. This house needed fresh air. It wasn't dirty—no chance of that, thanks to Frances's obsession with cleanliness—but it felt grubby somehow. *Contaminated.*

Miriam strolled into the kitchen, drying her hair with a towel, wearing grey cords and a maroon long-sleeved top. She looked surprisingly fresh-faced.

"I thought I'd take you out for lunch," Fenella said. "Do you fancy walking to the pub? Are you up to it?"

"Of course."

This was day one of Fenella's Plan For Miriam: the PFM. Two copies had been typed, printed and laminated. Miriam's future was shiny and wipe-clean, sturdy as a place mat. It would involve regular meals, long walks and small talk with strangers. On a Wednesday evening, Miriam and Fenella would attend a pub quiz. On a Saturday morning, they would have coffee in town. Miriam would purchase things by herself, small at first, like a croissant or some daffodils, working her way up to jeans and skirts. There would be milestones and rewards. Yoga, perhaps. Or an art class at the local college. Miriam could write the words I AM NOT MY MOTHER in buttons, sewed onto a giant piece of material. They could go on holiday, somewhere slow and easy and hot, with nothing to do but sit by a pool, read books and drink gin. At the very bottom of the PFM, two words in red: *job, boyfriend.* Beneath them, Fenella had scribbled a protective afterthought: *but everything in its own time.*

At the pub, Fenella bought Miriam a cheddar and onionmarmalade sandwich, French fries, half a cider. She revealed the PFM while Miriam was eating.

"There's no pressure, honey," she said, holding a toastie in one hand as cheese dripped onto her plate. "I won't give you a hard time if you want to take it slow."

Miriam smiled. She didn't feel pressured. Fenella's patience was infinite and puzzling. She ate her sandwich, drank her cider.

"Blimey, someone's got an appetite."

She was clearly in shock or denial. It was obvious. Fenella made a mental note and decided not to mention it. Shock and denial usually passed of their own accord, didn't they? No need to add them to the plan (which would have been difficult, due to the lamination).

"I'm going to treat myself to a laminator," Fenella said, eyeing her A4 plans, flapping them about, admiring their stiffness. "You can use it whenever you like."

"Do you need one?"

"That's not the point, really. I want one. It's good to indulge yourself, honey. Every now and then. It's good to want things."

"Is it?"

After lunch, they stood outside the pub and Fenella squeezed Miriam so hard it hurt. "I've got to dash to Pilates. Shouldn't really eat that much before a class, but hey-ho. Will you be all right?"

"I think so."

"Give me a ring soon."

Fenella jogged ahead, turning and waving before disappearing from view. Miriam strolled through the field, thinking about what she had found in her mother's wardrobe two days ago: an old shoe box, with the words POISONOUS CLEANING PRODUCTS scribbled on the top. It didn't contain poisonous cleaning products. It contained five letters addressed to Miriam, letters from her grandmother that she had never been given. *Your letters sound a bit unusual, dear,* Granny had written. *Are you all right?* In with the letters, an order of service from the funeral of Betty Hopkins, who had died when Miriam was eleven.

She had not moved to Spain.

She had not grown tired of her granddaughter.

She had died.

Frances Delaney was evil.

I lied, Miriam. And you swallowed my lies. You are full of them and full of me.

I hope they pick at your flesh, Miriam thought.

I will swim through your days and all of your nights.

The sky had darkened while they were inside the pub and Miriam hadn't brought an umbrella or a coat. She quickened her pace, tried to avoid the cowpats, noticed a rabbit watching as she sprinted past. Just as she approached the kissing gate it began to rain. She stopped, looked up, closed her eyes. *Let it wash away. That's right, mother. All of it. This is Miriam speaking. Can you hear me? I don't know how to live without you, not because you are no longer here, but because you never let me live.* She ran her fingers through her wet hair, walked through the gate and on to the woodland path.

She heard footsteps behind her. Slow at first, then speeding up. A jogger, probably. About to run past.

No, not a jogger.

Miriam knew this because the feet stopped running when they were right behind her.

He put his arm around her neck.

No.

This can't be—

Dragged her backwards. His free hand was on her stomach, her arm, her shoulder.

He dragged her across the path and pushed her down onto her knees.

It all happened so fast, the tangle of limbs, the pushing and the pulling, her chest hurt, he gripped her wrist and wouldn't let go, he clamped her down, he was heavy, his hands all over her, pulling at her clothes until—

Miriam saw her mother, just standing there, watching.

Dripping wet.

Seaweed in her hair.

Wearing a tweed jacket, black trousers and a bowler hat.

The clothes she died in.

She was grinning.

A man on her daughter's back and she was grinning.

Mum?

Miriam screamed.

The first scream since she was a baby.

Clouds were torn by the sound. Sky full of rags. Stories split in two. Like the story of Miriam Delaney, which ruptured as her elbow hit him in the chest and her teeth broke the skin of his left hand. She pushed herself against him, a human arch, twisting her body around, flinging her arms in all directions until they were face to face.

Then she scratched him. She cut his face deep.

Somehow she was behind him then—how did that happen?—his hands were over his eyes, her arms were a shocking necklace, her body a trailing pendant as he staggered forwards, trying to shake her off, shouting "What the fuck? Are you crazy? What the fuck have you done to my eyes you stupid bitch."

As he span around, Miriam span with him.

You asked for this, you bastard. He asked for this, didn't he, Mum?

(No reply.)

Mum?

(No one there.)

Miriam let go. She fell to the floor.

The man—his bloody face, his streaming red eyes—ran towards the woods.

Miriam—her bloody nails, her grazed knees—ran in the opposite direction towards town. When she arrived at 7 Beckford Gardens she opened the front door, ran inside, slammed it shut, locked and bolted it and hid in the kitchen. She sat on the floor in the corner, facing the window, holding her knees up to her chest, shaking.

She stared at the rainbow. An incongruous sky, untimely and cartoonish.

She waited for someone to come.

(Futile, hopeless.)

"I'm so sorry, Miriam," Ralph says. He wants to hold her hand. "Did the police find him?"

"I didn't go to the police."

"Why not?"

"Don't you see?"

"See what?"

"I was vile."

"But—"

"You don't understand."

"He could've killed you."

She tightens her grip around the Starbucks mug. "I might have killed *him*."

"Miriam, he—"

"You don't know what happened. What happened *inside me*."

"You mean your survival instinct? Fight or flight?"

"I was dangerous. Mad. Like my mother."

Ralph rubs his face. He is frowning, distressed, confused. "*He* was dangerous."

Miriam exhales loudly. Why doesn't he understand what she is trying to say? "I saw her," she says.

"Sorry?"

"During the attack. I saw her."

Ralph puts his hand on Miriam's.

"She was smiling," she says.

"You've been through too much," he says.

"Too much for what? Nothing compared to what some people go through."

"Were you too frightened to go back outside?"

"No."

"No?"

"I wanted to keep people safe."

"Other people?"

"I couldn't trust myself around them. When I got home I felt nothing. And I mean for months. I felt *nothing*. It was weird, like I'd used up all my feelings at once."

Lightning.

Thunder.

"Shit," Ralph says, standing up.

They pick things up—bags, buckets, cups, a camping stove, a guitar, a sleeping bag, spoons, teabags, UHT milk—and put them inside the shed before it starts to rain, which it does in no time at all. Fat drops of rain, water bombs bursting, heavier than any rain over the past fourteen months (by morning it will be on the news: two months' worth of rain in one night and more to come this evening, or words to that effect, words about localized flooding, sandbags, communities pulling together, drains unable to cope, rivers rising, cities underwater, and it's all because of the jet stream, *we blame it on the jet stream*; words accompanied by shots of dogs swimming, residents sweeping sewage from their kitchens, an abandoned car that should never have been driven down that waterlogged street, pensioners being asked if they have ever seen anything like this before).

Where were *you* in the storm? The storm that lasted half the night before it fell silent, the storm that reappeared the following evening.

Tucked up in bed, of course. For the first part, at least. Where else would I have been? Not in a rickety old shed in the woods, with water coming in through the roof and the ill-fitting door.

"This isn't good," Ralph says, as water drips onto the sheet, the sleeping bag, their piled-up belongings.

They look at the roof, which is starting to bow under the pressure of this cloudburst, this deluge. Ralph grabs Treacle and holds her under his arm in case the roof collapses. He directs his torch at Miriam like a question.

"Okay," she says, pushing wet hair back from her face. "Would you like to come to my house?"

"Is that all right?"

"Yes. Let's pack up what you need and leave the rest."

"I don't need most of this stuff," he says. "Can I bring the cat?"

"Yes," she says, putting her bag across her shoulder, picking up Ralph's guitar, wondering what this man is going to make of 7 Beckford Gardens with its brown and orange carpet from 1973, its cuckoo clock from 1958, its life-size cardboard cut-out of Neil Armstrong.

With a rucksack, a guitar, a bag and a cat, Ralph and Miriam head through the woods, through the darkness, their feet splashing through puddles, their clothes soaked, a cat bouncing in Ralph's arms, their laughter turning manic as they struggle to see, their legs covered in mud as they slip and slide.

Ralph shouts OH MY GOD at the rain. Gargantuan words, wild and robust. He opens his mouth and they are launched at the world, just like that.

Miraculous, Miriam thinks. It's *miraculous*.

22

PLASTIC FRUIT

A pineapple, a bunch of grapes, a pear. Hanging from Betty Hopkins's Christmas tree. The tree was real, the fruit was not.

"We need some new decorations," Betty said to her daughter. "Would you like to choose them?"

"What's the point?"

"Your father's coming home soon. It'll brighten the place up."

Frances shrugged.

They were at the market. So far, they had bought a new cobweb brush and some dishcloths. Now they were at the Christmas stall, an impatient man was dressed as Santa, he said what can I get you, what do you want, how about some baubles, how about some tinsel.

"My daughter is about to choose some decorations," Betty said. She looked embarrassed. "Aren't you, dear?"

"I don't think she is," the man said.

"Please, Fran. Just pick something. *Now*."

"These," said Frances, pointing.

"Really? You like the plastic fruit?"

Then she walked away, leaving her mother at the stall, fiddling with her purse, trying to pay quickly, saying hold on dear I won't be a minute.

Little Fran Hopkins. Fran the man, the boys said. You look like a man with that hair. Cut it myself didn't I, bet *you've* never cut anything, no limits to what I can cut, come here, I'll cut you, I will, I can.

Sitting in a car park, aged thirteen. An older boy soon to arrive. Sleet blew sideways, hit her in the face. The boy said he loved her. Real love, that's what this is. Do I scare you? she said. 'Course not, he said. She was sore for days, the soreness was precious, he held her tight, he wouldn't let go.

After that, he didn't know her. Boys in blazers, sitting on a wall, smoky throats. Fuck off girl, why are you staring at *me?*

I ache all over, she said to her mother. My stomach hurts my head hurts you don't care about me I don't need you.

Betty told the doctor, she spoke of holes kicked in fences, hair cut off, arms cut up, sleeping always sleeping, impossible to comfort and there are boys, I'm sure there are boys, she's going to get pregnant, tell me what to do. Frances sat in silence. They looked at her. Is this correct, are there boys? he said. No, she said. Discipline, Mrs Hopkins, that's what I prescribe, that's what *this* girl needs. If she's broken your resolve perhaps someone can assist you, just for a while, until you feel better. May I ask about your husband? Betty said he's taken to working abroad, he's away such a lot, and who can blame him, poor man. You're not alone, Mrs Hopkins, the doctor said. Take these Valium, buy some magazines, but do address this urgently, your girl's running wild, adolescence needs curtailing, shall we say. The only thing that will heal *this* mind is punishment, you mark my words, you can trust me, please stop crying.

That night, Frances overheard a conversation:

"I'm at the end of my tether," her mother said. "It's like she's not even mine. She's beyond me, she really is. She's breaking my heart."

She had heard it all before:

I don't know what to do with you.

You've driven your father away, that's what you've done.

Why do you hate me?

I love you but—

You're too much for me.

You're impossible.

I love you but—

You're beyond me.

(Mum says I'm beyond her, which means she's far away from me, which means she can't reach me, which means I am alone.)

Finally, at the end of a line of boys, stood Eric Delaney. He fixed cars, wore overalls, carved pretty shapes from old wood.

"Do I scare you?" she said.

"I'm not scared," he said.

"Tell me everything will be all right."

"Everything will be all right."

She wanted to believe him.

She set out to test him.

She asked him to hold her tight.

23

THINGS YOU ARE NOT SUPPOSED TO SAY

Central heating. Food delivered at regular times in a cereal bowl. Soft carpet (brown and orange, garish to some and retro to others, depending on your position, your vantage point, your mood at the precise moment of looking, all of which is shifting, so the brown and orange carpet is a magic carpet, pre-existing and conjured up). What else? Don't get this cat started—her magnificent list could go on and on. There's a garden to prowl through. There's Ralph anxiously calling her name. There are floors and walls and ceilings, a woolly blanket, the joy of rubbing against human legs while human mouths open and close to exchange the details of domestic life. 7 Beckford Gardens—it's heaven, that's what it is. To a cat, if not a human.

Treacle is on the dining-room floor, rolling and stretching, playing with the tassels of a yellow cushion. Ralph and Miriam are sitting at the table, eating Heinz tomato soup from cereal bowls. They have just finished a game of Monopoly (Miriam was the dog, Ralph the car). The game took a long time because Miriam had no idea how to play it. Now Ralph is talking about the Internet.

"How do you find it all?" he says.

"Sorry?"

"Being online."

"I just use Google," she says.

"Are you on Facebook or Twitter or anything like that?"

"No."

"You have no online presence?"

Is he suggesting that she doesn't exist? Surely it's hard enough for people to establish an *offline* presence, let alone another kind? How many presences can one person have?

"No."

"Well good for you."

"Why is it?"

"Well played, that's all I'm saying."

"I didn't do it on purpose. I didn't *choose* anything."

"You're off-grid, Miriam. Totally off-grid."

"What?"

"No one can find you."

"I'm not sure that's true."

"Oh it is," he says. "It really is."

The business of daily life has clearly changed for *proper* people. Activities like eating and sleeping and taking a shower are now thought of as being offline, incommunicado, absent, AWOL.

"I'd like to be on a grid," she says. "*Someone's* grid."

"Well I envy you, I really do."

"You envy *me*?"

"You have your privacy."

"I have nothing."

"My wife thinks it's acceptable to put the details of our private life online, but how does that differ from writing it on paper and sticking it on a lamp post? I feel like a character in her online stories."

"I'm sorry your wife is crazy."

"I don't think she can be classed as *crazy*, Miriam."

"Do you think you might be partially responsible?"

"For what?"

"Her stories."

The cheek. The audacity! "What do you mean?"

"Well, sometimes I pretend to be a normal person so I feel like one."

"You *are* a normal person."

"Sometimes you have to fake something to make it real," she says, quoting the book Fenella lent her about staying sane in a mad world. This special method of being is called "acting as if you already possess what you desire". *Act as if you're confident and confidence will grow. Act as if you're happy and...* It's amateur dramatics. Self-help theatre.

"I'm not sure what you're suggesting," Ralph says.

"Well, she could be telling stories about a marriage to make it *feel* like a marriage."

Ralph stares at Miriam. She is erupting. There is no other word for it. The excitement of learning Monopoly has made her erupt and he liked her better before, when she was less confident.

(She is only acting *as if*, Ralph. She is *pretending* to be confident.)

Treacle spots Miriam's slippers, white and fluffy, twitching under the table, and prepares to pounce. Ralph says something about a woman called Parsley. He says that sometimes he wonders if he should have married Julie Parsley instead of Sadie. Miriam sneezes, then says that she has never had the opportunity to marry one person, let alone two, and thank goodness for that really, because she wouldn't know what to do with a person who kept returning to her. Your plate is full, she tells him, and yet you moan all the time.

"Do I?" he says.

"Yes," she says, then wonders if this observation is one of the things you are not supposed to say. There is a list of these things; people like Fenella are born with it inside them.

She looks at his face—yes, something has happened. He has altered. She assesses her options. She could slap his face. No, that's not acceptable, so how do people navigate their way through these things?

"Do you like Tracey Emin?" she asks, watching him finish his soup and sit upright in his chair. "I do. I'd like to make a big neon sign, just like one of hers, with the words *audible smog* in lights."

"Do you do that kind of thing?"

"What kind of thing?"

"Are you artistic?"

"I'm not sure I'm anything in particular."

"Of course you are. We're all something in particular, but how possible is it to *know* what that something is? That's the question."

It's *a* question, Miriam thinks. Not *the* question. And being with another person is so complicated and difficult and maybe it's not worth the effort.

In the garden next to Miriam's, Boo Hodgkinson reaches the top of his ladder and finds himself glancing, staring, *gawping* at Miriam Delaney. "Holy crumpets," he says. It's a good phrase, holy crumpets, and Boo has always liked it. Why? Because crumpets actually have holes in them. Unlike so many exclamations (You're joking! My God! Fuck me!), this one is loaded with truth. It is a statement of fact.

As he balances on his ladder, trying to get a good look at what's happening in Miriam's dining room, he remembers reading about a woman whose entire life was overshadowed by an acute fear of crumpets. She suffered from trypophobia, a fear of holes that appear in small clusters, which is sometimes known as repetitive-pattern phobia. After ten minutes of intense Googling, Boo discovered that it comes from the Greek word *trypo*, meaning drilling or punching holes, and *phobia*. He also discovered that thousands of people across the world are horrified and repulsed and existentially challenged by beehives, ant holes, pumice stones, honeycombs, coral, meat, wood, muffins and bundles of drinking straws.

Boo is supposed to be cleaning out his guttering. His home is not simply his castle, it is one of the great loves of his life. He adores every bit of it, from its tiny basement to its brand-new roof, its double-glazed windows to its double garage, its summerhouse to its front porch. So when there is a storm, a freak midsummer storm that batters his house and thrashes against it, Boo pulls his waterproof trousers up and over his red tracksuit bottoms, clicks his tool belt into place and heads into the garden to assess the damage. He rests the ladder against the wall, climbs to the top and peers into the guttering with great tenderness and concern. While he is up here, flicking clumps of moss onto the grass below, filling a tiny crack with sealant, he spots Miriam in her dining room. Oh what a lovely sight. But what is *that*? *Who* is that? A man? Surely not? He knows that Miriam left her house but he hadn't seen her return (*with a man*). This can't be right. She's an innocent, not a floozy. Maybe he's a handyman or a plumber or a man who came to read the gas meter (*who ended up playing Monopoly, Boo?*).

Oh no, she has seen him. She is waving. He smiles, waves back. He throws his hands up in the air, it's a gesture about the craziness of the storm and he knows she will understand, she will read him correctly. She is nodding now, he is holding up a lump of moss in a dramatic way as if it fell from the sky, and he can tell she understands, she is following what he's saying about the impact, the damage, the aftermath. They are talking without words, attending to what is broken.

Miriam steps away from the window. Boo climbs down the ladder and goes inside. He takes off his waterproof trousers, makes a coffee, walks through to his living room and sits in a chair by the window. He is hungry but he doesn't feel like eating, tired but he doesn't feel like sleeping. Seeing Miriam in her dining room with a man has changed the atmosphere of his day. He wonders if his latest herbal remedy—a natural antidote to anxiety, acronymically named Anata—is making him oversensitive. (Anata is still in its trial period, which basically means that Boo swigs it from the bottle twice a day and scribbles observations in a Moleskin notebook.)

He is looking out of the window, watching the cars drive along the waterlogged street, when he sees something. A boy. Running up to Miriam's front door.

The letterbox rattles and Miriam hopes it's what she thinks it is—not junk mail, not proper post, just an unsigned card from an unknown person. Yes, she thinks. Yes yes yes. She picks it up, reads it, shows it to her house guest. On the front, a photograph of a tree. On the back, written in turquoise ink:

AT THE MARKET EVERY SATURDAY: A TREE OF
SIMPLICITY. THERE'S ONE WITH YOUR NAME
ON IT, MIRIAM

"Who's it from?" Ralph says.

"I don't know."

"You don't know?"

"They just come through the door."

"They?"

"Would you like to see the others?"

On the front of every card, a photograph. On the back, handwritten in capital letters, a statement. Ralph flicks through them:

OPTING OUT IS BEAUTIFUL, OPTING IN IS DIVINE
(on the front, a photo of St Ives)

WHEN IT IS TIME YOU WILL FIND US
(photo of a dog with puppies)

BEING ALONE IS NOT COMPULSORY
(photo of a sculpture by Barbara Hepworth)

THERE ARE MANY LIVES TO LEAD
(photo of a city at night)

THIS CAN BE YOU WHEN YOU'RE READY
(photo of a woman holding a white and red
megaphone)

YOU COULD SIT AND READ A BOOK IN A CAFE,
MIRIAM. YOU COULD CYCLE THROUGH THE
STREETS WITH THE WIND IN YOUR HAIR
(photo of a bike against the wall of a French cafe)

WHEN SOMEONE SPEAKS LOUDLY, IT DOESN'T
MEAN THEY HAVE FOUND THEIR OWN VOICE
(photo of a black cat)

"And these were all hand-delivered?" Ralph says.

"Yep."

"And they haven't freaked you out?"

"Why would they?"

"If I got postcards from a stranger it would freak me out."

"I find them comforting."

An incredulous sniff.

"I like what they say," Miriam says.

Ralph flicks through the postcards a second time, as if this will somehow disclose a name and address. "We were just seconds away from seeing who delivered this," he says, waving the final card around.

"Never mind," Miriam says, taking it from his hand in case he bends it.

"You like getting these, don't you? You actually like it."

"I do."

There is a knock at the door. Ralph stands up as if it's his house, *his* door, then pauses. He watches Miriam open the front door and say hello to a man in a red tracksuit.

"I chased," the man says, shaking his head. He pants and wheezes as he tries to speak. "No good, no good." Boo looks down at his legs, oily water on red velour, sartorial tragedy. "Oh no," he says. "I got *splashed*."

"Ralph, this is Boo. He lives next door. He's the one I was waving at just now."

"You were up a ladder," Ralph says, eyeing the man's thick moustache.

"And this is Ralph," Miriam says. "I found him in the woods."

Boo feels a little woozy, which rhymes with floozy, which makes him think of Miriam doing God knows what with this man from the woods and he can't believe what it makes him feel—how *physical* it is, how *acidic*. "Do you have any Gaviscon?" he says.

"You'd better come in," Miriam says.

"There was a boy," Boo says.

"A boy?"

"I ran after him—thought he might be the one."

"He was."

"Was he?"

"Yes."

"You received another card?"

"I did."

Ralph watches as Miriam feeds her neighbour Gaviscon on a plastic spoon and shows him the latest card, the one about a tree of simplicity.

"This is an invitation," Boo says.

"Do you think so?"

"I do."

The postcard and the boy and Boo's dirty legs—it happens like this.

"So are you in or are you out?" Matthew says, standing by the door of the bedroom he shares with his brother.

"I'm too tired," Alfie says, from one of two single beds. He is propped up on three pillows, reading a magazine called *Doctor Who Adventures*.

"Why are you in my bed?"

"It's more comfy."

"How can it be?"

"Dunno, it just is."

Matthew closes the door and walks over to his bed. This doesn't take long because their room is small. In fact, the whole house is small. This two-bedroom Victorian terrace may have high ceilings, but its rooms make non-violent animal-loving people declare that there isn't enough space to swing a cat. (Even when there are thousands of ways to say it, ancient words still rise from our mouths. Are the words inside us or are we inside the words?)

"I'll pay you," Matthew says, sitting on the edge of the bed.

"How much?"

"Five quid."

"What if she sees me?"

"She hasn't seen you so far."

"Why don't you do it?"

"I'm six feet tall."

"So?"

"I'm twenty-one."

"So?"

"You're less visible."

"No I'm not."

Matthew snatches *Doctor Who Adventures* out of Alfie's hands. "Please," he says. "I'll give you a tenner and that's my final offer."

The boy's eyes light up. "Do you love her?"

"What?"

"Do you want to go out with her?"

"Of course not. One day I'll explain, okay?"

Alfie gets out of bed. He needs the money for an Amy Pond action figure to go with Doctor Who and River Song. He also wants a Tardis and an army of Daleks, but he knows that he has to stop somewhere because I want doesn't get, money doesn't grow on trees and his parents are not made of it. He puts on brown trousers, his new shirt, a bow tie and a tweed jacket. "Do I look like Doctor Who?" he says.

"You look like a proper Time Lord," Matthew says.

"Thanks. Can I borrow your hair wax?"

"If you're quick."

A young man and a seven-year-old boy, driving through town. They sing along to Oasis in fake Manchester accents, something about lights being blinding. The man laughs. The boy laughs. Then the car stops.

"I'll wait here," Matthew says, handing Alfie a postcard.

"What if she sees me?"

"Just say hello."

"Okay. Give me the tenner."

"You can have it when you get back."

"Now or never."

Matthew slaps a ten-pound note on the dashboard. "Go," he says.

Alfie climbs out, walks along the street, turns the corner and enters Beckford Gardens. He wanders up to the front door of number 7, almost slipping on the wet pavement. *I'm doing this for you, Amy Pond. Soon we'll be together. I'll rescue you from Toys R Us. No, I'm not buying a Rory figure. We don't need Rory.* Without bothering to look at the photo or what's written on the other side (he has given up trying to read these things—the previous ones made no sense), he opens the letterbox and pushes the postcard through it. He turns and walks away and there are footsteps behind him, footsteps moving quickly. He stops. It's a bright-red man. Running after him. Shouting "Wait, please wait!"

Alfie begins to run. Matthew spots him, he must have spotted the man too because he starts the engine, opens the passenger door and reverses the car. Alfie jumps in, he struggles to close the door as Matthew puts his foot down on the accelerator. A three-point turn in the middle of the street and they're facing in the right direction, facing the bright-red man, and they feel bad as they speed through a puddle, sending water up and over him.

"Sorry, sir," Matthew shouts. He closes the car window and turns left.

"This is a rescue mission," Alfie says.

"Maybe," Matthew says.

"No, it definitely is," Alfie says, as they head for Toys R Us. He pictures Amy Pond, all alone in a cardboard box with plastic windows. "She must get so lonely," he says.

"Yes," Matthew says.

24

IT DIDN'T, IT COULDN'T, IT MUST

S adie is on the verge of buying a tent. She doesn't need or
want a tent, and she is not aware that she is standing on a
verge. The idea of sleeping under polyester in the wild outdoors
is, quite frankly, preposterous. Why would anyone want to do
that? Hotels were invented for a reason. But sometimes a tent
is not a tent: it is a justification for being where you are—for
just happening (*how strange*) to be (*after all these years*) in a
particular (*oh God, is that her?*) spot.

The spot: Grab&Go Camping.

As in: Grabowski.

As in: Alison.

The woman who was going to live in Manhattan, walk her
small dog through Central Park, fall in love with someone who
liked street art, Japanese food, James Joyce. So what happened?
Bessie is what happened. Bessie Bryant. Otherwise known
as Elizabeth Jennifer Bryant. Lover of the great outdoors.
Professional camper. Bought Alison a pair of waterproof trousers
for their anniversary. Romance isn't dead, it's alive and well,
you just have to grab it—Grab&Go Camping!

Sadie peers through the window, looking for a woman in a Smiths T-shirt, suede jacket and black jeans, smoking a roll-up. There is no woman of that description here. Her stomach hurts. She has eaten too many Werther's Originals on the journey. She has skipped lunch too, which always makes her murderous or depressed. And she's nervous. Will it feel like seeing a ghost? Will her beaten-up love for Alison spring from its crookedness like an old wooden doll coming back to life? *Oh déjà vu. Scared of my feelings again. Déjà fucking vu! Might as well be at university. Have I learnt nothing?*

And then

oh God,

is that her?

Sadie presses her nose against the glass.

It is, isn't it?

She is not wearing a Smiths T-shirt, suede jacket, black jeans. She is not smoking a roll-up. She is blowing up an airbed. Kneeling on the floor, blowing. Her hair is different (straight bob). Her body is different (less curvy). She is wearing combat trousers (green, practical, hi-tech) and a grey short-sleeved shirt with a tiny cartoon bear on the front (probably a logo, possibly Canadian, unless it's a badge, and let's hope it isn't, because what kind of woman wears a badge like that?). She is blowing and blowing and a young man walks over, he laughs and says something and hands Alison what looks like a foot pump, which she connects to the airbed, and now she's standing upright, pumping air with her foot, and all that's left for Sadie to do is assess Alison Grabowski's bottom, which is still the same bottom and not the same bottom at all.

They are dancing to the Wonder Stuff. I'm so dizzy, my head is spinnin'. Alison is jumping around in a ropey kind of jumper, denim shorts, black leggings, cherry Doc Martens. Her name is not Alison, it's Allie. She is drunk and laughing and dancing to the Wonder Stuff with Sadie Peterson, who is here with Ralph Swoon, who is chivalrous and thoughtful but not Allie Grabowski. It has taken Sadie several months to realize that Ralph is not Allie, despite the obvious anatomical differences, their contrasting dreams for the future, the fact that one has a fondness for melodrama and the other for pot plants. She watches Allie dancing, thinks oh shit, I really want you, puts her hand on her stomach, starts to cry.

Sadie Peterson is pregnant.

"You'd actually marry him? Ralph Swoon?" Allie says, a week later, in the art gallery's vegetarian cafe. Her eyeliner is smudged. Her face is pale. She hasn't touched any of her houmous and pitta bread.

"What choice do I have?"

"Do you love him?"

"I think so."

"Well you'd better marry him then, hadn't you? You can buy a nice house in the suburbs."

"Don't be like that."

"Like what?"

"Jealous."

Allie tears her pitta bread and dunks it in the houmous. "I'm not *jealous*, I'm disappointed. There's a big difference."

"Is there?"

Oh for God's sake, just spit it out. Tell each other how you feel. Turn this around. Make plans that involve talking to Ralph, finishing your degrees, moving into a terraced house with a tiny garden, just the two of you, asking the grandparents to babysit, getting by somehow, finding a way to be two mothers to two children who also have a father, three grandmothers, three grandfathers.

Sadie leans forward and wipes houmous from the side of Allie's mouth. They sit in silence, listening to Kirsty MacColl, drinking Diet Coke, waiting for something to happen. Months pass and Sadie grows bigger and Ralph proposes and Sadie says yes. They sit and drink Diet Coke and wait for something to happen. The caffeinated twins become fidgety. Someone says those lads are gonna be footballers, just you wait. When they are born, Ralph cries and Sadie screams and Allie goes to the cinema alone to see a subtitled French film about death, where she meets a woman called Bessie, who is also alone.

"Are you sure it's me you want?" Bessie says, six months into their relationship.

"Why are you saying that?"

"I don't know."

"You must know."

"Well I don't, all right? I don't know why I just said that. Shall we go for a long walk?"

There is a limit to how long someone can stand outside a camping shop, peering through the window, without attracting attention or becoming self-conscious. Sadie has a growling stomach and a confusing appetite. Old passions are stirring, but are they just that—*old* passions? Two figures stand beside her: Yearning on the left, Wistfulness on the right. She is the jam in a nostalgia sandwich, looking through the window and aching for what has gone. It's a satisfying ache, which is curious, because the ache is a symptom of dissatisfaction. Paradoxical longing. What has gone is still here, but only because it was never here at all. Unrequited love: the love that goes on and on because it didn't, it couldn't, it must. Its existence thrives on non-existence.

Sadie opens the door and enters the shop. A bell rings. She

strolls in, head high. Marches past the woman blowing up an airbed. Marches until she arrives at a wide selection of tents, fully erect. Hears footsteps behind her. Rushes into one of the tents, a dome all set up and ready for two happy campers to crawl into after a hard day of (what, exactly? What do campers do? Sadie has no idea) being outdoors. The sleeping bags have frogs all over them, lime-green smiley frogs, sitting on a black background. Is this a *child's* tent?

"Can I help you at all?"

Here goes nothing. Sadie doesn't turn around. She wants to, but it doesn't happen. *Déjà vu...*

Silence. The smell of plastic and perfume and—

Sadie can feel the woman's presence behind her in the tent. She is just standing there saying nothing, which, Sadie decides, is a rather *invasive* approach for a salesperson to take: *I watch over you, I take over you.* Are they lyrics from a song? She can hear them being sung by a woman—is it Juliana Hatfield? She wonders if tents always feel this erotic (maybe *that's* where the phrase happy camper comes from) or if it's the sudden memory of walking into a bathroom and seeing Alison in the bath, surrounded by candles, reading D.H. Lawrence and listening to Juliana Hatfield.

"This one's on offer," the woman says.

Sadie turns around. She exhales. The exhalation lasts for ever. She has been holding her breath.

Raised eyebrows and an open mouth. Shock reddens the woman's cheeks. She blinks, just once. Then she says one word. This word was on her lips before it fell from her lips. She says *Sadie.* It is a question.

"Sadie?"

"Hello, Alison."

She says it again, as if the first answer wasn't good enough, as if this woman called Sadie can't hear her and isn't really this close, because how *can* she be this close? "Sadie?"

"Yes." (It's me, I'm here.)

"Bloody hell."

"I know." (*What* do I know?)

"I can't believe it."

Sadie sighs. She has never been so full of air.

Alison is shaking her head. "Are you?—"

"Am I?—"

"Looking for a tent?"

Is she really going to talk about tents?

"Yes."

Yes?

"You don't live around here, do you?" Alison looks slightly afraid as she says this.

"Passing through."

Oh come on!

In Sadie's mind, high-speed deliberation. Two opposing sentences: *Actually, I came here to see you* versus *I need a two-man tent for my sons.* The truth versus a lie. Risk versus safety. Free versus £250. Instead of a tent, she decides to buy some time.

"Are you by any chance free for a drink after work?"

"Today?"

"Yes."

"Actually, I have plans."

Time is not for sale. It has sold out. Sadie remembers when it was free and all theirs. She wants to cry, but as usual this urge doesn't produce any tears. 'Songbird' by Eva Cassidy is playing in the shop, which isn't helping, because it always makes her emotional and it's strange, she doesn't even like the song, it's—

"But I could postpone," Alison says.

"Could you?" Sadie says.

25

They drink coffee while he mows the lawn.

"Why is he doing that?" Ralph says.

"He likes to be helpful," Miriam says.

"Isn't it a bit early? It's not even eight o'clock."

"A bit early for what?"

They watch through the kitchen window, then Miriam takes three small boxes of cereal from a cupboard and lines them up on the counter: Coco Pops, Cheerios, Crunchy Nut Cornflakes. It's not Ralph's usual breakfast—muesli with berries, nuts and pumpkin seeds.

"Help yourself," Miriam says, before leaving the room with a bowl of Coco Pops.

Cheerios it is, Ralph thinks. He tips them out, adds milk. Are these actually *edible*?

He wanders outside. "How's it going?" he shouts.

Boo stops mowing the lawn. He is wearing a short-sleeved denim shirt and faded jeans. To Ralph, this man looks sturdy and handsome and like a member of the Village People. "It's going well," he says. "I've nearly finished."

"You help Miriam out a lot, do you?"

"She has only just let me in."

"Let you in?"

"To her premises."

"Would you like to come in for a coffee?"

Boo tips his head and looks at Ralph over the top of his sunglasses. Who on earth does this man from the woods think he is? Talking like it's his house and his coffee and—

"I would, thank you."

In the kitchen, Boo watches Ralph move easily from cupboard to drawer to cupboard, knowing where things live. This exhibition of small knowledge makes him feel excluded. "Where is Miriam?" he says.

"I think she went upstairs." A pause, then: "She tells me you're a herbalist."

"That's right."

"I'm a psychotherapist. Well, that's open to debate right now. I'm not sure what I am. Having a kind of crisis, I think. If that doesn't sound too dramatic."

I only came in to see Miriam, Boo thinks. "I see."

"Anyway, I'm open to anything that will help, herbal or otherwise."

"What kind of crisis?"

"Well, this might sound a bit fanciful."

Boo stands completely still.

"I feel unknowable."

"Unknowable."

"Yes."

"To yourself or other people?"

"Both. I feel confused all the time, and like nothing matters. That sounds awful. My sons matter. I have two sons. But everything else feels like liquid."

Liquid?

Boo takes a deep breath. He was happy mowing the lawn—unquestionably happy. Now he is being bombarded and Miriam is nowhere to be seen. "Liquid?" he says.

"Things that were solid are now liquid. Do you have a remedy for that?" Ralph laughs. He knows that what he is saying is preposterous. Quick fixes don't exist, do they? He notices the doors on the kitchen cupboards, hanging crooked or about to fall off. Heinz tomato soup, sugary children's cereal, a man from the Village People—is any of this really helping? Is it serving any kind of purpose?

"Well, I'm trialling a remedy for anxiety right now," Boo says, "called Anata."

"I'm not sure it's anxiety."

"You don't feel anxious?"

"Not particularly."

"You look anxious."

"Great."

"Great?"

Ralph and Boo are two different types of men. Lock them in a room together and it would take months for them to bond. One values politeness, keeping busy, looking after what is his; the other is searching for a sign that something, anything, belongs to him.

Footsteps upstairs. Music from a radio (is that Chris Isaak?). The sound of a hairdryer.

"May I ask you a question?" Boo says. "And I'd like you to answer it quickly, without thinking."

"All right."

"Imagine you are completely free. You can do whatever you like. What are you going to do?"

"Oh that's a good one," Ralph says.

"Don't think," Boo says.

The hairdryer stops. Footsteps on the landing.

"Say it," Boo says.

"I don't know," Ralph says, feeling under pressure.

"Nothing at all comes to mind?"

"Not really."

"Your freedom is wasted on you," Boo says, his voice hushed by kindness.

Ralph is used to dealing with Sadie, two teenagers and numerous challenging clients. And yet now, in this scrappy little kitchen, he is flummoxed. He has gone too fast and too deep with Boo and he feels exposed. He remembers standing in a youth-hostel kitchen during a school trip—the other boys looked so stupid and untidy. He wanted to go home and he wanted to stay.

"I always let things drift," he says. "And I'm drifting now by being here."

"With Miriam?"

"Yes."

"You don't want to be with her?"

"Oh, you think—" Ralph shakes his head. "You think we're together."

"You're not?"

"No, not at all."

Such glorious words! Boo swigs his coffee and eyes the box of Crunchy Nut Cornflakes beside the kettle. He hears Miriam walking downstairs, her footsteps heavy and slow. He would like to fix her kitchen, clean out her pond, put up shelves in her garage, cook her a roast dinner with all the trimmings. He looks at Ralph, who is clutching a mug that says NO. 1 MUM.

"I must finish the lawn immediately," Boo says.

"Fair enough," Ralph says. He wonders where this man gets his energy from, suspects that it's probably herbal, and without his concoctions he'd be tired, lethargic, basically normal.

Across town, a boy has just woken up. "Good morning, Amy Pond," the boy says. "How are you today? Did you sleep well? I did. Are you hungry yet? Would you like some toast?"

From the other single bed, while pretending to be asleep, Matthew listens to his little brother talking to an action figure. He knows that in a few minutes' time Alfie will tumble out of bed in his *Doctor Who* pyjamas and carry Amy Pond downstairs to the breakfast table, where he will bend her legs (slowly, lovingly) and sit her down against a bottle of brown sauce ("Now *that's* what I call good posture," his mother will say). Amy Pond is new but she is already part of the family. Her comments (Amy is verbose) about an unforeseen assortment of matters are taken seriously, as are her requests ("I'd like to go swimming in the bath sometime," Amy says).

Today is Saturday. The day when Alfie's father sets up his stall at the market. Amy has offered to help, because that's the kind of woman she is. Matthew is coming too, which is unusual. He normally goes for a bike ride on Saturdays, or to the cinema in the afternoon with a girl. He never brings any of his girlfriends home, only sketches of their faces, which he shows his family after the evening meal (on a Saturday, fish and chips). They lean in close to look and there are *ooohs* and *ahhhs* and comments like *interesting expression* and *such sadness in her eyes.*

"You two had better hurry up if you want to help your dad," their mother says.

"You *three,*" Alfie says.

Matthew looks at his mother. "Are you coming too?"

"No, I need to go food shopping. Can you bring back some fish?"

By nine-thirty the market is chock-a-block with people carrying tote bags. The text on the bags ranges from NOBODY LOVES ME LIKE MY DOG to STAND UP TO CANCER, I LOVE THIS PLANET and PUGS NOT DRUGS. Alfie likes to read the wording on the bags, because when you are seven the messages seem deeply mysterious, extremely significant.

"I've just seen a woman with cancer," he says, running up to his father. Amy Pond's head is sticking out of his shirt pocket, bobbing up and down as he weaves through the crowd. "Does that mean she's dying?"

"What makes you think she has cancer?" Eric says.

"It says so on her bag."

"Where's your brother?"

"Parking the car."

The tote bags are bulging with organic meat, locally grown vegetables, jam with high fruit content, cheeses made by small producers using milk from their own herds. Some bags contain other items, like candles, second-hand books and small wooden objects. The objects are made by Eric, a wood sculptor who uses the stall to advertise his bigger creations. Today he is selling tiny swaying trees, a naked couple (face to face, their arms wrapped around each other), dragons, hares, a tiny violin leaning against a tree, a woman beating a drum. (Yes, people actually buy these things.)

Matthew turns up with two coffees and a lemonade. He picks up each of the carved wooden trees, one after the other, inspecting their bases. His father drinks his coffee and chats to his customers, finding the small talk easy. He notices the twitchiness of a woman's hands as she asks whether he might consider carving her a carriage clock, a wooden replica that she could give to her husband when he retires. She doesn't think his firm will give him a carriage clock. He's spent his whole working life expecting one, but he doesn't like the ticking of time, you see. He'd love one that is silent, wooden, *symbolic*—one that will fill an unpredictable gap. It's a tall order for a piece of wood.

"Are you really going to make a carriage clock?" Matthew says, when the woman has gone.

"How could I say no?"

"Ever made one before?"

"First time for everything."

Matthew looks around to see if anyone is about to approach the stall. He glances at Alfie, sitting on a stool, reading his comic. Now is a good time. "Dad?"

"Mmnn."

"Someone might turn up today. I mean, there's a slim chance—"

Eric turns to face his son. Is he finally about to meet one of his girlfriends? A living breathing woman instead of a line drawing? "Great," he says, rubbing his hands together.

"Well, hear me out."

Alfie starts humming the music from *Chariots of Fire*. A man walks over and asks for directions to the train station. He buys a wooden dragon. Says he'd rather have bought a horse. Says that Eric should make a giant Harry Potter. Leaves.

"You were saying?"

Matthew runs his fingers through his hair, pushing it in all directions. He looks his father in the eye and says, "I know about Miriam."

26

I, Sadie Swoon, feel wretched. Can Alison Grabowski see my wretchedness? I don't know which was worse: walking around with only the idea of you, or sitting here with the real person, who has now *replaced* my idea of you. (A seed of memory blossoms into an imaginary garden. We walk through it. We have never stopped walking through it.) But this is the story of us, isn't it? Loss and gain. It makes no sense. It's wretched.

I was thinking of you when I wasn't thinking of you.

You were there when you were here.

You were here when you were there.

I wish I hadn't ordered this glass of wine.

Sadie hadn't planned to drink. She wanted a clear head and the capacity to drive away from Alison Grabowski as soon as she needed to. *If* she needed to.

She sips pinot noir from a large glass and looks around. Red leather seats. White paintwork. A mirrored wall behind a long bar. Framed advertisements from the Fifties and Sixties. Black skirting boards. Skinny staff with asymmetrical haircuts. Lopsidedness is all the rage. (You know you're getting older

when you say *all the rage*.) The voice of Elvis, coming out of
four speakers. At the next table, three men who all resemble
Justin Bieber, eating steak sandwiches, plucking thin chips
from miniature steel plant pots. A tattooed girl, sitting by
herself, drinking a martini, reading *Ulysses*. Sadie envies the
girl, she doesn't know why. A young couple drinking beer,
eating pistachios, playing footsie under the table. A man on
his mobile phone saying don't do this to me, don't do this to
us. And Alison Grabowski, who is still wearing her hi-tech
trousers and grey short-sleeved shirt, but not the badge with
the cartoon bear on it, the one promoting a summer camp for
young carers, sponsored by Grab&Go Camping, which does
a vast amount for charity.

"So, where to start?" Alison says.

They are dancing to the Levellers. They are chopping vegetables
in the kitchen, discussing how easy it is to make a vegetable
lasagne as if they are the very first people in the world to discover
this. They are watching *Peter's Friends* at the Odeon; afterwards
they will buy two bags of chips and walk home while discussing
how brilliant Emma Thompson is. They are throwing snowballs
at each other in the park, and Alison says my God just stop and
look at this, look at how the snow makes everything beautiful.
They are eating bacon sandwiches in a cafe, reading *The Times*,
feeling grown up. They are washing Alison's first car, a red Fiat
Panda, and the man next door says oh girls you don't do it like
that, and he disappears inside his house and comes back out
with a special wheel-cleaning brush and a square of chamois
leather that looks impossibly stiff. They are sitting in the front
row of a Tori Amos concert, holding hands, and Tori Amos
is staring at them as she sings, she is really staring, and they
talk about this for days afterwards, how Tori Amos sang just

for them, they call it amazing and intense and they play the song continually, 'Cornflake Girl', the song that brought the three of them together. They are sitting around a dining table with Alison's parents, sister, auntie, uncle and grandmother, eating turkey and wearing paper hats. They are arguing about a women's studies lecture on a Friday morning, the one they were supposed to go to at nine o'clock, but Alison wouldn't get up so Sadie went alone and took pages of detailed notes and rushed home with croissants, feeling diligent, productive, generous, but Alison was still asleep, Sadie called her lazy, Alison woke up and said you're not my wife; she got dressed and drove off in her red Fiat Panda and stomped around the garden centre, wishing she'd stayed home and eaten her croissant. They are lying on Sadie's bed, Alison is smiling and running her fingers up and down Sadie's arm—she says we could have sex you know, just to see how it feels, and Sadie says yeah right, *as if.*

I, Sadie Swoon, am in agony. I lost you, and now I have lost you again by finding you.

"So, where to start?" Alison says.

She would give it all up to be with Sadie. Bessie, the business, their home. Yes, after all this time. She knows this now and she has always known it. The outcome is irrelevant. This is not about the future, only the past, the time when she was living authentically, expressing something that felt true and real. The time when she was most present in her own life.

"I hope you don't mind me turning up like this," Sadie says.

"Of course not," Alison says.

"I'm in a strange space right now. It's making me think about university."

"How's Ralph?"

"I have no idea."

Alison takes a sip of red wine. She checks Sadie's hand, looking for the wedding ring. There it is, plain and unbroken. Has she divorced Ralph and married someone else?

"He walked out a week ago," Sadie says.

"He's left you?"

"I don't think so. I have no idea. I kissed my friend Kristin in a cupboard. She's a printmaker. Designs book jackets too. Very talented."

Alison detests this woman called Kristin. Some things in life are simple. "So you're having an affair?"

"Oh no, I'm not having an affair. I've never been unfaithful to Ralph."

(Poor Beverley Smart. The woman who doesn't count.)

"Right. Why did you kiss her in a cupboard? Still slightly..." Alison pauses. "Inhibited?"

Cutting!

Sadie licks her lips and thinks about what to say. "So, are you some kind of rambler now?" she asks, eyeing Alison's outfit.

Touché!

"You know I always liked a long walk," Alison says.

Sadie nods. She doesn't remember any long walks. She remembers the short ones—around the park, to and from town, the cinema, the chippy—as if their feet had never stopped moving, left and right, side by side, walking through the years.

"Bessie's the energetic one," Alison says.

And Bessie jogs into the picture. Not literally, because Bessie is busy right now, running a summer camp in the Lake District. *Energetic.* Is that really the right word, Alison? She could have chosen so many others, like *driven* and *obsessed* and *jumpy*, but she has chosen *energetic* because it sounds better than the others, and Bessie is in competition with Kristin.

"Your partner?"

"In life and in business."

In life and in business? Did I actually just say that? Alison is grimacing and Sadie is drinking and 'All Shook Up' is playing on the stereo.

"Hold on, didn't you go on a date with someone called Bessie at uni?"

"Sadie, I brought her to your wedding."

"My wedding?"

"Don't you remember?"

"No."

She genuinely doesn't remember. She had two screaming babies, a brand-new husband and low-grade flu, according to her GP, who asked if she was happy and wished he hadn't when Sadie began to hyperventilate. Just breathe into this paper bag, the GP said. Breathe into this bag and everything will be all right. And it was, in a muted kind of way, because he prescribed her antidepressants, which she took for five years without telling a soul.

"I never understood why we lost touch," Alison says.

"It's not easy, having twins when you're twenty," Sadie says, as if this explains everything. "It was all right for Ralph. He finished his degree, he just carried on. I left with nothing."

"You left with a husband and two children."

"One minute we were dancing, then I had two babies."

"You sound like an advert for the pill."

Sadie looks up, says nothing.

"Would you like another drink?"

"Please."

I, Alison Grabowski, choose you, Sadie Swoon, even though you are not mine to choose. How dare you just turn up like this? You come walking into the shop, giving me no warning, no time to prepare. Do you think I'd be wearing these combat trousers and this shirt if I'd known you were coming? I would have washed my hair this morning, put on some make-up. But you gave me no time and no options. What's changed, over the years? I had no choices then and no choices now. We've been sitting here for less than an hour and already I know why you're here. The idea of life after Ralph has made you think of life before Ralph, and who was before him? I was. You were never in love with him and he must have known, yet he drifted along beside you like a boy. He's finally dropped you, that's why you're here. I hate you, Sadie. You were so cold. I've missed you so much. I'd give it all up to be with you now. I hate you.

They sit and drink wine and there is an arch of melancholy, it rises up and over their heads, their own private architecture, their own private world.

"Do you remember that band we used to go and see?" Sadie says. "Acquiescence?"

"Oh God," Alison says, laughing. "Acquiescence. The goths from Edinburgh."

"I loved those goths."

"I think you mainly loved the lead singer."

"She was fantastic. We would've been great together," Sadie says.

Alison doesn't answer. She holds her wine glass with both hands, clutching it as if it were a hot drink on a cold day.

"So, are you all right?" Sadie says.

"All right?"

"Are you happy?"

"Yes, I suppose so, in a way."

"That's good." Sadie pulls a food menu from a wooden stand. "Are you hungry? I haven't eaten for hours. Do you still like pizza?"

I, Alison Grabowski—the one wearing quick-dry technical trousers with built-in UV radiation and wind protection, advanced moisture control, cargo pockets for handy storage, anti-fungus and insect-repellent coating; the one wearing the *dullest* shirt I own—am sitting here with Sadie Swoon, eating pizza, listening to Elvis. I am thinking about *Take This Waltz*, a film I saw with Bessie last week, about a woman who leaves her husband and starts a passionate affair, and by the end of the film she is just as dissatisfied as she was at the beginning. That wouldn't be us, Sadie, because we are the original couple, the couple that never began, and we've been around long enough to know that the excitement turns into something else, and I want that something else with you. We can do this slowly if you like. We can dance around it. We can sit here talking about the old days, drinking red wine. You can ask me if I'm happy and I'll say yes, I suppose so, in a way. We'll just dance until we're tired of dancing.

27

THOUGHTS OF MURDERING ONE'S MOTHER
DO NOT MAKE A PERSON INSANE

In Miriam's living room, a cuckoo springs from a clock and *The One Show* begins. The programme is presented by a woman and a man, sitting close together on a green sofa. The woman tells us the man's name, the man tells us the woman's name. The camera pans to Sarah Millican, who is sitting on another green sofa, smiling. Ralph has never seen this programme before. As he eats his pie and mash, he marvels at this demented televisual creature, leaping from one topic to another, tame but reckless. Right now, the topic is a man in Wales who runs self-help groups for new mothers who are frightened of breaking their children. This is clearly a risky subject for *The One Show*, which would hate to suggest that not all women are instinctively maternal, able to produce a child and rise to the challenge as if the text from an innate Mother's Handbook had floated into awareness the second their waters broke.

"I ran a self-help group once," Ralph says. "I wasn't very good at it."

"I went to one for a few weeks," Miriam says, finishing her pie.

"Did you?"

"Fenella thought it would be a good idea."

"Who's Fenella?"

"My closest friend. You'd like her, she's very sane." Miriam shivers. It's the thought of the self-help group, the one organized by Anita Goodwin, who believed that madness had meaning and should never be stigmatized. Anita had no idea what she was letting herself in for. Miriam wonders what she is doing now—has she recovered from Pam Croft?

"I'm an artist in residence," Pam Croft announced. Her latest exhibition had just opened in her living room.

"I don't think that's what it means," said Rudy. "You can't be an artist in residence at your own house."

"Why on earth not? No wonder you're mad if you live by rules like that."

"We don't call ourselves *mad*, Pam. It's politically incorrect."

"We leave that to other people, do we?"

"We call ourselves *challenged*."

"Challenged?"

"Yes."

"So what's *your* challenge?"

"I find being with other people a challenge."

Anita Goodwin, psychoanalyst and group facilitator, waved her hands in the air. "Let's take it in turns to speak, shall we?" she said, like a lollipop lady without a stick, trying to stop the flow of conversational traffic in a soothing tone of voice that others found belittling.

"And where are the *real* mad people, if we're not mad?" said Pam.

"In institutions."

"What?"

"Extreme cases. Dangerous people. Chronic and acute," said Rudy, who had tears in her eyes.

"I used to think about murdering my mother," said Miriam, as she unwrapped a Snickers bar. "Yum."

"Yum?"

"I was talking to the Snickers bar."

"And who are you?" asked Anita Goodwin. She had forgotten the first rule of groups: the opening round, in which people introduce themselves, one by one. (How can she have forgotten that? Well, life was complicated for Anita Goodwin, whose husband had started wearing her clothes while he did the weekly food shop at Waitrose. She didn't mind him wearing them—she was quite open to the idea of subverting the performance of gender roles. What she minded was the number of compliments he received, the way their friends, neighbours and acquaintances seemed enraptured by his feminine presence, his taste in clothes, his new identity. She had done the weekly food shop for *years* in those clothes, floating through the aisles, invisible, *unappreciated*, and now she felt like screaming, like ripping every blouse, like pulling the sleeves off every fucking lambswool jumper.)

"Thoughts of murdering one's mother do not make a person insane," said Cliff Richard, whose full name was Cliff Richard Jones. "It just makes you human."

"I used to write my name on my legs with a compass," said Mary.

"Is this a competition? It's starting to feel like one," said Pam.

"Well why not?" said Mary. "Why not? It'd probably be the first time any of us had the slightest chance of winning a bloody competition!"

"Mary, please," said Anita. "No swearing or shouting. The Buddhists are next door, trying to empty themselves."

"I drove my brother's Fiesta into the front of our local Asda," said Chris. "I thought their bread was infecting people with racism. But I'm over that now."

Anita Goodwin ran the group for six weeks before quitting all of a sudden due to ill health. By *ill health* she meant *a terrifying sense of inner chaos*. She had discovered that Pam Croft was stalking her from inside a Morris Minor, but it was hard to press charges because Pam actually lived in the Morris Minor, so technically all she was doing was sitting in her own home, looking out of the window, and where's the crime in that?

"That group sounds amazing," Ralph says. "Anarchic."

"You think anarchic is good?" Miriam says.

"Sometimes," he says, with the fettered dreaminess of an orderly mind.

"I'm never going to another self-help group," she says, staring at the TV. "And I've had my fill of anarchy."

On *The One Show*, they are discussing a boy who was adopted in 1971 and has just been reunited with his birth mother. On screen now, the man and his mother. His arms are around her, he is pressing her head to his chest as if she were a child. The mother is sobbing. The man looks unfazed, numb, absent. This is accompanied by a bastardized pop song, slowed down and stripped of lyrics, a mawkish version for emotional effect.

"This is disturbing," Ralph says.

Miriam jumps to her feet and switches off the TV. "Enough," she says.

Later that evening, the phone rings.

Twelve miles away, a man had been watching *The One Show* with his wife and eldest son. Two days had passed since they had a long and difficult conversation about a daughter, a sister, a stranger. The conversation took place on Saturday, after fish and chips and mushy peas, as soon as Alfie and Amy Pond had gone to bed. The eldest son: "I overheard you and Mum, years ago, talking about my *sister*." The father: "I had no choice." The eldest son: "I got Alfie to put postcards through her door." The father: "You've been to her house?" Two days later they are watching *The One Show*, on which a man is reunited with his mother, and after three glasses of brandy Eric Delaney stands up and says: "All right, I'm ready to do this."

Miriam believes that her father is dead. It's a reasonable thing to believe, when you consider the fact that Frances told her he was dead. But facts are often fictitious. Lies are often true. This fabricated world, dressed in perplexing cloth.

"He had an aneurysm," Frances said. "Dead as a dodo. Dead dead dead." She felt guilty for a while, until she began to believe her own story, which went like this: "He was a loud, booming man. A simple man. He died of a brain aneurysm while hanging out the washing. Yes, just like that. Who could have seen it coming? He was hanging out my pink beach towel. He left behind a wife and a baby daughter. That baby was you, but you didn't really notice. You were just a baby, weren't you? Babies don't notice when a person disappears."

This story changed as the baby turned into a toddler, a girl, a teenager, a woman. Sometimes the man was hanging out a petticoat when he died, at other times a yellow Babygro. The one constant in the story was his death. So that must have happened, right?

Wrong.

Miriam's father is not dead.

He has been alive all the time, which is more than Miriam can say about herself.

Where has he been?

In a small terraced house twelve miles up the road.

Once, without knowing, they travelled on the same bus.

Once, without knowing, they passed each other in a supermarket (by the frozen sprouts and frozen peas).

Once, without knowing, they sat in the same waiting room, waiting to see the same dentist. The dentist leant into the room and nodded at Miriam. I'm ready for you, the nod said. No names were spoken. No identities were revealed. It was a top-secret highly confidential manoeuvre that kept a father and daughter apart. He watched her walk over to the water cooler. She watched him pick up a copy of *Country Life* magazine. He watched her stand up and leave the room when the dentist nodded. And that was that. The emptiness remained inside them.

Somewhere, Miriam knows this. Not the fine details, not where and when and why, just the broad strokes of his presence, brushing up against her sometimes, out there in the world, still out there.

I zigzag my way through.

I listen out for you.

(I am always listening out for you.)

A world of white noise, congestion, muzak.

(Still I listen for you.)

I don't know that I'm listening.

(I know in a way that is out of reach.)

I love you without loving you.

(I see you but you have never been here.)

In 7 Beckford Gardens, the telephone rings.

"Hello?" Miriam whispers.

Before speaking, Eric Delaney turns to look at his wife and son. He nods. They nod.

"Hello?" she whispers again. She is about to put the phone down when she hears a man's voice.

"Is this Miriam Delaney?"

"Yes."

"Miriam, my name is Eric. This will come as a terrible shock, so please forgive me. I'm your father, Miriam. This is your father speaking. Mr Eric Delaney."

28

THE ALLURE, THE MAGNETISM

Miriam Delaney is saying no, I don't believe you, my parents are both dead, where's your proof, what are you after? As she whispers, her heart races and her palms sweat. Hope surges through her, she tries to stop it surging but this hope has a mind of its own.

Ralph Swoon is listening to Miriam on the phone, wondering what's going on, wondering who is making her whisper slightly louder than usual. He strokes Treacle's head and glances at the cuckoo clock.

Sadie Swoon is eating a gluten-free pizza with blue cheese, roasted onions and potatoes, spinach, tomato and mozzarella. She is looking at Alison's mouth, thinking what now, what the hell happens now?

Alison Grabowski is eating a smoked-ham and pineapple pizza with extra chillies. She asks if Sadie has seen a film called *Take This Waltz*, and Sadie says no, she hasn't seen a film in ages, in fact she can't even remember the last time she went to the cinema with Ralph or anyone else, and it's a long answer, it goes on and on, and Alison just watches her, she doesn't look away.

Arthur Swoon is watching *Breaking Bad* on Netflix. He hasn't left the sofa for five hours. Last night, he dreamt he was swimming through a river and the water was cold, unbearably cold, but his body was warm, the swimming was easy and his mother was standing at the side, shouting words of encouragement, egging him on as if it was some kind of race but there was no one else in the water.

Stanley Swoon is kissing Joe Schwartz in the kitchen. Under the grill, bacon is curling. On the hob, a frying pan is warming up. Three plates, three knives and three forks have been placed on the work surface. The absence of his parents over the past few days—his father gone completely, his mother coming and going—has awakened a sense of personal authority. This house feels like *his* house. He walked Harvey this morning, fed him this evening, opened a tiny tube and poured it over his neck to protect him from bloodthirsty fleas. He went to the supermarket and brought home the bacon that is curling under the grill. Right now, his iPod is sending music into three different rooms—a new playlist called Our Summer. He is filling this house in a way his parents never could and it's exciting, it's uncomfortable, it makes him feel alive.

Kristin Hart is at home with Carol, watching *The Good Wife*. She is missing her friend Sadie, who has blanked her since that night in the cupboard on the landing—since the kiss that should never have happened, the kiss she can't think of without feeling furious, the kiss that flutters through her days and nights like a tiny fantastical bird.

Boo Hodgkinson is attempting to invent a new herbal remedy. His kitchen is a laboratory and he is a scientist and Vivaldi's *Four Seasons* is playing on his Bose music system. Fuelled by steak and chips and a bottle of ale, he flicks through his books and hums to the music and admires his own reflection in the window: his thick moustache, his rugby player's physique, his rampant hairy chest.

Eric Delaney is listening to his daughter. She is accusing him of wanting to steal her inheritance. Her whispers race around him like a breeze and the breeze smells of his dead ex-wife—Chanel No. 5.

Alfie Delaney is asleep in bed. He is wearing *Doctor Who* pyjamas. Amy Pond is lying on the pillow beside Alfie's head. He is dreaming about the neighbour's Jack Russell, white and brown and black, running in circles with Amy in its mouth.

Matthew Delaney is listening to his father, who has just finished speaking to Miriam. She whispered at me, Eric says. Oh sweetheart, his wife says, sitting beside him, stroking his hair. It is imperative that Matthew meets Miriam, he can feel it, deep in his bones—skeletal knowledge. He wants to draw her face. He wants to draw his father's face too, right now in this moment, the way sorrow has made it crumple and give way. Why anyone would want to draw a smile is a mystery to Matthew—it's sorrow that has the allure, the magnetism.

29

WHOSE LIFE IS THIS?

"I don't believe it," Ralph says, staring at Miriam. "Are you all right? Shall I make some tea?"

He moves towards her and she shudders.

A pot of Yorkshire Tea. A plate of Rich Tea biscuits. A bar of Kendal Mint Cake—why not? Miriam is clearly about to embark on an expedition of sorts—anyone can see the huge familial mountain, rising higher by the second, shouting *climb me climb me you know you want to climb me*.

Side by side on the sofa. He puts his arm around her shoulder. Her body is stiff, stubborn.

"He says my mother told him to leave and never make contact," she says, her face even paler than usual.

"But why would he agree to that?"

Miriam gives him a sharp look and rolls up her sleeves.

"If Sadie told *me* I could never try and see the boys, I wouldn't agree to it," he says.

"But Sadie isn't my mother."

"No she isn't."

"My mother told him she would hurt me if he turned up."

"And he believed her?"

"You never met my mother."

"He could have gone to the police."

"She got there first. Told them he was aggressive and she'd forced him to stay away."

Ralph sips his tea. Whose life is this? Sitting on a sofa eating Rich Tea biscuits with a woman whose father played dead? It's not *his* life. It's *never* his life.

"This is a lot to take in," Miriam says. She looks at him expectantly.

"It is," he says.

"I probably just need to sit quietly," she says.

"Yes."

"By *myself.*"

"Oh—"

"Do you mind?"

"Of course not."

His presence is neither comforting nor helpful. It's humiliating.

"To be honest, you've been sitting in this house for days," she says.

"Mmnn."

"You're going to turn into me if you're not careful."

"I'll go for a walk," he says.

"You could go to the pub for last orders."

That would be a first—wandering to a local pub for last orders. Quaint.

"Boo often does that," she says. "Actually, he'd probably like to join you."

"And you wouldn't mind?" he says. He never asks Sadie if she would mind him going out. He just comes and goes and she just comes and goes and—

"Definitely not."

Boo doesn't answer the door. He can't hear it above the sound of Vivaldi's *Four Seasons*. Ralph just stands there, feeling partly like Miriam has kicked him out and partly like he has abandoned her.

He walks through the streets until he reaches the Crown. Inside, people stare at him. At the bar, he orders a pint and a bag of crisps. In his peripheral vision he can see a woman getting up from her seat and walking over to where he is standing. She says her name is Sandy. She says would you like some company? She is wearing an orange boob tube and tight stonewashed jeans. She asks what he does for a living and he says he's a psychotherapist. She says what's a psychotherapist? He says it's someone who's paid to listen and help people make sense of their interior worlds. She says what's an interior world, are you talking about hanging pictures and stuff? And he says no, I mean the interior of a *person*. She laughs and calls him a psycho. Her teeth are a shocking white. She leans in and tells him that people have paid a lot of money to enjoy the benefits of *her* interior world, and is he interested, does he know what she means? He says thank you for your kind offer, but no thank you. She says it's not a kind offer, you prick, I'm not doing this out of the kindness of my heart. He says I'm terribly sorry, I didn't mean to offend you, I'm just here for a quiet pint. Need a break from your frigid wife? she says. I bloody knew it. It's written all over you. Bet you can't even remember what to do with it. Bloody useless, you are. Give us a crisp it's the least you can do.

Fucking hell, Ralph thinks, as he leaves the pub. He walks around the corner until the Crown is out of sight, and hesitates

before heading back to Miriam's. Does she want him there?
Does he want to be there? And if not there, then—

He looks at his phone. No messages or missed calls today.
He dials a number.

"Well I never," a voice says.

"Hello."

"Finally bothered to make contact, have you?"

"I'm sorry."

"Are you really."

"I'm sorry, Sadie."

"Do you think it's acceptable to just walk out on your family?"

"Not really."

"I've reported you missing to the police."

"Oh God, you haven't."

"No, I haven't."

"Why not? Anything could have happened to me."

"Something told me you were fine. Are you fine?"

"I suppose so. How are the boys?"

"They're good. Look, can we talk another time?"

"It's late, I know."

"It's not that. Do you remember Alison Grabowski?"

"From university?"

"Yes."

"Why?"

"I'm out with her right now."

"Where are you?"

"In a car park."

"What?"

"Look, I have to go, Ralph. We're about to get a taxi."

"Where to?"

"Alison's."

"Are the boys with you?"

"They're hardly boys any more, are they? They're sixteen."

"So they're home alone."

She sighs. "They're *sixteen*."

"Did Alison contact you?"

"Why?"

"Did she?"

"No, I Googled her."

"You Googled her."

"That's what I said. Look, I'll call you tomorrow, okay? Alison's waiting. I'm glad you're fine. We'll talk soon."

Beside a street light, on a row of white terraced houses, Ralph stares at his phone and says *Jesus Christ*. Sadie is out with Alison. She isn't at home, worrying about him and their marriage. Did he expect her to be? Probably. Or she might have been out with Kristin or Beverley. But *Alison fucking Grabowski*. He hoped she had become fat and boring. How mature, Ralph. Oh fuck maturity. Fuck it all. Even Miriam's on the move, she's on her way up a mountain, climbing suspiciously and hopefully towards a man who claims to be her father. But what about *him*? He is just standing here by a street light, in a part of town that can only be described as insalubrious, and earlier tonight he was rejected by Miriam, then the man from the Village People whose light was on when he knocked on the door, and now his wife sounds drunk and silly and he could hear the smile in her voice. Google did that. It made the smile happen. Not Alison herself. Maybe Google could do something for him too? He would need to use Miriam's computer. Does she have a computer? She must have, everyone has one.

Oh you idiot, Ralph. You have Google in your hand, don't you? He rolls his eyes at his own technological naivety. Smart phone, dim user. He has never used his phone *properly* before— he's had no need to visit websites or send emails on the go. But now his life is permanently on the go. So *where* is he going? This question is unexpectedly vast, a construction of letters the width of Amsterdam, with its own canals, bikes and tulips, its own galleries and red-light district, and a bar in which a woman called Julie Parsley is singing about how the past never ends.

If Sadie can do it, why not him?

Ralph has a competitive streak and tonight it gives him a purpose and direction, even if that purpose is beating his wife in a game of Win Back an Old Flame.

(Childish, Ralph.)

(And you don't even know how to access Google on that phone.)

Game on, Sadie, he thinks, as he jogs all the way back to Miriam's.

"You can't drive," Alison says. "You've had too much wine."

"Neither can you," Sadie says.

They stand in the multistorey car park, fiddling with keys. A jingle, a chime, the scanty sound of indecision. Alison rubs her thumb against a key ring—a plastic case containing a photograph of a beagle.

"Is that your dog?" Sadie says, looking down at the key ring.

"This?"

"Yeah."

"No, it just came with the key ring."

"You're supposed to put your own photo in it."

"Who says?"

A teenager steps out of the darkness. White trainers, blue jeans, a red T-shirt, pink hair.

"Nice hair," Alison says.

"I need money for the night shelter," the boy says.

Sadie asks if he's homeless.

"Why else would I be begging for money?"

A woman appears, carrying a bag that says Fusion Noodles.

"Kevin, for God's sake," she says. "We've been over this haven't we? Just get in the car." The woman and the boy get into a black BMW. Doors slam, an engine starts. The passenger window is wound down and raised voices can be heard as the car pulls away.

"So I was thinking," Alison says. "You can stay at mine if you like. We can collect the cars tomorrow."

There is a lump in Sadie's throat. Alison is in control—that's how it feels. It brings a lump to her throat and she looks away, embarrassed. She feels her phone vibrate in her handbag and checks to see who it is.

"Do you mind if I take this?" she says. "It's important."

"Of course not, you go ahead. I'll call us a taxi."

"Well I never," Sadie says. "Finally bothered to make contact, have you?" Then "Are you really" and "Do you think it's acceptable to just walk out?"

Alison phones for a taxi, while trying to listen to what Sadie is saying.

"So you Googled me did you?" she says, as they walk out of the car park.

"How else was I supposed to find you?"

"Creepy," Alison says.

"Like you actually mind," Sadie says.

By the time the taxi arrives they are holding hands.

A cardboard monkey hangs from the rear-view mirror—on its chest, the words *I smell of banana, baby.* But the car doesn't smell of bananas, it smells of aftershave and beer.

The driver is from Cornwall. He tells them this while they sit in the back and look out of the window. St Ives, he says, well it's the great love of his life, that's what it is, there's no other way to put it, and if anyone says you can't love a place like you love a person they're talking absolute bollocks.

"You ladies love any place?" he says.

"Not really," Sadie says.

"If you love St Ives, why are you here instead of there?" Alison says, which makes the driver fall silent. He shakes his head, stares at her in the rear-view mirror, and the monkey spins as he slams his foot down hard on the accelerator.

"You fucking women, you're so *smug*," he says.

"I beg your pardon?"

"Think you can say what you like, do what you like."

What?

Alison takes Sadie's hand.

Too fast. Wrong turning.

This is *not* the way to Alison's house.

They speak at the same time.

Sadie says look I think you're.

Alison says pull over right now I.

The driver says shut the fuck up just shut the.

Straight over a roundabout.

Straight through traffic lights.

Drove me out of St Ives didn't they, he says. Her new bloke and his mates. I mean *come on*, for what, the odd drunken shag with my *own* wife? Stop the car, Alison says. Please pull over, we want to get out. And the man says lady I'm *talking*. He says you have no manners, anyone ever tell you that? Then he's back on St Ives, saying he loves its roads its curves the sound it makes at night. Wrote a poem about it once, had it published, pretty good eh ladies?

He turns up the radio. 'Take My Breath Away'. As in *Top Gun*.

For a second, Sadie just remembers the film. She remembers Tom Cruise and Kelly McGillis. Then she is back in the car with Alison Grabowski and a man saying let's go somewhere quiet, what do you think, I know the perfect spot, I know the perfect place.

31

THERE ARE SOME THINGS YOU JUST KNOW

While Miriam and Ralph are sleeping, the telephone rings. Usually it's just Fenella, or someone wanting to know if Frances Delaney is at home. The people who ask for Frances are selling things, and Miriam knows this for certain because her mother only had one friend and his name was the headmaster.

It is not Fenella on the phone. It's a man.

"Hi, is this Miriam Delaney?"

"It might be," she whispers slowly, "or it might not. Are you aware that it's one o'clock in the morning?"

"Is it? Oh God, I'm so sorry. I lost track of time. I—"

"Who is this please?"

"My name is Matthew Delaney."

Now everyone's a Delaney. Madness of a new kind. Does it ever stop?

"Are you about to tell me you're my father?" Miriam says.

"Actually, I'm your brother."

There is a long pause.

"Hello?" the man says.

Miriam takes a sharp intake of breath as though she is about to speak.

"Are you all right?"

"I don't know what to believe," she says.

"I think that's a solid way to live," he says.

"Why?"

"Better than being gullible."

"You don't know if I'm gullible or not."

"That's true."

They sit there for a while, together and apart. She can hear noises in the background, like he's moving his belongings from one place to another, books and magazines, that kind of thing. It's a good guess, because he's opening a sketchpad, putting it on his lap and letting the first few pages flop down over his knees. In his left hand, a phone; in his right, a stick of charcoal.

He's more believable than Eric Delaney. Miriam couldn't say why, he just is. Maybe this is a big scam and maybe it isn't. She is curious and afraid. "Are you really my brother?"

"I'm your half-brother. You have another one too."

"I have two brothers?"

"I'm twenty-one and Alfie is seven."

Miriam tries to picture them, a man and a boy, connected to her in some way that has yet to be seen. She wonders which features they share, which characteristics, if any at all. "Do you have a mum?" she says.

"I do," he says.

"Is she nice?"

"Most of the time."

"Mine's dead."

"I know. I'm sorry."

"Don't be. I thought both of my parents were dead. Now I'm supposed to believe one is alive."

"It's a mad world," Matthew says.

Miriam remembers Fenella saying this once. She remembers her singing about finding it kind of funny, finding it kind of sad, then saying the whole of life was a bit like that, and she might put it on her gravestone. *Here lies Fenella Price. She found it all kind of funny, she found it all kind of sad.* Miriam takes the phone through to the living room, opens the curtains, sits on the sofa and puts a blanket over her legs. "Sometimes I think it's too much," she says.

"My dad's a good man," Matthew says, which seems like an ill-fitting response, but who is the judge of what fits and what doesn't and what does a good fit look like?

"How do I know you're who you say you are?" Miriam doesn't really need to ask this question, because Matthew's voice is unlike any voice she has ever heard. They are connected. She can feel it. There are some things you just know.

"Dad has your birth certificate."

"Really?"

"He took it with him when you were a baby."

A congested silence.

"What do you do?" she says.

"Do?"

"For money."

"I work in a cinema."

"You watch a lot of films?"

"Loads. I also draw sorrow and go on long bike rides."

Miriam walks over to the window. She looks into the darkness, the bluish star-studded darkness. "I have a lot of sorrow," she whispers.

"I'm sure," he says, soft and deep.

"I used to work in a supermarket."

"Did you like it?"

"I was on the deli counter."

They talk about cheese, cold meats, what it's like to work with the public. They discuss what his house is like (small) and what hers is like (dated but very clean). Miriam makes a hot chocolate, Matthew makes a Horlicks and they sit back down. The call goes deeper into the night until:

"I'd like to meet you," he says.

"What about your dad?"

"*Our* dad."

A pause. A sniff.

"Would you tell him?"

"Of course. Are you free today at all?"

Treacle strolls past the sofa. Miriam reaches down, makes a kissing sound, rubs her finger and thumb together, but Treacle ignores her. This cat is not a fan of Miriam Delaney, who looks at the cuckoo clock and imagines smashing it to pieces with her old hockey stick. This clock is partially to blame for everything that happened—it called time, hour after hour, without ever calling time. It was reliable and ineffectual, rather like her hockey stick, which lasted for years and never hit a ball.

"Today," Miriam whispers.

"Why wait?"

"All right then. Where and when?"

Twelve miles away, a man is talking to his sister and she is right here, beside the window in the front room. She has been here all along.

I don't know which is most terrifying, she thinks—believing you're alone in the world, or discovering that you're not.

32

GAMES

The phone wakes him up and he lies in bed, listening. He looks at the alarm clock, it says 01.12 a.m., which can't be good. Someone must have died, but who is there in Miriam's life to die? Only Boo and Fenella, otherwise it's all about the one who has returned: the *undead*.

Ralph remembers trying to play some silly zombie game on Sadie's iPad, for which he showed zero aptitude. He was better at racing games, he said. He had never played a racing game, but how hard could it be?

He wonders how long it will take Julie Parsley to reply to his email. Was it even the *right* Julie Parsley? This anticipation feels good, like having something written on the calendar—an event, a plan, lurking in the future, inviting him to move towards it.

Julie Parsley, a lifelong insomniac wearing Moomin pyjamas, is staring at her laptop screen. She puts a Hotel Chocolat pistachio praline in her mouth. This email from Ralph Swoon came as a shock. Where did he find her email address? Can anyone find it? Is she a sitting duck, a target for stalkers and crackpots, or is this just the way of the world? *Ralph Swoon, goodness me.* She saw him in B&Q at Easter but he didn't see her. He was wandering around the shop with his wife, who looked more beautiful now than when Julie saw them ten years ago—*Much Ado about Nothing*, an outdoor performance in the park. Ralph has done well for himself, if one goes by appearances, which most people do.

Julie eats another chocolate and thinks for a long time. She doesn't like meeting new people. All those questions going back and forth, not to mention all the inevitable answers. An information highway, most of it bullshit, let's be honest, come on, we all know it. She finds it hard enough to relax with friends, let alone people she doesn't know. Ralph is a stranger. His knowledge of her is out of date. They're not teenagers any more. They've had shit to deal with. Piles and piles of shit.

She decides not to write about the piles of shit. Instead, she invites him to the Nordic Coffee House—her territory, her turf. A quick coffee and a pastry. It'll be over in an hour. It's the polite thing to do. It's honouring a past that she can't even remember.

He replies straight away, which unnerves her. She pictures him sitting in front of a screen in a dark room, which shouldn't be unnerving, because this is precisely what she is doing. He says he's off work, no commitments, any time is good, *as soon as possible?*

Might as well get it out of the way, she thinks. It'll be good to cross it off the list, even though it isn't actually on the list yet. The list exists in her mind: Things I Have To Do That I Don't Want To Do. Otherwise known as Daytime.

33

The taxi driver is *drunk.*

He is talking about St Ives again, saying he would buy every damn house, shop, gallery if he could, which would make him the *fucking King of St Ives*. He loves every inch of that place, but St Ives is a whore, *a filthy whore*, and when Alison asked why he was here instead of there she had no idea that she was pressing a button, flicking a switch. His disappointment, all over the dashboard. His despair, all over the passenger seat.

Now he is driving at fifty-seven miles per hour through a residential area. The front windows are open, and he can't hear his passengers protesting behind him.

Sadie and Alison reach into their bags for their mobile phones but there's no time to call the police. The car is swerving. The driver is shouting. They speed through four gardens and smash into a tree.

The driver jumps out, runs across the grass.

The surrounding houses begin to light up, windows and doors open, people rush outside. They were asleep, watching TV, arguing, making tomorrow's packed lunch, having sex and, in one case, reorganizing a knicker drawer by colour and style, and now they are standing in their porches and front gardens staring at a taxi, a bent tree, a man running away.

Alison opens the car door. Without thinking, she also starts to run.

Sadie doesn't register this at first. She is looking under the passenger seat for her mobile phone, which flew from her lap when the car swerved and crashed. She hears the door open, hears footsteps, has a horrible sense that something precious has gone. She fumbles in the dark, reaching as far forward as she can until her fingers find something hard, something rectangular.

A man's voice: "You all right, love?" He is peering in, looking at a woman with her head between her knees, assuming that she is badly hurt.

Sadie straightens up, puffs out air as if she were in labour, holds up her phone. "I'm okay," she says, breathless, "but only just." And this, she realizes at that moment, is the story of Sadie Swoon. She is always okay, but only just. And what happens when you are only just okay? People take no notice, no one rallies round, nothing happens. This is middle-of-the-road life, a life of moderation, checklists (*feed dog, pick Stanley up at six, buy padded bra*) and as many raw vegetables as possible to extend this life of moderation, to make the endurance test go on and on.

"I always thought of myself as subversive," Sadie says. "What a *joke*."

"Right," the man says. He is wearing stripy pyjamas.

"I bought him flowers all the time. I was always in charge of the barbecue."

"I see," the man says. This woman is clearly concussed. She is babbling. He turns away for a second to beckon his wife with a frantic wave.

"I'm the most sociable person you'll ever meet," Sadie says, "and mostly I dislike other people." She buries her face in her hands but the tears she is expecting don't come. She is emotionally constipated, has been for as long as she can remember. She is *bunged up*. Must've been those bloody antidepressants. Do they make laxatives for the psyche? What's the emotional equivalent of a prune? She looks up at the man, who has been joined by a woman in a burgundy dressing gown.

"I've called an ambulance, dear," the woman says, leaning in to take a good look. She sees something in Sadie's face, a kind of anguish, a desperation that makes those five words seem grotesquely inadequate. She tightens the belt of her dressing gown and gets in the car. "You're not alone, dear," she says, pulling the door shut.

Sadie examines the stranger's expression—warm and full of pity. Where is Alison Grabowski, the one who was here first, just moments ago? She leans forward, trying to see past the stranger's massive breasts, wide shoulders, enormous hair, but all she can see is the woman's husband, who seems to be drawing circles in the air with a sparkler but there is no sparkler.

"He wants me to open the window," the woman says, expelling warm breath that smells of brandy. "But I see no need."

Sadie feels sick. The woman's perfume, body and breath are filling up the car, eating the air. Soon they will both suffocate. This woman has the power to do that. She is the sort of person who would hold a pillow over someone's face and then potter off to bleach some cups when the deed was done. Oh yes, Sadie is completely sure of this. She sneers and shakes her head. "You should be ashamed of yourself," she says.

"You're concussed, dear," the woman replies, smiling. Her mouth seems to bulge as if she has too many teeth.

"No," Sadie says. It's the same *no* she uses on Harvey

when he pulls socks off the clothes horse and shakes them as if they were a rabbit. She opens the car door and gets out. An ambulance arrives, paramedics dive into the car and start assessing the woman in the burgundy dressing gown, and she goes along with it, she says I feel shell-shocked and strange, and her husband watches, knowing that his wife's cumbersome tendency to snatch attention from anyone and everyone is gradually making him hate her—*really* hate her. She is the Pac-Man of middle-aged women, forever munching. *That's* why her mouth seems to bulge—it's full of what she has taken from other people and is incapable of digesting.

Sadie moves towards a small crowd on one of the front lawns. Huddled together in nighties, pyjamas, shorts and vests, they are watching Alison Grabowski, who is chasing the taxi driver from one immaculate lawn to the next. Someone says look at her go, she's got balls that girl, but Sadie can't tell where the voice is coming from. *Look at her go, she's bloodywell got him, she's on top of him. Give the girl a round of applause!*

And she is. She is on top of him. It looks sexual but it isn't (although one can never be sure).

"Quite a woman," says the man in stripy pyjamas, whose Pac-Woman wife is now sitting in an ambulance with a blanket around her shoulders.

"Yes," Sadie says, but the word breaks, splits in her mouth, tastes like metal.

The man hears it break. He checks his pockets for a tissue to give to this woman, but there are no pockets—just flappy pyjamas, big blue buttons, flannelette. He feels useless, underdressed.

A woman's voice: "Are you crying?" It's Alison. A word accidentally slips from her mouth: "Darling?" she says.

"I don't cry," Sadie says.

34

A BICYCLE BUILT FOR TWO

Miriam is early. Ninety minutes early. She is sitting on the grass in the park, waiting for a man who is a stranger and not a stranger. This is new—waiting in the outside world for someone who *wants* to see her. Perhaps other people are used to this kind of thing? It's highly likely. Other people are used to all kinds of things that Miriam has never tried. Lovers' tiffs. Holidays. Bowls of pasta in Italian restaurants. *Sex.* She wonders if Matthew has had sex. It's a little odd, thinking about your brother's sex life, but having a sibling is another thing Miriam isn't used to. Is the conversation between siblings different to other conversations? Can they read each other's minds?

"Imagine that your head is a glass box," Frances said to her ten-year-old daughter. "I can always see what's inside it."

"No you can't."

"I can. Your thoughts aren't private, Mim."

That afternoon Miriam bought a bobble hat to cover the glass box, and wore it every day until her mother flushed it down the toilet, which caused a blockage.

"Is this a bobble hat?" the plumber said.

"So what if it is?" Frances said. "What a woman flushes down the toilet is her own business."

"Well I never. Can I take a photo?"

"No you cannot take a photo. Do you have a perversion?"

"Do *you*?"

Miriam realizes something. She doesn't actually know what Matthew looks like. How will she recognize him? Her eyes will dart from man to man. Are you my brother? Am I your sister? She has no idea that Matthew will recognize *her*. He knows that she stayed inside her house for three years. How does he know what he knows? He talks to people. Like his father, he makes talking look easy. He's a conversational pickpocket. It's dialogical pilferage. It's fancy talk.

She sits and waits and wonders what she will do for the next ninety minutes. She needed to get out of the house—Ralph was driving her mad with all his Parsley this and Parsley that and he wasn't even cooking.

Matthew is spreading butter and raspberry jam on a slice of toast. He looks at his father, who is unusually quiet. They are all unusually quiet, even Alfie, who has just been informed that his dad was once married to another woman, and thanks to this horrible confusing out-of-the-blue union, he has a sister who is really really old (thirty-five). He's already been to her house. He put postcards through her door. 7 Beckford Gardens— remember, Alfie? Matthew knew about the sister but didn't tell him. He did this for Alfie's own good because their father was waiting for the right time, even though there's no such thing.

"Time has a life of its own, like the sea," Matthew says.

"How did you know about her?" Alfie says.

"I overheard Mum and Dad talking about her before you were born."

"Before me?" he says, because time before Alfie is inconceivable.

"Before you."

"What time was it?" Alfie says, squinting at the kitchen clock.

"Sorry?"

"What time did you hear it?"

"I have no idea. It was late, though. Late at night."

He was sitting on the stairs, holding an empty glass, and they were discussing a girl.

"I can't imagine how that must feel," his mother was saying.

"It's awful."

"Perhaps it's not too late?"

"You haven't met Frances. It just feels wrong, letting Matthew believe he's an only child when he has a sister."

A sister?

Silence. Matthew sat perfectly still. He shivered. It was January. He had only come downstairs for milk and a Wagon Wheel and now he had a sister. So where was she?

"When she was a baby she had this toy penguin. She held it so tight. She was scared, Angie, even then, I'm sure of it. Her little knuckles would turn white."

"Don't, Eric. You're just upsetting yourself. You did what was best."

"Did I?"

"You were only eighteen."

"That's hardly an excuse."

"Did you get your Wagon Wheel?" Alfie says.

"No, I don't think so."

"Why not?"

"I think I just went back to bed."

Alfie looks at Amy Pond. The look says: "Help me, Amy. Call Doctor Who. Take me back in time to erase the lady who is not my mum."

"I can't do that," Amy says. She is soft and kind and Scottish. "Doctor Who doesn't *erase* people unless they're a threat to the human race."

Alfie sighs. Naughty Amy! What a silly answer. Can't she see he's suffering? Under threat? And he's part of the human race. He's a small human being with a big problem and that problem is called *turbulence*. He knows what turbulence is, he saw it happen to an aeroplane on TV and now it's happening to him. ("Is turbulence the same as flatulence?" he had asked his mum, shortly after the programme. "Well, they both involve wind," she said, "but no, they are *not* the same thing.")

"I'm going to meet Miriam today," Matthew says.

"Why?"

"Because she should be part of our family."

"Steady on," Eric says. "She may not want to be part of this family."

"Are you going too?" Alfie says.

"No," Eric says. "Matthew arranged this himself."

Eric and Angelina exchange a look of powerlessness, gratitude, bewilderment.

"Why?"

"Because I want to buy her a cup of tea," Matthew says.

"Doesn't she have tea at her house?"

"I have no idea."

"Is she nice?"

"She sounded nice on the phone."

Alfie stabs a block of butter with a knife.

"Alfie, please," his mother says, grabbing the knife.

"Are you going to swap me?"

"What do you mean?"

"Is she going to take my place?"

Eric stands up. He asks Alfie to do the same. Father and son face each other in the middle of the kitchen. Matthew and Angelina watch and eat toast as Eric picks Alfie up and spins him around. He tickles him, turns him upside down, says that's the daftest thing I've ever heard you crazy crazy boy, you're stuck with us for life, do you hear me? They play the human aeroplane game, even though Alfie is a bit old for this now, and it's a smooth flight with no turbulence at all, and the plane is giggling, it's giggling really loudly, because the pilot is brilliant and he's going nowhere.

And then Matthew has gone and the room is too quiet and no one is giggling any more.

"Maybe you could draw Miriam a picture?" his mum says.

"Why should I?" Alfie says.

He sees her in the park, cross-legged on the grass with her hands on her lap. He walks over and stands beside her, staring at the top of her head. "Miriam Delaney?" he says, rather abruptly.

She jumps to her feet, startled.

His arms are wide open. After years without physical affection, he is the second person this summer to offer her a hug. Before she can make up her mind he lowers his arms and steps forward to kiss her on the cheek.

He is six feet tall. Wiry. Messy light-brown hair, brushed forward, long over the ears. Clean-shaven. Earnest.

"Hello, Miriam," he says.

"Hello," she whispers, forgetting that he already knows what kind of sound she makes. She waits for him to respond, to say *sorry?* or *what?* or *speak up*, but he doesn't.

"Would you like a cup of tea?" he says.

"That would be nice."

In the cafe near the park entrance, he chooses a table by the window and pulls out a chair for her to sit on. They order tea and egg sandwiches from a waitress in an old-fashioned uniform who is solemn and frilly.

Through the window, they watch two men playing tennis. Words do not come easily—this is not like the phone call a few hours ago.

"That was a good shot," Matthew says.

"It was," Miriam says.

"Do you play tennis?"

"No."

"Me neither. I'm not very sporty."

"No?"

"No. Do you have any hobbies?"

Miriam looks at him blankly. The silence is awkward, vertiginous, it feels like falling.

"I like box sets," she says, finally.

"Me too," he says.

They say something and nothing. They drink tea and eat sandwiches. A baby screams and they roll their eyes, pretending to mind the noise. (Miriam notices how his eyes are brown like hers.) They are shy and lost but Matthew has a plan, a way to bring them together.

"Would you like to go for a bike ride?" he says, when their plates are empty.

Miriam has never ridden a bike. She doesn't own one. *A bike ride?* What an odd thing to suggest at a time like this.

It's disappointing too, because now she is feeling like she so often feels in the company of others: stupid, alien, out of her depth.

"I don't know how," she says.

"That's okay. I'll do the work."

He'll *what?*

"Would you like to see my bike?"

Not really, she thinks. I'd rather have a piece of cake and ask about your father.

Matthew leads the way across the park. It's a relief to be outside, not face to face under bright lights in a room full of insistent waitresses who want to know things. (Would you like tea or coffee or cake or sandwiches? *I don't know I don't know I don't know.*)

Miriam buys a Mr Whippy with a flake for Matthew and a lemonade lolly for herself. As they walk past a small lake, she imagines that he is five and she is nineteen. Is this the sort of day they would have shared? A stroll in the sun, an ice cream, talk of bicycles? But he is not five and she is not nineteen. It is sixteen years later and he is telling her that he likes art, bikes, Oasis. He makes it look effortless, this listing of things, as though his self is solid and fixed and easy to explain. What else does he like? Charcoal, George Orwell, life drawing, *Wallander*, roast dinners and postcards.

He stops walking. "I sent you eight postcards," he says.

"They were from *you?*"

"Yes."

"Why?"

"I was trying to make contact."

"You could have picked up the phone."

He blushes, looks guilty. "I got Alfie to post them while I waited in the car."

A high-pitched whisper as his words sink in: "You've been to my house?"

He freezes. She looks so sad.

In her mind, Miriam shouts: *This was a mistake. You're crazy. I need Ralph. He'll take me home. I need Ralph.*

"I just wanted to reach you," he says. "That's why I sent them. And why I brought you this." He rummages through his bag and pulls out a small wooden tree. He holds it upside down and points at the base. "Tree of Simplicity, see? Dad made it years ago. I kept it for you."

Miriam takes the tree from his hand and inspects the wording: TREE OF SIMPLICITY. It is beautiful. Intricate. The tree is crooked. It has one tiny leaf, painted orange.

They walk on in silence, following a footpath along the edge of the park. As the path curves, it opens into a parking area for bikes. Right in the middle of the row, secured by two locks, is a tandem: two handlebars, two sets of pedals, two seats.

"What do you think?" Matthew says.

"There are many bikes," Miriam says. "Which one is yours?"

"This one," he says, tapping the tandem.

That cumbersome thing? A bicycle built for two?

"I can't get on that."

"Why not?"

"People will stare."

"So?" he says, unlocking the bike.

What is he doing now? She watches him bend down and look inside his bag. He pulls out some kind of music player and a massive pair of red headphones. Miriam has never seen such ridiculous headphones. She would feel self-conscious wearing those, but he doesn't seem to worry about such things. He—

Excuse me?

is putting the headphones on her head, adjusting them until

they are tight. He presses something on the music player and slips it inside her pocket. Now she can't hear anything. The world is silent. It's nice. Until—

My God that's loud!

He smiles at the tinny sound coming from the headphones. "Come on," he shouts. He is sitting on the front seat, gesticulating towards the back. He wants her to get on. To get on *now*. "Come on!"

She does what he says. She gets on the bike. *And they're off.* Four feet on four pedals. He's steering, they've left the park, they're cycling down the main road. Now they're turning left, heading downhill and it's so bloody fast, the wind is in her hair, he's yelling woohoo! and she can just about hear him over the sound of Oasis, 'Don't Look Back in Anger', and there's another woohoo, it's wispy and small but definitely there, in her throat in her mouth, making its way out as she closes her eyes, as she kicks out her legs, and the woo is a whisper but the hoo is something else, it's richer and bigger, part whisper part song, and this is her secret, just hers for now, the woo and the hoo and the speeding downhill on a bicycle built for two.

35

I PREFER MOOMINS TO PEOPLE

Ralph can't find the coffee shop. Julie Parsley is close but he can't locate her. He stops a passer-by, a woman pushing a toddler in a buggy. The buggy seems to be covered in wraparound plastic—can the child actually breathe in there? Is this woman attempting to suffocate her son? It looks like it was designed for mud, snow, treacherous conditions, not a summer's day and a quiet street in an artisan quarter of town.

"Excuse me," Ralph says.

"I can't stop," the woman says. Put together, her facial expression and tone are a cryptic duo—a blend of Charlotte Rampling and Kenneth Williams.

Ralph notices that inside the plastic cover the toddler is unseasonably dressed in a bobble hat.

"I have to make and do," the woman says.

"Make and do?"

"I made this bobble hat," she says, tapping the boy's head through the plastic, waking him up. He begins to cry. "Today is knitted animals."

"I see," Ralph says, but all he can see is a camp and mysterious woman, an intrepid buggy, a red-faced child.

"Don't cry, honeybun," the woman says to the toddler. "You're *always* crying."

"Why the cover?"

She scowls, shakes her head. "Surely you realize that he isn't *safe* without the cover?" Then she rushes off, pushing the buggy as fast as she can. In her mind she is racing against a troop of mothers, trying to keep up, longing for a time when life doesn't feel like a competition. The mothers fill the streets but Ralph can't see them. He can only see his own ghosts, his own projections, dancing around him, shadowy.

The door of a bike shop opens and a young man cycles through it on a mountain bike. He cycles up the road and back again, turning this way and that way. It's a test drive. Try before you buy. As he freewheels towards him, Ralph holds up his hand.

"Excuse me, do you happen to know where the Nordic Coffee House is?"

The squeak of new brakes. "Julie's place, you mean?" the man says, getting off the bike.

"Is it?"

"What?"

"Julie's place?"

"Julie P," he says, bending down to inspect the bike.

"Does she own the Nordic Coffee House?"

"It's part of her shop."

"I see."

(Today is a day of seeing and not seeing.)

"It's just up there on the right, next to Make and Do."

"That's great, thanks."

"No problem."

Julie's place. For a moment there is a kaleidoscope of butterflies in Ralph's stomach. They have J and P on their wings,
black on yellow, fluttering initials, beautiful. It's been so long
since he spoke to someone who knows Julie Parsley, who
speaks of her with warmth and familiarity. This could have been
his life: dropping her off at work in the mornings, getting to
know the people who run the bike shop, the delicatessen, the
hairdressers, the shop selling minimalistic music systems with
a wood-grain finish. As he walks along the street he pictures
himself having a trim in the salon, buying bread, cheese and
chocolate from the deli, waiting in his car while Julie sets the
alarm and locks the door of the Nordic House—a store selling all things Scandinavian, with a cafe at the back called the
Nordic Coffee House.

He wonders what his life might have looked like if he had
chosen Julie. What *he* might have looked like.

*Chosen Julie? That's a convenient way of remembering it,
Ralph. Easier than the truth: you were too intimidated to make
a move.*

As he opens the door and steps inside, Ralph finds himself face to face with a giant Moomin in a black hat. It's
Moominpappa—the romantic, the adventurer. Ralph used
to read Tove Jansson's books to Stanley and Arthur and he
remembers them well, but he has never been *face to face* with
a Moomin. (He recalls the huge gnome in B&Q, the one he
walked into when he last saw Julie. Is she destined to make
his world a cartoonish place, populated with fictional figures,
their lively rigidity both charming and disturbing?)

Behind Moominpappa there is Moomin world: mugs, tea
towels, cards, badges, plates, tablecloths, tote bags, spoons.
Once you've passed through Moomin world you arrive in a
room full of Scandinavian chairs, lights, clocks, plates, glasses

and candlesticks, accompanied by catalogues full of similar objects. A young woman with red hair sits at a desk in the corner. There's a cash register, a tiny Moominmamma, an iMac, a pile of paperwork.

"May I help you?" the woman asks, glancing up from the iMac.

"Just looking for the cafe," Ralph says.

The woman points at a large sign above a door. She smiles. The smile says: "How could you have missed that?" She doesn't realize that missing what is obvious is Ralph's forte.

He rolls his eyes. The rolling says: "I'm so stupid sometimes."

He walks up to the door. The door to *what*? His past? His future?

An excited voice: "I'm instant messaging a woman in Finland," the voice says.

Ralph turns to look at the woman with red hair, who is beaming at her iMac.

"I still find it amazing, you know? She's in Finland, and it's like she's sitting on my lap."

"On your lap?"

"If only," the woman says, squeezing the tiny Moominmamma.

Ralph opens the door to the Nordic Coffee House. The first thing that hits him is the music. He used to own this album— *Hips and Makers*, Kristin Hersh. The walls of the coffee shop are either wood-panelled or covered in red tiles. There are seven tables, an abundance of stools, an industrial coffee machine, plates full of pastries, cookies and cakes covered with glass lids that look like upside-down bowls. At one of the tables, a woman is writing in a notebook. She has short black hair and olive skin. She is wearing grey sneakers, green linen trousers and a long-sleeved T-shirt, its three top buttons undone. She doesn't look up as Ralph walks over. On the table, alongside her notebook, there's a pencil case, an empty coffee cup and a plate covered with crumbs.

Now he is right beside her.

She is looking up, smiling, rising to her feet, pulling headphones from her ears.

He goes to kiss her on the cheek but she moves first, kissing one side of his face, then the other.

He could cry, so easily and for so long, but he doesn't.

Julie Parsley is sitting in the corner of her cafe, eating a Danish pastry, listening to Kate Bush on her iPod. The album is all about snow. Julie would happily live her entire life in snow, because snow is a departure, a cover-up, a slowing down of what is usually too fast. She turns up the volume and scribbles in her notebook. This scribbling is something to do while she is waiting for Ralph. It will make her look busy and diligent and less self-conscious than usual. She writes the words *waiting for Ralph*, which inflates the significance of the waiting and makes her feel self-conscious. The scribbling has backfired, but Julie is used to how this feels. *C'est la vie.*

Ralph goes to kiss her on the cheek but she moves first, kissing one side of his face, then the other. He asks if she would like another drink and she says no, you sit down, what would you like, I'll get these. He says some kind of pastry would be nice. He is starving. He didn't eat breakfast this morning. He sat and watched while Miriam devoured a plate of eggs, bacon, tomatoes, mushrooms and toast. When she is nervous she eats. When he is nervous he fails to see what is in front of him, and considering the fact that he is often nervous (low-level edginess, normalized by its own longevity), he spends most of his life blinkered.

A few minutes later they are looking down at a latte, a macchiato, a cinnamon and raisin swirl.

Ralph says the word *so*, it comes out loud and quick.

"So," Julie says.

And so it begins, their afternoon together, which opens with coffee and closes with a surprising announcement.

"I can't tell you how good it is to see you," he says.

"I'm sure you could if you wanted to," she says.

His cheeks flush. He mutters something about the pastry being delicious.

"If Kate Bush can think of fifty ways to describe snow, I'm sure you can tell me why it's good to see me after all this time."

"Kate Bush?"

Julie sips her macchiato. The years that have passed since they last met have stolen her ability to make small talk. They have stolen other things too. More important things.

Ralph sees that he has two choices. He can be as direct as her, or he can pull back with questions about the shop, the cafe, what she has been doing all this time. Deep or shallow, sink or swim. Fuck it, he thinks, tapping his feet to the beat of Julie Parsley. Some things clearly haven't changed—she's still sharp, candid. *Fuck it.*

"I've thought of you so often over the years," he says. (It's a BFL. It's a *big fat lie.*)

She bursts out laughing. Not the *best* response.

He laughs too, like it's funny, like it didn't really mean that much.

Silence.

She rubs her chin.

He eats his cinnamon and raisin swirl.

The man behind the industrial coffee machine watches them.

"Why are you here?" Julie says.

"Sorry?"

"Why are you here?"

"You don't mess about do you?"

"I can't be bothered with messing about. I've done too much of that already and where did it get me?"

"Where *did* it get you?"

She sighs. "I married a man with big hips," she says, "that's where it got me."

Ralph grimaces. "Big hips?"

"It was the great tragedy of his life, being hippy instead of hip."

"Are you still together?"

"Fortunately not. By the end of our marriage he had two chins."

"Oh."

"He was a musician. I couldn't stand him. We never had children—couldn't be sure we had enough love to offer. When we divorced, I bought the shop and a flat and *thousands* of Moomins."

Ralph thinks of Miriam, who believes she is crazy while everyone else is sane.

"Do you still sing?" he asks, sipping his latte.

"Only at the beach when no one's around. I swim in the sea three times a week. Apart from that, I work. I prefer Moomins to people. Tove Jansson is my muse. I also do yoga and look after my father."

"Right."

"You didn't answer my question. Why are you here?"

"I'd been thinking about you. I wondered how you were."

"And now you know."

Well, sort of, he thinks.

"Your turn next," she says, impatiently.

"What would you like to know?"

"Married? Children? Employed?"

"Okay, well, I'm married to Sadie. We have two sixteen-year-old sons, Stanley and Arthur. I'm a psychotherapist—a bad one, because I've taken an early break without giving any notice. I haven't seen my family for a week and a half. I just walked out."

Interesting, Julie thinks. If this conversation were a walk down the street she would now be on his back, her legs around his waist.

"Where did you go?"

"To the woods."

"The woods."

"Yep."

"What happened in the woods?"

"I found a cat and slept in a shed."

"What else?"

"I met a woman called Miriam."

"She was in the woods?"

"No, she just arrived. It rained so much we couldn't stand it so we ran back to hers. It's purely platonic, though."

Julie leans forward. "What about the *cat*?" she says.

"I took her with me."

"How did you carry her?"

"In my arms."

"And where is she now?"

"At Miriam's."

"Good."

Ralph nods. He is out of breath.

Julie looks at her watch. "Do you have somewhere to be this afternoon?" she says.

"No, why?"

"I just wondered if you'd like to go to the beach."

"Now?"

"Yes."

He thinks for a moment, or pretends to. "Okay."

"I need to feed my father first."

Before Ralph can ask why her father needs feeding, Julie is sweeping her things into a rucksack. She tells him how much better she feels now he has explained why he's here. "You're lost in the woods," she says.

"What?"

"You're stumbling around in the woods."

"Er, no—"

"Oh yes," she says, making her fingers run across the table. "You're like one of Tove Jansson's little characters, scurrying through dead leaves. I wonder how it will end."

"How what will end?"

"The story of little Ralph Swoon."

Who is she calling *little?* Has she been speaking to Sadie?

The butterflies in his stomach have gone. Now he is just full of pastry and hot milk. He looks down at her tight-fitting top to make himself feel better; she sees him looking, her eyebrows are raised and she is smiling. The atmosphere changes, just like that, and he walks behind her, feeling calmer, feeling tall.

They enter the room full of Scandinavian objects. The young woman with red hair is laughing.

"She's Skyping Annika," Julie says. "They Skype at the same time every day."

"That's quite a commitment," Ralph says, following her through Moomin world and out into the street.

"What a strange thing to say."

"Is it?"

"I think so. It's lovely that they speak every day. They have no one else."

"Not the healthiest way to live," he says.

"What a smug psychotherapist you are," she says.

She blows hot, she blows cold. These are erratic conditions. Julie is as volatile as ever and Ralph strolls beside her past Make and Do, the shop selling minimalistic music systems, the hairdressers, the delicatessen, the bike shop. The sun is shining and his arms are covered in goosebumps.

"I really don't think I'm smug," he says.

36

WE ARE NEVER COMING DOWN

A woman's voice: "Are you crying?"

It is Alison Grabowski. The hero. The forty-year-old girl with balls. She is breathless, red-faced. The drunken taxi driver has landed and who brought him in? Alison Grabowski. *Take a bow, madam. Don't mind if I do. Are you some kind of vigilante, Ms Grabowski? Well not until now. I don't know what came over me to be honest, I think it was probably just adrenalin, the body talking, fight or flight. Well it's quite a victory, Ms Grabowski—quite a conquest. I must confess that it's not the conquest I was aiming for this evening. The King of St Ives is not the prize I had in mind...*

In Alison's mind there is champagne and clapping and for she's a jolly good fellow. But alongside the self-congratulation there is something else. Sadie Peterson (no, Alison, she's a Swoon remember? She's Sadie Swoon) is crying and it hurts Alison Grabowski, it actually hurts. When Bessie Bryant cries, Alison's responses range from irritation to wanting to fix the problem, but it's *never* particularly uncomfortable. What does this mean?

"Darling?"

"I don't cry," Sadie says, more breath than voice.

Alison assumes that all this *upset* is about the taxi driver and tonight's near-death experience (she has always been overdramatic), but she is wrong. Does it matter? Probably not. This innocuous misinterpretation is the first of many that will happen between them over the next three decades. If it were visible now—this misreading of the other's mind, this relational blunder—it would be something they could refer back to: *Do you remember the first time you thought I was thinking one thing when really I was thinking another? We were standing on a stranger's front lawn—you'd just sat on a taxi driver, do you remember? I was crying, but it had nothing to do with the taxi driver. I was crying because I loved you—not my husband, not Kristin—and the fact that I'd been able to put those feelings away was devastating. If I could repress something as vital as that, what else had I repressed? How could I trust myself? How much time had I wasted?*

"It's okay," Alison says, putting her arm around Sadie's shoulder.

"Where to, ladies?" a policeman says.

"Sorry?"

"I'm taking you home."

If I start to cry I might never stop. You hear people say this sometimes, when they're in so much emotional pain that crying feels like a trap instead of a release. Sadie, on the other hand, has been snared by an *inability* to cry. It's hard to remember the last time tears flowed from her eyes—the birth of her sons, perhaps, and since then, nothing. She has howled, moaned, made her breaths quick and jagged, scrunched up her face. *Zilch.*

And now she can't seem to stop.

She tells Alison this, between sobs—how she gets what people mean now, when they say that thing about not wanting to start.

Alison says I'm sorry, darling, I can't make out what you're saying, why don't you just breathe, sit quietly, try to breathe.

Two strangers, impelled to call each other *darling*. Nothing else needs to be said.

Sadie buries her face in a tissue. When she finally emerges she tells Alison to take a shower.

"You want me to take a shower?"

"I just need a few moments," she says, "to compose myself."

"Oh, I see. I thought you were trying to tell me something."

Sadie shakes her head. The tears are coming again, another wave rising.

"I do fancy a shower," Alison says.

"You go."

"All right."

Sadie sits up straight, places her hands flat on her thighs, talks to herself silently.

Jesus Christ. The embarrassment, the *shame*. Weeping all over her like that. I'm a soggy wreck of a woman. *Disgusting*. Why have I longed for *this*? This outpouring of God knows what.

Deep breaths, there we go.

Think of something uplifting. You can do it. Imagine Alison in the shower. There we go. That's better. No need to sit here crying is there?

That's it.

Everything's all right.

She gets up, takes a CD from a shelf and sets it playing. The voice of a woman fills the room: intense, urgent, American. Then a guitar that sounds as though it's being played in someone's bedroom: squeaky and monotonous.

you
are a spell and I
am a lesson and you
don't need a teacher and I
don't need a magician but

She sits back down and closes her eyes until it's time to see what is in front of her.

Alison is fresh-faced, bespectacled, her hair damp from the shower. She is wearing a red and grey skirt and a silky black top. A silver heart hangs from a chain around her neck. This is not the same Alison Grabowski as the one Sadie ate pizza with a few hours ago. That one could be guarded, distant, a little suspicious. And this one? Sadie eyes her up and down and watches her fill two glasses with whisky.

"Feeling any better?" she says, joining Sadie on the sofa.

"Bit calmer."

"That's good."

"I'm sorry."

"Don't be."

"It's just that—"

"It's okay," Alison says.

"Is it?"

Alison leans in.

(There are so many ways to say *yes*.)

She leans into a first kiss that has taken eighteen years to happen.

A kiss with history.

Sadie's mind is empty.

Her thoughts have flown.

It's a respite, a reprieve from

No.
Stop.
Who cares what it's a reprieve from?
That was then and this is

a skyscraper, a tower
we walk high above the city
we use stars as stepping stones
we are never coming down

And Alison says you're beautiful, I must have told you that, way back when. You're just, I don't know, *you're just.*

And Sadie says I'm not playing games, this is serious, Alison—do you know what you're letting yourself in for?

And Alison says I used to live with you, remember? I know what a complete pain you can be.

And Sadie says this is serious, okay, *I am really being serious.*

And Alison says I know, so am I, don't worry.

And Sadie says I made a joke, years ago—I was glib and stupid and everything was a joke until it wasn't.

And Alison says stop, you'll make yourself cry again. I really think it's time to stop talking.

From the bedroom, Sadie can hear a car alarm, two men shouting, a woman singing, footsteps on a pavement.

"That singing sounds really close."

"It's Leonora. She sings with her window open."

"She's good—sounds like Tracey Thorn."

"She does, doesn't she?"

Alison's body is pale and slim. She has muscular arms and narrow shoulders. Sadie can't stop looking. It makes Alison laugh.

Then they are not laughing.

(This is *serious*.)

Leonora is singing about a knife, rusty and cold.

If I can't have you baby, no one can.

The car alarm is still going off.

Feet are still walking along the pavement.

The men are no longer shouting.

If I can't have you baby, no one can.

A candle flickers and goes out.

This is then and this is now.

After breakfast, Sadie calls Ralph's parents.

"I beg your pardon?" Brenda says. She has a knack of making Sadie feel incomprehensible.

"I said I've had to go away at short notice. Could you possibly keep an eye on Stan and Arthur? You know I wouldn't normally ask, but things are difficult right now."

"Ralph called us this morning."

"What?"

"He told us the boys are home alone."

"They're sixteen, Brenda. They're absolutely fine. But it might be nice if you and Frank went round to see them, that's all I'm saying."

"Where are you, Sadie?"

"Sorry?"

"Well it's not as if you're working. Unless you've finally got a job?"

"Can you call in or not?"

There is a pause. Muffled voices. Sadie is sure she hears the word *bitch*.

"We've already discussed this with Ralph," Brenda says. "And we're moving in for a while."

"That's really not necessary, Brenda. There's absolutely no—"

The phone goes dead.

What just happened?

37

J ulie Parsley drives a red Fiat 500. It holds the road better than Ralph thought it would. He tells her this but she doesn't reply. Maybe it's boring. Maybe she's thinking about something else.

"Julie?" he says.

"I don't like to talk while I'm driving," she says. "Life and death are only separated by a cat's whisker you know."

"A cat's whisker?"

"That's all," she says.

Ralph looks out of the window. He pictures Julie singing 'Move Over Darling' on stage at the King's Head. He remembers the evenings they spent together at the Maypole Social Club for teens—the way he used to watch her. How could she seem so experienced when she was only fifteen? She knew things about the world that he didn't, and the things she knew made her distant and gloomy. It was a solemn kind of maturity, a dark sensuality that made her irresistible to older men. They stared at Julie. They offered to buy her drinks. Eat your heart out Doris Day, they said. She's going places that one, they said. But the places they had in mind were not where Julie wanted to go. Her sultriness was not for the pleasure of her friends' pitiful fathers—men who spent every other night in the King's Head.

As a teenager, Ralph had a plan. He was going to woo Julie Parsley. How? By going to university, of course. By going away and coming back. His absence would make her miss him and then he would turn up, less boyish and naive, full of talk about seminars, lectures and bars, and he would say so then Julie Parsley, how about I buy you dinner at that Italian place by the river? And she would say fine, if you want to, because Julie was the Queen of Understatement.

But he didn't come back wearing a new jumper and new shoes.

By then, he was married with children.

"What are you thinking?" Julie says.

"I thought you didn't talk while you're driving?"

"I don't have a problem with listening."

"But you won't respond?"

"No."

"Not much of a dialogue then."

"I can respond afterwards."

"You're talking and driving now by the way."

Both hands on the wheel, looking ahead all the time, she says: "Ralph Swoon, when did you become so prickly?"

"First I'm smug, now I'm prickly."

She smiles.

"Maybe you bring it out in me," he says.

"Maybe I do," she says. "So what were you thinking?"

"I was remembering you singing at the King's Head. You were gorgeous back then."

"Oh thanks very much."

"You know what I mean."

"I'm not sure I do."

"You were gorgeous then and you're gorgeous now."

Cornered, Ralph. You're *always* cornered. (Will you ever come out fighting?)

She takes her eyes off the road, just for a second, to look at him.

It's true, he thinks. You were and you are. But you're different now. Of course you'd be different now.

"Here we are," Julie says, parking the car outside a bungalow.

"Is this your father's place?"

"It is."

Mr Hugh Parsley. Retired artist. Hugely successful in Europe. Ralph hasn't seen him for years. Whatever happened to Mrs Parsley, the voice coach who developed an insurmountable stutter at the height of her career?

"And your mother?"

"That's a sad story," Julie says. No explanation follows.

Hugh Parsley is watching *Starsky & Hutch* on a gigantic television. "David Soul!" he shouts as they enter the room. "Paul Michael Glaser!"

"He likes to state the names of actors," Julie says, glancing at the moving picture on the living-room wall.

"And who are you?" Hugh asks.

"This is Ralph Swoon, a friend from school."

"You're still at school?"

"No, Dad, from my *schooldays*."

"And his name's Swoon?"

"That's right."

Ralph walks up to Hugh's chair and holds out his hand. Hugh kisses it, then inspects Ralph's nails.

Julie's expression doesn't change. She has clearly seen this a hundred times before. "Fish fingers?" she shouts.

"Fish fingers?" Hugh shouts back. "Don't mind if I do, dear."

"In a sandwich or with chips?"

"Fish-finger butty with gherkins, if that's all right."

"On its way."

Julie wanders off into the kitchen, leaving Ralph alone with Hugh Parsley and the gigantic television.

"Have you come to ask me for her hand in marriage?" Hugh says.

"Oh no, nothing like that. I'm already married."

"To a man?"

"To a woman."

"Got any pets?"

"One dog." Ralph pauses. "And a cat."

"Don't you like the cat?"

"The cat's new. I forgot about it for a second."

"Why don't you sit down?"

"Actually, I think I'll give Julie a hand in the kitchen," Ralph says, noticing the pile of magazines on the sofa. One in particular catches his eye: *Make Your Own Helicopter*.

"Baby Ralph," Hugh says, laughing. "You always were a big baby. Are you aware that I'm not the actor Hugh Bonneville from *Downton Abbey*?"

"I am aware of that, yes."

"It's just that people tend to get us mixed up."

Despite the twenty-year age difference?

"Right."

A perfume advert appears on the TV and Hugh shouts: "Brad Pitt with long hair! When did he turn into a country singer?"

The three of them eat fish-finger butties and watch the news.

"Do you know what's going on in the world?" Hugh says to Ralph.

"Not *everything*," Ralph says. He is finding his fish-finger and gherkin butty surprisingly tasty. He has never had a butty before. A sandwich, yes. A roll, yes. But never a *butty*.

"Don't you watch the news?"

"I normally do."

"Self-obsessed?"

"I'm sorry?"

"Don't be sorry. Some people are just born that way," Hugh says, before summarizing the news at the same time as the newsreader on TV is also summarizing the news. Noise upon noise. Two announcements colliding.

"We're going to the beach this afternoon," Julie says.

"Why would you drive so far? You hate driving."

"For a change of scenery, Dad."

"Are you eloping? He's married already, to a man. They have a cat."

Julie kisses her father on the cheek. "I'll just wash up, then we'll be off. Don't forget to watch the Channel 5 film at three."

Ralph's phone vibrates. It's a text from Boo Hodgkinson: Hello there Ralph, I hope this message finds you well. I've decided to fiercely pursue Miriam. What do you think of this please? Best wishes, Boo X

"That's from his lover," Hugh says, before choking on a gherkin. Once he has recovered and wiped his chin, he asks Ralph another question. "Can you play the guitar, Ralphy boy?"

"He can," Julie says. "He used to play all the time."

Hello? I can speak for myself you know. And my name is not *Ralphy boy*. "Why do you ask?"

"Go get it, Julie," Hugh says, clapping his hands.

"Dad, we haven't got time."

"One song, Jules."

Raised eyebrows, tight lips, stiff back. Ralph imagines David Attenborough observing Julie from a distance: "And when the female Parsley is irritated, she displays this quite clearly by pushing out her stomach and stiffening her body from the waist upwards. Her eyes are fixed on the father, and any minute now she will—"

"One song and that's it," Julie says.

Hugh has a request: 'Little Boxes'. It's one of his favourites. Julie sings it for him sometimes, when she calls in to deliver his Monday evening treat—a hot chocolate with marshmallows from the local cafe. On Tuesdays he gets a Chinese takeaway. On Wednesdays a coffee flavoured with syrup. On Thursdays and Fridays he gets nothing, but that's life. Take what you can get and be grateful (Hugh's motto).

And so Ralph plays 'Little Boxes'. His performance is clumsy, what some might call *experimental*, but Julie and Hugh can see that he's trying and that's what matters. What Ralph lacks in ability he makes up for in effort, which is not something that can be said for the rest of his life.

Julie sings. She still has it. Fantastic. Just *fantastic*. Ralph's mood brightens as she sings. He can feel it, the regeneration, the renewal. She is making him new. Her voice is a glitter ball. It's disco time. Let's dance. No, calm down, keep playing the guitar. Hugh is clapping again. The news is still on. Such discord. Cacophony. He winces, even though he's having fun. This moment is it. What? Just *it*, he thinks.

The song is over too soon.

On the gigantic television, a trailer for *Downton Abbey*.

"Well if it isn't Hugh Bonneville!" Hugh shouts, and bursts out laughing.

"Do you need the toilet, Dad?" Julie says.

"Don't mind if I do," Hugh says.

Julie speeds into the beach car park, sending a cloud of dust into the air. They sit and watch as four young women run past. Julie opens the window. They can hear the women saying can you believe it, I can't believe it can you?

"What's going on?" Julie calls out.

"There's a man on the beach, *naked*," one of the women says.

"So?"

"Well it's not a nudist beach is it? It's not a beach for dangling his *you know what*."

Julie laughs. She likes these women. She imagines having them as friends, then quickly losing them. This is what happens, she's careless like that, clumsy when it comes to people, just drops them, oops, *there goes another*.

"He's got some cheek," a woman says, which makes the rest of them squeal.

"We found him queuing for an ice cream."

"What did he get?" Julie says, enjoying the way their voices are getting faster and higher, a symphony of gossip.

"It looked like a Mini Milk lolly."

"It wasn't the only thing that looked like a Mini Milk lolly."

They squeal again, their bodies convulsing, and one of the women slaps her friend's bottom out of sheer delight, which stops the laughter for a second, then it begins again, carrying the words *deary me* and *stop it I need the loo*.

"Bye ladies," Julie says, winding down the window.

"Do you know them?" Ralph says.

"Never seen them before in my life."

"They certainly cheered you up."

"What do you mean?"

A blanket, a towel, a flask, a Kit Kat Chunky. Ralph sits cross-legged on the blanket, grimacing at the seagulls hopping about on the sand, while Julie Parsley strips down to her underwear and runs into the water.

Matching bra and knickers, duck-egg blue, revealed to the world, just like that.

He watches her swimming, an eastwards front crawl, then back again. She's a strong swimmer, fast and steady. She floats on her back, her feet poking out of the water, looks in his direction and waves.

Now she is standing in front of him, dripping. It's not the *worst* view he's ever seen. She hides inside a grey towel and the matching bra and knickers fall to the floor. The towel is a damp dressing room. He looks away, stares at the sea as she steps into her linen trousers and pulls a long-sleeved T-shirt over her head. He is watching without watching, looking without looking, and she knows what he is doing and she doesn't mind. This is nice, she thinks. It's *interesting*.

He pulls two plastic cups from the top of a flask and unscrews the lid. "Tea?" he says. Then: "I didn't expect to see your underwear *quite* so soon."

She laughs. "So you expected to see it, did you?"

"Who knows," he says.

On a blanket, side by side, they drink tea and watch teenagers learning how to surf.

"What *were* your intentions?" Julie says.

"I rarely have any intentions."

"I knew you were going to say that."

"No you didn't."

"You haven't changed that much."

"*You* have."

"You might be happier if you had firm intentions. You need to visualize what you want."

"That's very New Age, Julie."

"Not really. I'm not talking about magical thinking. You just don't seem to care what happens to you."

He thinks it over, but he is tired of thinking, so he stops.

"Your life," he says. "It's not the one I imagined you'd be living."

"None of us lives the life we imagined we'd be living."

"But yours is so..."

"So?..."

"I don't know." He wants to say *mundane*. He wants to say that he had expected her to be doing something extraordinary—something that would inspire him.

"I'm a carer," she says. "I'm single and I work in a shop. Is that what you're trying to say?"

"No, not at all. You're a businesswoman. You're *independent*."

She rolls her eyes. "I would describe you as handsome," she says. "Amongst other things."

"Really?"

"Don't look so surprised. Surely your wife must say it?"

Is she winding him up? Flirting with him? He just can't tell.

"Sadie doesn't really go in for compliments."

"Cold?"

"No, she's not cold."

What are you talking about, Ralph? She's as cold as they come.

"Just not very warm?"

"Can we not talk about my wife?"

Julie sips her tea. She looks at where the sea meets the sky.

This meeting is an illusion, a meeting of the mind. "Are you her favourite person?" she says.

What kind of question is that?

"Well, she married me. We tend to marry our favourite person don't we?"

This statement hangs between them, sandy and stupid. How did she know to ask that question? *How did she know?* She is opening him like she always did, but he isn't sure that he likes it. The trouble is, Ralph doesn't really know *what* he likes. He's been confused for so long that murkiness is his natural territory and it's hard to separate good feelings from bad ones. (How handy—a psychotherapist who has no idea what he feels.)

"When you walked out, what did she do?" Julie says.

"What do you mean?"

"Did she look for you?"

"Of course not. She's too level-headed for that."

"But you didn't say where you were going. Wasn't she concerned?"

"I feel a bit interrogated," he says.

Way to go, Ralph—you've identified a feeling. Only "interrogated" isn't actually a feeling is it?

"Interrogated?"

"I came to see *you*, not talk about Sadie."

Every time she mentions Sadie he feels something in his stomach. It feels like loss, or longing, which is clearly a misinterpretation, because he can't be longing for Sadie, he just *can't*.

They were standing outside the cinema, about to buy tickets and popcorn.

"There's something I need to tell you," said Sadie.

Ralph wondered if she was about to finish with him. He stood completely still. Perhaps doing nothing would resolve the situation? She seemed to be having the same idea, because she was also standing still and they were two statues in leather jackets with wide collars, his and hers, hers and his, bought together from the indoor market, the one all the students shopped at, the one that sold brand-new clothes which looked really old.

"Can we just go for a drink?" she said.

"Are you going to dump me?"

"Of course not. Why would you think that?"

Why *would* he think that? Things had been good, incredibly good. And yet there was something about her that he couldn't grasp. A remoteness, maybe. A reserve.

In the pub, he asked if she'd like her usual whisky and Coke and she said no, I think I'll have an apple juice.

"Since when do you drink apple juice?" he said, placing their glasses on the table and sitting beside her.

"Don't box me in," she said.

"What?"

She rolled her eyes.

He made a mental note: don't comment on what she eats or drinks. In fact, don't comment on *anything*.

"So you wanted to tell me something?" he said.

She brought the glass to her lips and began to drink. The drinking went on and on until the apple juice was gone. She burped. She smiled. "I'm pregnant," she said.

A young man with an open mouth.

A young woman with a fake smile.

"Say something," she said.

"Well blow me," he said.

"I *really* wish you wouldn't use that phrase."

"It's perfectly harmless."

"Oh come on."

"It is. My dad says it all the time. It's just a shortened version of blow me down. You know, as in blow me down with a feather duster."

"I've never heard *anyone* say that."

"You must have."

"I haven't. Anyway, I think your version is misogynistic."

"How on earth is it misogynistic?"

The argument went on for half an hour. It was a high-speed cart, hurtling around the edges of the pregnancy, avoiding it completely. They jumped in, held on tight, threw words at each other. The cart shook them about, kept them busy, then tossed them back into the room with red faces and churning stomachs.

"So what do you want to do?" he said.

"I could murder a veggie burger," she said.

"I meant about the baby."

"Oh."

"Whatever you decide, I'll support you."

That's what you're supposed to say, isn't it?

"I want to keep it."

"Do you?"

She nodded. But what about him? Did she want to keep *him*?

They walked to the American diner and ordered two burgers, one fries, one special coleslaw. They ate in silence for a while, watching other customers, looking at the Edward Hopper prints on the walls.

"Sadie," Ralph said. "Sadie, I—"

"What's so special about this coleslaw?" she said. "Why did they call it *special*?"

That evening, he phoned his mother. He told a story about a man with an open mouth, a woman with a fake smile.

"Why did she have a fake smile?" his mother said.

"I think she was nervous," he said. "We're students, for God's sake. The timing is terrible."

"She needn't be nervous around you. You're a good boy."

He flinched. "Don't call me a boy."

"You're a good man. You'll do what's right, I know you will. Things happen when they happen. What's she like, this Sadie?"

"She keeps her cards close to her chest."

Brenda thought for a moment. She had expected him to say *pretty* or *lovely*. "Well as long as you're playing the same game," she said.

He had no idea what that meant. "We are," he said.

"Well that's marvellous."

"Is it?"

"Absolutely. We weren't sure you had it in you."

"What do you mean?"

"Well, you're a bit *cerebral*, aren't you? I can't wait to tell your father. He's at the car boot sale. Maybe I should ring him, he could pick something up for the baby, what do you think?"

Eight months later: *twins*.

A chubby boy, a scrawny boy.

Double the screaming. Double the clothes and food.

Sadie was cheerful with other people and miserable at home. "I *love* these boys," she said to her friends. With Ralph she cried, ate HobNobs, used words like *delirious* and *overrated*.

"I don't think you're delirious," he said.

"I am. I'm so tired I'm fucking delirious. It's all right for you. You get to have conversations about something other than babies. I mean really, why do people find it so *absorbing*?"

Ralph became her audience. It was a well-worn track. He had been his parents' audience too.

I listen. I respond. I listen. I respond.

(The hefty shadows of other people.)

I have no idea what I like and don't like.

Missing: the true feelings of Ralph Swoon. Reward will be given to anyone who can uncover them.

Once more with feeling, Ralph. You can do it. You can feel joy like your parents' joy. All you need to do is try harder.

His parents visited and expressed their concern.

"You need fattening up," said Brenda, at the twins' fourth birthday party. "Eat some of this cake, go on."

"You do look a bit pale, if you don't mind me saying," said Frank.

"I'm fine. Sadie's the one who's tired."

"Do you buy her flowers?" said Brenda.

"Sorry?"

"Flowers."

For fuck's sake!

Ralph took a deep, slow breath.

"I'm working every hour there is," he said.

"So stop going out."

"What?"

"When we had you, we didn't go out all the time. Restaurants cost money. Babysitters cost money. Did you really need to go to the theatre last week? We played Scrabble. We counted our blessings."

Ralph laughed.

His mother looked hurt.

Sadie was not a woman who counted her blessings. She knew that in order to have a good life you had to keep moving, searching for new experiences, putting in the effort. She didn't stand around, marvelling at what was simply there in moments of foolish optimism. He admired her appetite. Day after day, she was empty.

How exhausting, Ralph.

(How sad.)

"Do you two even *own* any board games?" said Frank.

On a blanket, on a beach, Ralph gazes at the sea. He takes a handful of sand, lets it run through his fingers.

Julie Parsley offers him a Kit Kat Chunky.

"No thanks," he says. "Will you sing something?"

"Here?"

"Yes."

"Now?"

"Why not? Sing something from the old days. Doris Day?"

She grins, eyes him with mock suspicion, ruffles his hair. "Oh all right."

But she doesn't sing Doris Day. She plumps for Joni Mitchell, 'A Case of You'. Is this for *him*? What is she trying to say?

Here we go again. The regeneration, the renewal. Her voice is all over him. How different she looks when she sings, like she hasn't changed at all. This is *it*—a feeling he can easily describe. It feels like aliveness. It feels like vigour. A sharpness of mind. A *firm intention.*

His intention, in this moment, is to kiss her.

They could spend years playing the guitar, singing, selling Moomins.

There are worse ways to kill time.

And just *imagine* what might happen if this aliveness stuck around, if it actually gathered momentum. His clients could make use of him—they could internalize a vigorous presence.

Aliveness is contagious. It passes from one person to another as easily as—

His lips are on her lips.

It silences her.

He would rather she kept on singing while they were kissing, but that would be creepy. A passion killer, in fact.

If he had a recording of her singing, he could have his cake and eat it.

Yes!

She could perform all the songs she sang when they were teenagers and he could record her.

Now *that's* a good idea.

This kiss is long.

It makes his thoughts race.

It starts to feel exhausting, all this vigour and regeneration, all this thinking while kissing and kissing while thinking.

Kissing usually makes the thinking stop.

What does it mean?

It means he's just not that into it.

Isn't that the name of a film?

He's Just Not That into You, that was it. Romantic comedy, chick flick, Sadie went to see it with Kristin.

These lips are not Sadie's lips.

This kiss is not the kiss he is used to.

But Julie seems into it.

At least that's something.

His lips land on hers while she is singing and she kisses him back.

Oh God, she thinks. One kiss, out of politeness, just for old time's sake, but I'd rather be reading a book. I'd like to bake some muffins for Dad, tidy out my desk, watch another episode of *Homeland*. I should never have told him he was handsome. I'll just say Ralph, that was nice, but I'm not looking for anything right now. To be honest, I just want to be alone.

Julie's tongue is in Ralph's mouth as he remembers Sadie Peterson, pregnant with twins, saying yes I'll marry you, go on then, let's do it.

As they shared the news with friends and family, he wanted to ask her about that remoteness, that reserve, but he was too frightened of the answer. His fear should have given him a clue—it meant that he already *knew* the answer. He wasn't her favourite. It was known and unknowable. No wonder things were right and not right. No wonder he felt confused. There was a gap in the marriage and they had fallen right through it. (*Mind the gap*—that's what his mother should have said.)

Ralph pulls away from Julie, who looks drunk.

He makes a surprising announcement: "I'm so sorry, but all I could think of then was my wife."

"Well that's honest," she says.

"Don't get me wrong, it was lovely but—"

"But what?"

"I want my wife."

"Is that a firm intention?"

"I think so."

"You think?"

"I know."

"Guess what," she says.

"What."

"I was thinking about *Homeland*."

"You were not."

"I was."

"That's really insulting."

"Sorry."

M iriam is thinking about the woo and the hoo. Well, largely the hoo. It was a slip of the tongue, a free-wheeling vocal experiment. The woo was run-of-the-mill, your everyday whisper, maybe a little more excited than usual but essentially just a whisper. And the hoo? *That* was something else. Not a hoo-ha, you understand—let's get this straight right now, because a hoo-ha would have been exactly what Miriam is used to. Her life has been one extended hoo-ha.

What's a hoo in the grand scheme of things? A drop in the ocean. And who dropped in the ocean? Her mother did. Frances Delaney. One thing leads to another. It just does. That's the chaos and the simplicity of life, the way all things are connected, the way every place takes you somewhere else, like it or not.

Ralph is downstairs, talking to the cat. Miriam can hear him talking. He wants his life back, that's what he's saying. Everything was fine only he just couldn't see it—the flaw was *inside* him, not outside. It had been inside him all the time.

If he were to delve into the details, the nitty-gritty of all this, he would discover that what he's thinking is untrue. If you can't *see* that something is fine, then it isn't fine at all.

But now is not the time for technicalities. Miriam is trying to look up from the nitty-gritty to the bigger picture. In fact, she's going to be creating one today—a big picture of her own. Or, to be precise (she can't help it—precision is her thing), a massive piece of art made of buttons. Yes, buttons. Her entire collection. It's coming out. Thousands of them. Buttons and buttons. From her grandmother. From Scarborough, Skegness, Torquay. From cardigans and coats. From here, there and everywhere. All shapes, sizes and colours. She's going to glue them to a background, the nature of which is currently undecided (artwork takes time—there has to be a *gestation* period), but what *is* decided is what these buttons will be doing. They will be spelling out words. Speaking. Okay, so it's not a neon sign. It's not Tracey Emin. But it's honest, confessional *noise*.

This afternoon, Miriam is going to meet her brother at a gallery. They've signed up for an art class. It's spontaneous—the kind of thing Miriam has heard people refer to as *last-minute*. Matthew loves Tracey Emin. Can you believe that? Miriam can. She believes in hardly anything but she believes in this.

Next week, he's taking her to the cinema to watch a film while no one else is there. It's a perk of the job, he says—free showings and popcorn. The week after that, they're going to London on a train to hear a lecture about George Orwell and the state of the nation. Miriam has never been to London before. She has never been anywhere. Matthew didn't find this strange when she told him. He asked if she'd like to travel in first class, with peace, quiet and free cups of tea, and when she asked why he gave her three words, *you* and *deserve* and *it*, which sounded like a slogan from an advert on TV and made no sense to Miriam at all.

But before all this, she will meet her father.

He will be outside the gallery at four o'clock.

Waiting for his daughter and her buttons.

Buttons that make noise.

Downstairs, in the kitchen, Ralph drinks black coffee and tries to think of an appropriate grand gesture. Arriving home with flowers just isn't going to cut it. So what is?

He spots Boo, up a ladder in his garden, and remembers the text he sent him, the one about *pursuing* Miriam. He unlocks the back door and wanders outside.

"I'm really sorry," he says, standing by the fence that separates Miriam's garden from Boo's. "I completely forgot to reply to your message."

Boo moves three steps down the ladder. "Not a problem," he says.

"What are you doing up there?"

"I'm cleaning the guttering."

"Didn't you do that a couple of days ago?"

"Of course," Boo says, proudly. "So what do you think?"

"I think it probably doesn't need cleaning that often. I've never done mine."

"I was referring to the other matter."

"Oh."

"I'm very keen."

"Right. Shall I quiz her about it?"

"Quiz?"

"Test the water. See how the land lies."

"You speak in the vaguest of languages."

"I'll report back later."

"Please try to be subtle."

"I will."

"Your assistance is much appreciated. I'd better get back to the guttering."

"Do you ever stop doing things?"

"Things?"

"I'm sure you could let some of these jobs slide, if you wanted to."

"Absolutely not," Boo says, with such force, such precision. Ralph looks up, inexplicably awestruck.

Back in the kitchen, with Treacle in his arms, Ralph quizzes Miriam.

"You know Boo?"

"Mr Boo?"

"Your neighbour, Boo Hodgkinson."

"How funny. I've never thought of him as Boo Hodgkinson."

"Anyway, do you like him?"

She thinks for a moment. "He's polite and generous."

Ralph looks at the clock. What is he doing? He needs to see Sadie, and instead he's playing matchmaker for Miriam and her hyperactive neighbour. This is *not* the time for subtlety.

"He has strong feelings for you."

Her big brown eyes widen. She reaches out to the work surface to steady herself.

"Feelings?"

"He fancies you."

Fancies?

Miriam laughs. She laughs at how silly this is. *He fancies you* is the kind of statement that gets bounced from normal person to normal person in a giant game of Hooking Up. It doesn't get passed to Miriam Delaney—can't Ralph see that?

The bouncing stops here. She can't catch it, this statement, because she doesn't play for the normal team. The teams were picked in childhood and she wasn't chosen. Get it, Ralph? *That's* why she's laughing.

Her stomach flips.

She glances at a loaf of white bread and wonders if she should eat it immediately to stop the flipping.

"He's a nice guy," Ralph says.

"Yes," Miriam says. She is realizing what happens when one human is informed that another human fancies them. A reaction, regardless of whether the desire is reciprocated. Such a *fascinating* reaction.

"I need a marmalade sandwich," she says.

"Are you sure that's what you need?" he says.

Upstairs, while Ralph is packing his rucksack, Miriam phones Fenella.

"Hello, honey. How are you? Still living with that therapist?"

"He's about to go home."

"You okay?"

"Fenella, I need to ask you an urgent question."

"Go on."

"What do you think of Boo Hodgkinson?"

"Boo who?"

"Don't be silly."

"I wasn't."

"My next-door neighbour."

"Oh you mean Tracksuit Man."

"Yes."

"I think he's nice. Why do you ask?" Fenella slurps. She is drinking a banana milkshake.

"What's that noise?"

"Sorry, I've just been to Shakey Shakey."

"Shakey Shakey?"

"Stupid name, isn't it? It's new. They were giving away free milkshakes if you said you loved Shakey Shakey shakes into the camera."

"What?"

"It's not important. What have you been up to with Tracksuit Man?"

"Nothing. I'm not capable of doing anything."

"Of course you are. Do you think you might want to do something with Boo?"

"Oh God."

"What?"

"I haven't told you, have I? I have a father and two brothers."

"I beg your pardon?"

"I have a cat too. Her name is Treacle. I'm not sure she likes me, but she seems to like the house."

It's finally happened. Miriam has gone mad. Conjured up a ready-made family, a cat, a potential boyfriend. "I'm coming over," Fenella says. "I'll be there in half an hour. Don't worry, honey. You don't need to worry."

"Actually, I'm going out."

"You're what?"

"To an art class."

"Miriam, are you telling the truth?"

"I am," she says. "You can come too if you don't believe me. You can meet the missing people."

The missing people are back, only Miriam hadn't known they were missing. Her grief had been indecipherable—a nonsensical poem, bending through her soul.

39

I'D LIKE TO LAMINATE SOMETHING FOR YOU

Fenella jogs into Beckford Gardens. She runs straight past Miriam's house and knocks on Boo's front door.

"Hello there," he says. He has met Fenella several times, mainly out in the street, but he can't remember her name. "You're Miriam's friend."

"Fenella."

"Oh yes, of course. I'm Boo Hodgkinson."

"That's right. May I have a quick word with you in private?"

"Of course, come in. Please excuse the mess."

Fenella follows him through the hallway into the dining room, where he offers her a seat. "What mess?" she says, sitting down. "This place is immaculate."

"If only that were true," he says.

"It is true."

"You're very kind. Can I get you a cup of tea or coffee?"

"No thanks, I'm on my way to Zumba."

"Zumba?"

"It's an exercise class—you dance to music."

"Do they play Chumbawamba at Zumba?" he says, then

blushes. It's a silly joke, a *bad* joke, he has no idea where it came from. He doesn't even *like* Chumbawamba—too much swearing. They look at each other for what feels like a long time, their faces serious. Then Fenella laughs as though she is blowing air through her lips while trying to keep her mouth closed. In the air, saliva and song. She sings about getting knocked down and getting up again, it must be a Chumbawamba song, but Boo doesn't know it. He strokes his moustache, a moustache with many purposes—a transitional object, a hairy comfort blanket, a symbol of masculinity (or so he believes, which is the important thing), a bit of curly fun.

"I can't wait to tell my Zumba teacher about this," she says. "They should start every class with that song."

"Mmnn," he says.

"Anyway, I'd like to talk to you about Miriam."

The room smells of lavender. Recently polished, the dining table reflects their faces.

"Is she all right?"

"She's not like other women."

"That's true."

Fenella eyes the red velour tracksuit hanging in the kitchen and wonders if it would suit her. "She tells me you have feelings for her. Is that correct or is she confused?"

"She told you that already?"

Who pressed the turbocharge button on my slow-motion life?

"So you do like her?"

"Yes."

"Right. Well, the thing is, Miriam's never had a relationship before."

"I see."

"She's *unusual*."

"I know, that's why I like her."

"If you're going to ask her out we need a plan."

"A plan?"

"I'm Miriam's planner." Fenella sniffs, sits up straight, leans forward. "I laminate things," she says. "And I'd like to laminate something for you."

Boo looks nervous. Is she *hitting* on him?

"Project M&B should be slow and delicate. I'm thinking that phase one could be consistent friendliness and compassion—you need to show her you're a good person."

"I've completed that phase. I cleaned her windows and mowed her lawn."

"Okay, so straight to phase two: old-fashioned courting. Do you think you can do that?"

Boo snorts, which Fenella finds comforting. "Was that a yes?" she says.

"Courting is my middle name," he says.

"Oh really."

"Yes really."

Fenella pauses. She mentally undresses Boo from the waist up. Funny what's in front of you all the time. Funny how she never really noticed him before. He's an old-fashioned tin of boiled sweets and other men are loose jelly babies. He will do nicely for Miriam.

"Well, I was thinking that you could take her to an exhibition or an Italian restaurant," she says. "She likes cheese and cold meats."

"All good ideas," he says.

"If things go well, we could start to improvise."

"How many of us will there be in this relationship?"

"Think of me as a silent partner."

"You are very caring, but also slightly disturbing."

Fenella beams. "I think this could work," she says.

40

Sadie Swoon @SadieLPeterson
Today my head is full of songs by Barry White. Need I say
more? #myeverything

Kristin Hart @craftyKH
@SadieLPeterson Excuse me?

Sadie Swoon @SadieLPeterson
@craftyKH Why what have you done?

Jilly Perkins @JillyBPerks
@SadieLPeterson My Great Dane loves Barry White

Beverley Smart @bearwith72
@SadieLPeterson I take it your husband is home then?

Stanley Swoon @stanswoon96
The world is an unhinged place. The answer? Pavlova

Joe Schwartz @CanadianJoe6
@stanswoon96 I thought I was your answer

Beverley Smart @bearwith72
I'm eating beans on toast with cheese grated on top

41

GO FORWARD BY GOING BACK

She is carrying a holdall full of buttons. He is carrying a rucksack containing felt, charcoal, pencils, pens, scissors, glue and a sketchbook. She is standing outside the art gallery, counting the buttons on people's clothing. He is approaching the gallery, wearing brown shoes, flared trousers and a yellow T-shirt.

"Good morning, sister."

Miriam pauses. This will take some getting used to. "Good morning, *brother*," she whispers.

The art teacher is called Marianne. She has long ginger hair and black glasses. She shakes Miriam's hand, holds on to it for a few seconds, lets it go. Brave, Miriam thinks. You could catch anything by holding on to a hand for that long. She watches Marianne shake Matthew's hand and wonders if everyone in this class will have a name beginning with M. The answer is no. There's a Penny, a Seth and a Benjamin. A Lance and a River. A Lisa and a Dominic. Plus a garrulous Peggy from the Isle of Man who has three children and six chickens (she shares this information with the class as if it's poignant, relevant, vital to their combined artistic endeavour).

"I'm just here to guide you," Marianne says, "with whatever you want to do. Please remember this is a workshop, a class, *not* a competition."

"Can I draw your face?" Matthew says to his sister.

"Mine?"

"Yes."

"I'm not sure." It feels dangerous, the idea of someone looking at her face for a long time. If he sees what is really there and catches it on paper, will it *always* be there?

"Please?"

After a lengthy discussion, mediated by Marianne, they decide that Matthew will sketch Miriam while she works, instead of staring at her face. This feels safer. Strange but good. So Matthew draws and Miriam glues buttons and she asks if he's ever seen a film called *The Awakening*.

"I have," he says. "Incredibly sad."

"All about a brother's love," Miriam says, then blushes.

"Murderous love, wasn't it?"

"How's it going?" Marianne says. She is holding a cup of tea and eating a Lion Bar. She glances at Miriam's sheet of blue felt and reads what she has written in buttons. "This is deep," she says, "really deep." She stands beside Matthew and looks at his sketch. He has drawn an owl. "Interesting interpretation," she says. She touches his back, notices the warmth of his skin through his cotton T-shirt, then walks off to find out why loud-mouthed Peggy is trying to pull the legs off a table.

Mr Eric Delaney. Wood sculptor. Husband. Officially the father of two. Unofficially the father of three. Waiting outside the gallery. Standing where Miriam's feet were standing three hours ago while she counted the buttons on people's clothing.

He paces. He waits. They are late. He is holding a bunch of gerberas. Say it with flowers. Say *what*, for goodness' sake?

He spots Matthew, rucksack on his back. He smiles and waves. Then a woman. She is behind him, coming into view. Something under one arm, a holdall in the other. Long hair, light brown, wavy. First impressions? Not what he was expecting. She looks relaxed, for a start. He expected edgy, nervous, eyes darting from left to right. She is laughing, presumably at something Matthew has said. She looks like her mother.

"Dad, this is Miriam."

She holds out her hand for him to shake.

Shakey Shakey milkshakes. Shakin' Stevens. My hand is shaking. Is he going to take it and shake it or not?

Thirty-four years have passed since he last held her hand.

Her hand was tiny then.

He can still remember it.

She remembers nothing.

She has never seen him before.

(If she can't remember, was he ever there?)

"Dad?" Matthew's voice. Perturbed.

Eric takes his daughter's hand. Shakes it. Smiles. He is lost but she mustn't know this. It's time to step up, not be lost again.

Dad. His warm hands, his rough fingers. I recognize you. I don't remember you at all and yet I do. I know you, Daddy. I don't know you.

"Hello," she whispers.

That whisper. Like on the phone. Damage. Devastating. His fault.

Matthew glares. *Dad? Are you going to say something?*

Social abandonment.

(So many ways to abandon each other.)

Miriam takes the sheet of felt from under her arm and lays it on the floor in front of Eric's feet.

In buttons: HOW COULD YOU LEAVE?

The buttons have spoken, said their piece.

The answer opens in Eric's mind.

Memory: a pop-up theatre whose actors never age.

He feels a sharp pain in his head.

"I can't do this," said Frances, opening and closing the oven door, checking the roast lamb. "You need to move out."

"We've only just moved in," said Eric, washing the oil from his hands in the kitchen sink. He glanced at the baby, sleeping in a pram in the corner.

"This isn't your house."

"I know. It's *our* house."

"Dad bought it."

"It's our marital home, Frances. What are you talking about?"

"You're an oaf."

"I beg your pardon?"

"You make too much noise. I need to be alone."

Eric dried his hands with a tea towel. On the tea towel, the words HAPPILY EVER AFTER. "Do you need to see the doctor again?" he said.

"You can eat this roast dinner, but that's as far as it goes," she said. "If you try to see her, I'll push her in the canal. I'll say it was an accident on an icy path. I'll say my chest hurt and I thought I was dying. The pram raced down the slope and ran into the river and my heart went with it, my precious little—"

Eric grabbed her shoulders. "Frances, for God's sake."

"That's it, go on, give me some bruises, that's exactly what I need."

He recoiled, stepped backwards, stumbled into the pram. The baby began to cry. He lifted the woollen blanket and picked her up.

"Enjoy it while you can."

It?

His mother had warned him about Frances Hopkins, but he hadn't listened. She told him her family was wealthy and her nails were clean, but her mind was dark. Dark like the winters in Norway, he said, and talked about the magical northern lights. We haven't brought you up to be fanciful, his mother said. You need your wits about you, otherwise her winter will be your winter. That's what love does. You could lose yourself.

Eric held Miriam in his arms, jiggled her up and down, made up a song on the spot about a father and a daughter. She stopped crying. She smiled. He held her in the air as his wife marched towards them.

"Now give her to me," she said.

"No."

"Hand her over."

"You need to see a doctor. There's something very wrong with you."

"You sound scared."

"That's because I *am* scared."

Frances huffed and stomped over to the oven. She took out the lamb and put it on the hob. "I don't care how old she is," she said, taking the lid off a bubbling saucepan, "if you try to contact her I'll kill her. And if you tell anyone about this conversation, I'll show them the burns you gave me."

"What burns?"

She removed the saucepan from the electric hob and placed her arm where it had been.

She grimaced, her eyes were half shut.

The skin on her arm was stuck, hard to pull free.

Eric held the baby tight. He thought about running, taking Miriam with him, but how could he look after a baby by himself? All he had was a job at the garage.

"I won't hurt the child," she said.

"You say that now."

"It's a promise. I'll keep her safe. As long as she's quiet and she lives by my rules, I'll keep her safe."

Eric looks down at the buttons: HOW COULD YOU LEAVE?

It's a relief, actually, to see those words. It's not small talk or pretending.

The words are made of circles.

He looks up from the floor, looks into Miriam's eyes, holds out the bunch of gerberas. "We have a lot of talking to do," he says.

Miriam picks up the felt, says nothing.

"I think I'll give you two some space," Matthew says, as he spots Marianne walking down the steps of the gallery, carrying a suitcase. "That okay?"

Miriam blinks three times.

Is that a yes?

He rushes over to Marianne, says something with a look of great seriousness and takes the suitcase from her hand.

Eric has an idea. He's not sure if it's a good one. The idea involves driving his daughter to the botanical gardens and sitting on a bench. A bench with a memorial plaque. FRANCES DELANEY, LOST AT SEA. Yes, they could do something lighter, more superficial, like drink tea and ask questions about hobbies and work and their favourite things, but his gut instinct is telling him that something else needs to happen. *Go back to where this started. Go forward by going back.*

No one has ever bought Miriam flowers before. She is busy smelling them. She won't tell him this is her first bouquet, because her own gut instinct is to withhold, refuse, deny.

He says something about his car and a bench and the botanical gardens. He assumes she has been there before, but he's wrong.

In the car, she watches his hands on the steering wheel. He has big hands, worn and wide. They held her when she was a baby. Lifted her up. Stroked her wispy hair. Apparently. *Daddy, is that you?* She wants to love him but she doesn't.

"I don't love anyone," she says. (Better out than in.)

He bites his bottom lip, flicks the indicator, turns left. "That's a shame," he says.

She frowns.

"Did you love your mother?"

"She's in the sea," is all Miriam can think of to say.

Dead monster, my monster, devil you know, devil I know.

"I read about it in the papers."

"Before that she was all at sea, so what's the difference?"

He stops at a pedestrian crossing, waves at a woman walking past the car with her dog. The woman waves back. Miriam notices that his wave is simple and brief while hers is frenzied and eager. She wonders if they always wave like this, every time they see someone they know, or if the waves fluctuate, depending on how pleased they are to see the other person. Does Eric sometimes wave in a frenzied, eager way? Who makes him do this?

"Did *you* love my mother?" she says.

He takes another left turn and looks for somewhere to park. "She was my first love," he says.

They walk around the botanical gardens, looking for Frances Delaney.

Someone is sitting on her. A man with greasy hair, eating a pork pie. Piggish man. A bloated obstruction. These are cruel thoughts, and Miriam hates being cruel, but he is sitting on her mother and she doesn't like it.

Eric walks up to the man. He says something, they glance at Miriam, the man gets up and moves to another bench.

She wonders how he just did that—how he made someone walk away. Is it really that easy?

"Ladies first," Eric says.

Then they are side by side.

There is a gap between them.

Frances Delaney is in the gap, her name in sunlight.

They just sit there, looking ahead, looking at their feet, the plaque, each other. They sit for ten minutes, saying nothing. It feels uncomfortable at first, like a failure, like the worst kind of loneliness, but as the silence deepens it becomes something they are making together, as yet unbroken. It belongs to them.

Miriam tells herself that *he* will be the one to break it. Eric worries that she is feeling abandoned again, or lonely, or like she's sitting with a man who has no idea what to say. But her father is a man of the gut, not of the mind, and his gut tells him to sit beside her and wait. *She* will be the one to break it.

(Stubbornness. It runs in the family, but they don't feel like family yet, so there is nowhere for the stubbornness to run.)

Then there is a breakage.

"Excuse me, do you have the time?" a woman says. She is wearing a red raincoat. Her hair is tied back so tightly it must hurt. "Where is the zoo?"

Eric tells her the time. "There is no zoo," he says. "Well not around here. Obviously there is a zoo *somewhere*."

Miriam smiles. Of all the breakages she has experienced, this isn't such a bad one.

The woman asks what he means about the zoo. "No zoo?" she says.

"No zoo."

"What about a tapas bar, is there a tapas bar nearby?"

"I really don't know," Eric says. "There are pubs and cafes."

The woman sighs. "No zoo, no tapas," she says.

"Sorry," Eric says.

"It's not your fault."

Then she is gone.

"Would you like to meet your other brother?" Eric says.

Other brother from another mother.

"Where?"

"My house."

"Your house?"

"My wife will be there too. Angelina."

"Angelina?"

"Yes."

"Her name's Angelina?"

He nods. Small questions. Easy.

"That name is so full of possibility," she says.

"Sorry?"

"Is she an Ange, Angie, Angel, Lina or Geli?"

He laughs.

"Why's that funny?"

"*Geli?*"

"It's the centre of Angelina."

"Not *my* Angelina."

"What's she like?"

"She's very patient. A whizz in the kitchen."

So *this* is what they will talk about after all these years? Angelina? Eric hadn't expected Miriam to be interested in his wife. He describes Angelina Delaney in as much detail as he can and she listens, captivated, as if it's the most exciting thing she has ever heard.

As they stand up to leave, Miriam lays the bunch of flowers on the bench, just beneath the plaque. He doesn't want to make this gesture any bigger or smaller than it is, so he pretends not to notice, and she asks him something else about Angelina, and they walk away from Frances Delaney, whose name is no longer in sunlight.

42

B oo parks his car in Ralph's drive and looks up at the house. "Very smart," he says. "I like your guttering and your black front door."

"Thanks."

"Shall I help you carry these things in?"

Camping gear, a guitar, a rucksack. They place them by the front door and Boo gets back in his car.

"Thanks," Ralph says, not wanting to invite Boo inside. "And thanks for the lift."

"See you soon," Boo says. It's a command, not a social nicety.

Ralph looks at the guttering and the black front door. He never notices these things. They are just there, like the piece of stained glass above the door, like the willow tree and the roses.

Sadie is not returning his calls. She's in regular contact with their sons, he knows this from talking to his parents, but the flow of information ends there. It's ridiculous, silly, it has to stop.

He opens the front door and is assaulted by his mother's voice, singing along to Cyndi Lauper, 'Girls Just Want to Have

Fun'. He hasn't heard her sing that loudly for years—not since she went through her phase of singing 'I Want to Break Free' over and over again, usually while doing the hoovering. (She went through a 'Steamy Windows' phase too, but Ralph has chosen to forget her Tina Turner impersonations. They disturbed him. They disturbed everyone.)

Harvey appears, jumps all over him, licks his face. "Well this is a nice welcome," he says, rubbing the dog's head. "Good boy, Harvey. Who's a good boy?"

On the table in the hallway, a bunch of fresh tulips. In the air, the smell of baking bread.

This is not his house. It is and it isn't. It smells like his parents' house.

He pokes his head into the living room. "Hi, Arthur."

Arthur is lying on the sofa in his pyjamas, watching *Breaking Bad*. That's more like it—a familiar sight. "Dad?" he says, turning around. He stands up, points the remote at the TV, switches it off. Ralph has never seen him do this before. He's seen him switch the TV on a thousand times, but never off. *Breaking Bad* has gone, mid-episode. *Gone*. Arthur's hands are deep in his pockets and he is staring at his father. "Are you all right?" he says.

"I think so."

"That's good. Where have you been?"

"I've been camping."

"Right."

"I needed some space."

"Right."

"Have you heard from your mum?"

"We spoke to her first thing."

"This morning?"

"Yeah."

"And?"

"Maybe you should give her a call."

"Is she all right?"

"She's good. Would you like a cup of tea?"

Does he even know how to make a cup of tea? What's going on?

Ralph wants to say bloody hell I should go away more often, but he doesn't. Arthur's politeness is serious, tentative. His concern is like a multicoloured coat, garish and strange on his back. On his brother it would be a lambswool V-neck jumper. Anyone would think Ralph had just been discharged from hospital or had returned with broken bones. Why is he so concerned?

Footsteps on the stairs. Not one set of footsteps, but two.

"Dad?"

"Mr Swoon?"

Stanley and Joe, red-faced. They throw their arms around Ralph, who has never experienced a group hug before. He resists the urge to dive onto the floor and put his hands over his head.

"You okay, Dad?"

"I'm just fine."

"Good to see you, Mr Swoon."

"Please, call me Ralph. You're making me feel old."

Three teenagers, standing in the hallway, staring.

"I'll make a pot of tea," Arthur says.

Ralph glances at Stanley, expecting him to respond with surprise or sarcasm, but his face is quiet and kind.

Eerie. That's what it is. This house is fucking eerie.

The boys move towards the kitchen but Ralph doesn't follow.

"There's a loaf in the oven," Stanley says.

"Blimey," Ralph says. He looks at the black TV screen, the vase of pink tulips.

More footsteps on the stairs. His parents this time. He sees his mother first, smiling and freshly permed, like a cartoon that a child would draw of a curly-haired woman: tight ringlets, indistinct face.

"You're back," she shouts. "Oh how *lovely*."

"Yes I am."

Brenda hugs her son, Frank pats him on the back.

"Are you all stoned?" Ralph says.

"What on earth do you mean, dear?" Brenda says. "We're pleased to see you."

Is that *pity* on her face?

In the kitchen, on the breakfast bar, *How to Be a Domestic Goddess* by Nigella Lawson has been left open on a page about meringues. Beside the cookbook there is a home-made pavlova.

"I'm going to call your mum," Ralph says.

The Swoons look at one another.

"We'll be here," Brenda says.

Upstairs, on the bed, he calls his wife. "Oh, I didn't expect you to pick up. How are you? *Where* are you?"

"I'm at a hotel," Sadie says.

"Where? And why?"

"Oh Ralph."

"I'm back," he says.

"In what way?"

"I'm at home. Everyone's here."

"I doubt that very much."

"No, they are."

"*Your* everyone, maybe. Not mine. Anyway, if you're back your parents can leave."

"There's no rush."

"Oh there is."

"When are you coming home?"

"I don't know."

"What do you mean?"

"Why don't we meet somewhere? Somewhere neutral."

"Why would we want to do that?"

"Look, I'll call you tonight. We're about to go for a walk."

"We?"

"Yes."

The line goes dead. He lies down, closes his eyes, wonders what to do. He could find out where she's staying, drive to the hotel, bring her back.

Footsteps again. So many footsteps. Then he is surrounded. They are standing by the bed, his parents, his sons and Joe, looking at him as though he's a broken man, a man who can't move and needs nursing. Arthur puts a tray on the bedside table, there's a mug of tea, a croissant, a glass of juice.

"What?" Ralph says. "What are you all looking at? Why are you being so *nice*?"

43

IT JUST IS

M iriam Delaney is walking into a house she has never
been to before. A woman called Angelina opens the
door and invites her in. She says hello there, I've been looking
forward to meeting you. Miriam wants to ask why, because
what reason could someone have for anticipating *her* arrival?
She looks Angelina in the eye, holds out her hand, puts great
effort into the appropriate kind of smile.

Ralph Swoon is eating Stanley's home-made pavlova while trying
to explain his recent absence to his family. He is using words
like *space* and *time* and *blindness*—a sketchy kind of language.
As he talks, he finds himself riveted by the presence of Joe
Schwartz, who looks so happy, so joyful. Is Stanley partially
responsible for this joy? If so, how did he learn to do that, to
make another person feel glad to be alive?

Sadie Swoon is walking through the grounds of a country hotel
with Alison Grabowski, making plans that involve the words
divorce and *separation*. I know what you should do, Alison

says, grabbing Sadie's hand. You should go back to university. A silence follows, overcrowded with thought. Sadie squeezes Alison's hand. She wonders what might have happened if Ralph hadn't walked out during his party. Would she ever have contacted Alison? That thought frightens her, makes her think about the weight of decisions, the heaviness of a *no* and a *yes*.

Arthur Swoon is sitting in the kitchen, trying to look like he's listening to his father, but he's thinking about *Breaking Bad*. He's been polite all day and he's exhausted. How do people do it? *Why* do they do it? He feels sorry for his dad, and that's exhausting too, it's really *uncomfortable*. Poor Dad, stupid Dad—should he be hugged or punched in the face? It's all too much. Arthur needs to watch TV. He needs the reassuring company of Walter White.

Stanley Swoon is listening to a story about *space* and *time* and *blindness*, full of words that don't seem to mean anything. This is his father's style: the more he explains, the murkier things become. He's the opposite of Stanley's hero, Nigel Slater, who explains what he's making and why it works, and isn't afraid to be spontaneous sometimes—to forget the what and the why. His father could learn a lot from Nigel Slater. Stanley's mind drifts into a culinary world. He thinks about toppings for bruschetta—broad beans, mint, ricotta. He thinks about how making good food for someone transforms their mood, actually *transforms* it, so why hadn't his parents taught him this essential fact of life? His father's words are still coming: *confusion, unknowable, revelation.*

Kristin Hart has received a text from Sadie. (Hi K. I'm so sorry for kissing you then going slightly nuts. It wasn't about you if that helps? You're my closest friend, don't want to lose that.

Can I explain soon? xxx) This text has made her furious. *Not about her?* Oh that's charming, that's really charming. Who *was* it about then? In a quiet carriage on a train to London, Kristin curses under her breath. *Jesus fucking Christ.* The woman sitting opposite looks up from her copy of *Horse* magazine. Tut-tut, she says. Kristin slams her phone on the table, says really, you're really tut-tutting me? I wouldn't tut-tut me again if I were you—just read your *Horse* magazine and keep your fucking tut-tuts to yourself. The woman gathers her things and moves seats, leaving Kristin alone to stare out of the window at the fields and the hills as she thinks of Sadie and Carol and why she can't stop swearing all the time.

Boo Hodgkinson is in Paperchase, looking at postcards on a spinning rack. Fenella told him that Miriam loves postcards. She has quite a collection pinned to the noticeboard in her kitchen. So he spins the rack and peruses all the cutesy cards, the apology cards, the cards saying let's talk, let's do lunch, let's always remember we're the best of friends. Which one would Miriam like? Not this photo of a panda. Not this photo of a cowgirl (Boo selects this for himself). What about *this* one? He pulls a Banksy postcard from the rack—two children playing catch with a No Ball Games sign. Yes, this is *perfect*. He doesn't know why it's perfect, it just is.

Eric Delaney watches his wife introduce Miriam to Alfie. Alfie edges closer, eager and reluctant. He stops and he starts. He holds Amy Pond out in front of him. Miriam kneels down, says hello, Amy Pond, how are you today?

Julie Parsley is watching *Starsky & Hutch* with her father. He says what happened to that big baby? She says what big baby?

He says Ralph Swoon. Oh *that* big baby. He's gone, she says. Good riddance, he says. They drink coffee flavoured with hazelnut syrup. They eat pizza. Then Julie's father asks if she knows that he's not Hugh Bonneville from *Downton Abbey*, and she says yes, Dad, you're Hugh Parsley, and I will always know who you are. She kisses him on the cheek.

"Hello there," Angelina says. "I've been looking forward to meeting you."

Miriam isn't sure why, but she feels like she's meeting some kind of rock star. All she knows about this woman is she's very patient and a whizz in the kitchen.

"Hello, Mrs Delaney," she whispers. She holds out her hand and smiles.

Mrs Delaney—what a strange thing to say to someone who is not her mother. It's like addressing an actor who is playing the part of Mrs Delaney. But she is not an actor, she's an ordinary woman, an A instead of an F.

"Call me Angelina," the woman says.

"Angelina," Miriam says, and the woman laughs, which is unbearable for a second, until Miriam realizes that there is nothing sharp inside the laugh.

"And this is Alfie."

A boy steps out from behind his mother's legs. He is wearing jeans, a blazer, a shirt, a bow tie. He is clutching a doll, which he holds out in front of him.

Miriam kneels down. "Hello, Amy Pond. How are you today?"

"Amy's very well thank you," the boy says.

"That's good," Miriam says.

Wow, Alfie thinks. She knows Amy Pond. Who else does she know? "Would you like a lemonade?" he says.

"Are you having one?"

"I am."

"Then I'd love one, thank you."

"All right."

Alfie leads Miriam into the kitchen, leaving Eric and Angelina by the front door.

"Are you okay?" she says.

"I think so. Is Matthew back?"

"He's upstairs."

"Right."

"I made a fish pie. Do you think she might like some?"

"I have no idea."

They stand in silence and she strokes his face. He is trying not to cry.

"It's all right," she says.

He shakes his head, grits his teeth.

"It's all right," she says, wiping his tears with her thumb.

They sit around the dining table, Miriam Delaney and four brand-new Delaneys. It's not the kind of thing that should scare a person to death, but it does.

Miriam feels freakish, exposed.

Can they hear her heart inside her chest?

Surely everyone can hear it.

She blinks. Blinks again. The other Delaneys are still here, but that doesn't mean they are real.

Maybe she has imagined them.

Maybe this isn't really happening.

The mind is a fairground of unearthly rides. Intrapsychic theme parks. The constant rattle of ghost trains.

Is this an alternative reality, made by her own mind?

Welcome to the Normal Family Life amusement park, Miriam. Please leave your shoes by the entrance.

Oh no.

What if...

What if she is still sitting at home with her mother and there was no visit to the cinema, no Florence Cathcart, no men in the woods looking for three metal tins, no Ralph, no cat, no Boo. What if the agile fingers of anxiety have weaved this new world. All of it, up to this moment, her mother's tapestry. A sick joke. A machine plugged into her brain while her body stays still.

She wants to run.

To never see another person again.

But there is a voice. It says, "Would you like some fish pie, Miriam?"

It's the rock star speaking. She is holding an orange casserole dish.

"Are you having some?" Miriam says.

"I am."

"All right then. Thank you."

Calm down, Miriam. Think of Fenella. Think of something nice, like The Bridge. *Think of Saga in that greenish-brown Porsche. Wouldn't it be nice to take a drive in that car?*

If Fenella were here now she would say nice one, honey— ten out of ten for self-soothing.

"This must be weird for you," Matthew says.

"It is."

"I can imagine," Angelina says.

"Can you?"

"Of course. It must be quite nerve-wracking."

"Yes."

They nod, all of them, even Alfie and Amy Pond are nodding. Telling it like it is. Saying it's weird and nerve-wracking. Which is interesting, because this makes it less weird and nerve-wracking. Is this what Fenella has been trying to show her—how stating the obvious *changes* the obvious?

"Why do you keep whispering?" Alfie says, just as Angelina puts a spoonful of fish pie on Miriam's plate.

"Alfie, that's really rude," Eric says.

Miriam cups her hands together on her lap. "No, it's not rude," she says.

Alfie says he's sorry and looks down at the table.

"Whispering kept me alive."

Alfie thinks for a while about what this means. "Like you'd die if you didn't?" he says.

"Sort of, yes. Or that's how it felt."

He looks at his mother, his father, his brother. He bends Amy Pond's legs into a sitting position, gets off his chair, walks around the table until he reaches Miriam and places Amy in front of her, just beside the plate full of fish pie and peas. He returns to his chair, sips his lemonade, picks up his knife and fork.

They talk about the art class and the art teacher.

They talk about how Angelina went swimming today and did twenty-five lengths.

They talk about what Eric does for a living—how he used to be a mechanic, *way back when*.

Way back when you were my dad, Miriam thinks.

Matthew opens a bottle of red wine. He thinks about the sketch he made of Miriam earlier today, wonders why he drew her as an owl.

"I'm having a really late night," Alfie says. "I'm allowed, though. Mum said so."

"Have you shown Miriam what you made?" Angelina says.

The boy's eyes widen. "Can I get it now? Can I get it?"

He has gone and now he is back. The boy is fast. Super fast. "I drew you a spaceship," he says. "It has four bedrooms and two toilets and this is a room just for rabbits and this is a room for playing games in and this is where the driver can sit."

Miriam inspects the drawing. "This is the best spaceship I've ever seen."

"Is it?"

"I want to get in this right now," she says. "It's perfect."

"*I* want to get in it."

"May I keep this?"

Alfie nods.

"Thank you."

Matthew has something for her too, but he doesn't want to overshadow the spaceship. He drinks wine, eats fish pie and waits for Alfie to be sent to bed, which takes ages, because Alfie has become hyperactive. He's asking Miriam about *Doctor Who*. What's your favourite episode? Who do you like best? Do you find it scary? Do you like my bow tie? Why don't *you* get a bow tie?

Finally, he looks tired. His lips are still moving but his eyes are red.

"Time for bed now, Alfie."

"Not yet."

"Alfie."

"Will you be here when I wake up?" he says.

"Depends when you wake up," Miriam says.

"Where are you sleeping?"

"In my house."

"I've been to your house."

"Alfie, go and get in your pyjamas. I'm not saying it again."

"I'll go with him," Matthew says.

A kitchen cupboard opens, but it's not a cupboard, it's a dish-washer. Miriam has never seen a dishwasher before, especially one that looks like a cupboard. She asks how it works and whether it's noisy. Angelina shows her how they put in cups, plates and cutlery, then a capsule of powder and liquid. That's about it really, she says, as she closes the door and sets the cycle.

"Clever," Miriam says.

"Yes," Angelina says.

There is a pot of coffee. Chocolate biscuits. Angelina asks Miriam if she likes where she lives and she says yes, it's okay, my neighbours are nice.

Matthew is back. He tells them Alfie is awake but at least he's in bed. He drinks his coffee, eats a biscuit, says he's just going to get something for Miriam, won't be a sec. His parents look puzzled. He returns holding a box wrapped in glossy pink paper.

"For you," he says.

Miriam takes it. A gift? For her? "But I've already had a spaceship," she says. She feels full of panic. They are watching her. What should she do with her face while she opens the gift? What's the required response? The tempo of social life is so hard to get right. *Don't be too loud, don't be too quiet, don't be too reserved, don't be too excited.* It's such a performance.

She tears the paper.

You can do this.

Opens the box.

Almost over. Don't squeal, don't cry.

Lifts out her gift.

A white and red megaphone.

"It's a thing of beauty," she says, because it is, she's not lying, she doesn't have to pretend.

"I thought so too," Matthew says.

Later that evening, Miriam's mind and body become unbearably heavy. She is not used to this much conversation all in one day, or this many people all in one room. "I'd better be going," she says.

"I'll drive you home," Eric says.

"I can get the bus."

"Definitely not."

"You could stay over?"

"I don't have my pyjamas and toothbrush."

"I have spare ones," Angelina says.

Goodness me. Doesn't she know that it's *way* too soon to step into another woman's pyjamas? There is a limit to how many new things a person can do in one day, and Miriam reached that limit hours ago. "Actually, I have to feed my cat."

"No problem."

"Do you mind if I step outside for a few minutes?"

"Are you all right?" Eric says.

"I just need a little air," she says, picking up the megaphone from the coffee table and clutching it to her chest.

Eric unlocks the back door and watches his daughter step outside. He's about to ask if she would like some company but something stops him. He closes the door.

Upstairs in bed, Alfie is unable to sleep. He sings a lullaby to Amy Pond, who has just had a nightmare in which everyone she loved disappeared. He listens to the voices coming from downstairs, hears the back door open and close. Someone has gone outside.

He climbs out of bed, rushes to the window, wonders what's happening in the back garden. The outside light has come on. He can see his Swingball, his racket, his shark and his new sister. He grabs Amy Pond and runs downstairs.

Miriam walks across the grass.

She passes the Swingball, the lime-green tennis racket, the rubber shark.

She looks up at the sky.

Lifts the megaphone to her lips.

Whispers into it.

"Testing, testing. This is Miriam Delaney. Is anyone there?"

She looks back at the house and sees four faces peering at her through the kitchen window.

"Testing, testing. This is Miriam Delaney."

45

CONTRACTION

I t was a humid day in July and Frances Delaney was out shopping for milk, onions and liver.

In the supermarket, she was served by a girl who looked too young to be working on a weekday.

"Shouldn't you be at school?" she said.

"I left school three years ago," the girl said, eyeing Frances's tweed jacket and black bowler hat. "Did you find everything you need today?"

"I beg your pardon?"

The girl's face reddened. "Did you find everything you need?"

"What kind of question is that?"

"It's what we're told to say."

"Well don't. You have no *idea* what I need."

"Screw you."

"Excuse me?" said Frances, but she liked the girl better now. She let her pack the shopping into a bag without saying anything more.

Outside, she walked along the high street, sat on a bench opposite the church and pulled a can of Coke from Miriam's old rucksack. It hissed and she drank and it tasted the same as everything else she put in her mouth these days. Hearing footsteps behind her, she turned her head and saw a skinny man. He had grey slicked-back hair and was wearing a black suit, white shirt and black tie. She squinted as he came closer.

"My God."

He sat down beside her. "My wife will be here in a minute," he said.

What kind of greeting is that after twenty-two years?

"What are you doing here?"

"We're back for a funeral."

"Who died?"

"You won't know him."

"I might."

"You don't know anyone, Frances."

"I knew you didn't I? Before you *left* me."

"Your daughter gave us no choice. Stupid girl."

His mouth was full of *we* and *us*. Revolting.

"Don't talk about Miriam like that," said Frances.

A pompous laugh, full of spit. "Did you just *defend* Miriam?"

"What's it to you?"

A woman walked past. It was Mrs Thomas from the chemist, a dainty woman with a thuggish face. (Heaven help those who asked why their prescription was taking so long.)

"Blimey, she hasn't got any prettier," the headmaster said.

"Who was she?"

"See, you don't know anyone," he said, rolling his bloodshot eyes. "Anyway, since when did *you* care about Miriam?"

"What?"

"You never loved that girl." He took the can of Coke from Frances's hands, wiped it with his sleeve and drank for a long time. "She would've been better off with me."

"You?"

"Yes, *me*."

"She hated you."

"I don't think so," he said, staring ahead at the church.

"You wound her up."

"Oh I did much more than that."

She looked him in the eye, but was distracted by the amount of hair coming out of his nose. That's what the years had brought him: less hair where he wanted it, more where he didn't. "What?" she said.

He put his hand on her thigh. "Don't pretend you didn't know."

"You wound her up, that's all. You *taunted* her."

He moved closer, whispered something into her ear: "I went into her room while you were sleeping."

His mouth just there, his breath inside her, she would have been lying if she said it was unpleasant. He was putting something into her, it didn't matter what.

Until it did.

Words. Evil. Despicable.

"What?" she said, wanting him to stop and go on but mainly to stop.

"Night after night," he whispered.

"No you didn't. I would've heard."

He pulled his face away and spoke in his usual voice. "You slept like an old pig, snorting in the dark. You wouldn't have known if the house was on fire."

Where was this hatred coming from? After all these years, surely he could manage some pleasantries? Like: Hello, Frances, how lovely to find you here on this park bench. Like: I can't believe how fast time goes, has it really been twenty-two years? How are you keeping? How has life treated you? Like: It really is lovely to see you.

But no. Not even a hello. He had appeared from nowhere and *accosted* her. That was the word, and there was another word too: *ambushed*. He wasn't the only one with words to push inside someone else.

"What's happened to you?" she said. "You're not the same man. You never would've ambushed me like this before."

He lit a cigarette. "Miriam loved my little visits," he said, sucking smoke into his mouth.

Frances could hear traffic, spiders creeping across the ground, twigs falling from trees, fish swimming in the sea. She could hear the grunts of arm-wrestling boys, clouds drifting through the sky. Noise, coming from everywhere. Nothing but noise, inside and out. The amplified echoes of the world, turned up to full volume.

"But—" she said.

"But *what*?"

She felt a pain in her stomach. I know this pain, she thought. I will *never* forget this pain. I'm having contractions. Here and now on this damp wooden bench. *Contractions*.

She wanted to push. Push this baby out. Get it out of me, I can't do this, I'm not made for this, why can't people see? I'm not good enough. I'll put it in a blanket and leave it outside the hospital. *It it it*. Get it out out out.

"Oh for God's sake," the headmaster said. Typical Frances. Squirming around. Hamming it up. Look at her, bent double, having some kind of *fit*, making a show of herself.

She moaned, leant forward. The pain was unbearable. She tightened her muscles, closed her eyes. Contractions on top of noise on top of contractions on top of noise.

"I promised to keep her safe," she said.

"Safe?" he said, standing up. He kicked her rucksack, knocked it onto its side. "You're joking aren't you? You wouldn't know how to make *anyone* feel safe."

She opened her eyes and watched him walk towards the churchyard. He looked like a matchstick man in a Lowry painting, monochrome and creaky.

"Miriam," she said. It was the last word to come from her mouth.

She staggered to her feet, picked up her bag, made her way to the bus stop. Her stomach still hurt, there were spasms inside her, she wanted to *push*. The bus stopped and its doors opened. She dropped change into a tray without saying where she was going. The driver looked at all the coins. You want an all day ticket? he said. Her body landed fast and heavy on the first empty seat she could find.

She had seen it on the news, what happened to a person who jumped from that spot. Or what *didn't* happen. They didn't come back.

Smell that? Almost makes you want to live, doesn't it?

Frances breathed deep until her lungs were full of the ocean.

She stood there for a while, just watching, breathing in and out, listening to the waves.

This is a nice way to spend your last half an hour, she thought. Then the contractions started again.

She took five steps backwards. Stopped. Waited.

Then she ran and she jumped and it was over.

On the surface of the sea, a black bowler hat.

On the floor, at the cliff's edge, Miriam's old rucksack. Inside it they found a purse, two onions, a pint of milk, a pig's liver.

He thought it would feel good, dangling a lie in front of Frances Delaney, like twisting the tail of a live rat through her hair and watching what it did.

But it didn't feel good.

It felt like betraying the one person he didn't want to betray: Miriam Delaney. "I loved that girl like she was my own daughter," he once said to his wife. "That freaky whispering girl?" she said. "You *disgust* me."

As he entered the church, he thought about turning around. Frances couldn't have gone far. He would take it back, say I'm sorry, I was lying, I *did* go into her room but only to talk. I've been so angry, Frances. You'd never believe how angry I have been.

But he didn't turn around. His wife was here now. They were sitting at their friend's funeral, dusted with death. Streaming eyes, sore throats, nothing in the air but death. He listened to the vicar, reducing a stranger's life to a litany of headlines. Dear friend, he thought. You are diminished in death and I am diminished in life.

As he watched the coffin being lowered into the ground, he glanced at the empty bench. The desire to find Frances had gone. She didn't seem important any more.

46

A COIN, A COUNTRY SONG, A VIENNESE WHIRL

It is autumn. Summer has passed, that Russian-doll summer when every encounter opened to reveal a smaller version of itself, connected but separate, and if you put the moments together all you were left with was a wooden doll.

"I carved this for you," Eric said, handing Miriam a parcel.

"Really?"

"Open it."

Wrapped in brown paper, a small wooden Miriam.

"Is this me?" she said, holding it up.

"I hope you don't think it's silly."

Miriam looked at herself in miniature.

"I was thinking about how you don't always see yourself," he said. "You don't see yourself as a real person. So if you put this somewhere in your house, you can't forget that you exist and we can see you."

This morning, the real Miriam pats the wooden Miriam on the head as she passes by. She feeds the cat, takes a shower, dresses in baggy jeans and a sweatshirt. It's time for work.

Imagine a woman, digging in the dirt. Imagine a man, digging beside her. They are Swoon & Delaney Garden Services, with an old Land Rover and a frenetic black spaniel.

While she is looking for her boots, Miriam hears the letterbox rattle. Something has landed on the mat. Another postcard. On the front, a koala wearing an orange Aran jumper. On the back, in big blue writing:

Dearest Miriam,

Thank you for finally agreeing to go for dinner with me. I had a wonderful evening. Would you like to do it again? Please give this some thought. I will knock on your door soon to hear your answer.

Yours in anticipation,

Boo Hodgkinson

She pins it to the noticeboard, next to the postcard of a woman holding a megaphone and the drawing of a spaceship.

Working side by side in the misty rain, they trim dead leaves and branches, pull roots from the soil. Harvey joins in with the digging, sending dirt into the air, then rushes off to bark at a pigeon.

"Harvey, come here," Ralph says. He rubs the dog's head.

He asks Miriam what she's doing this evening. She says she's going to Fenella's to watch the second series of *The Bridge*. Before the box set, they will be eating what Fenella refers to as her signature dish: Fenella paella.

"Sounds like a nice evening," he says.

"What about you?"

He grimaces. "Sadie's coming round to collect more books."

"I'm sorry."

"It's okay."

"It isn't."

"No, it isn't."

Miriam pushes her hands deep into the soil. Unlike Ralph, she doesn't wear gloves while she works. She wants proof under her fingernails—proof that she was out here, having a normal kind of day like a normal kind of person. Soon, someone will uncover the truth. "That Miriam's a fake," they will say. "She's not one of us." But for now there is dirt and fresh air and days that involve getting in a car and going somewhere.

When they stop for lunch, she tells Ralph how she is expecting someone to tap her on the shoulder.

He stops eating his ham sandwich. "Imposter syndrome," he says.

"Pardon?"

"It's when people feel like frauds or fakes, waiting to be found out." Then he says something about the importance of internalizing good experiences and how her brain is plastic. "You can do this," he says.

He doesn't mean the design and upkeep of this garden. He means life. The be-all and end-all. The being in it without ending it. At least she *thinks* this is what he means.

"What do you mean?" she says.

"You know what I mean." He pours her a cup of tea from his Thermos and offers her a Viennese whirl. "So, what about Boo?" he says.

"What about him?"

"Are you going out with him again?"

"Maybe."

He rolls his eyes. "Miriam," he says, mock stern.

"Shall I tell you what I've learnt about love?" she says.

"Go on then."

"It's one part illusion, two parts anxiety—a magic trick and a personality disorder, rolled into one. You've taught me that and I'm grateful."

"That's *not* what love is."

"No?"

"Don't use me as an example. I made the classic mistake of marrying someone who didn't love me."

"What did that feel like?"

"Sorry?"

"I'd like to make sure I never do it," she says.

He thinks for a moment. "You know when you walk into a room to get something, and by the time you arrive you've forgotten what you were looking for?"

"Yes."

"Well it feels a bit like that."

They drink tea. They eat Viennese whirls.

Ralph reaches into his bag, pulls out an edible green toothbrush and holds it in front of Harvey's nose. The spaniel runs off to eat in the sun, and a few minutes later he is rolling on his back, rolling on the damp grass, all four legs in the air. He releases one high-pitched bark, a bark of silliness and joy.

They work quietly for a while, alone with their own thoughts.

Ralph is still losing what he has lost. *What has gone can't really be gone.*

Miriam is still finding what she has found. *What is here can't really be here.*

Two sides of the same coin, spinning between them.

"A penny for them," he says.

She stands up straight, stretches her back. "I was thinking about Fenella," she says. "One minute she's jogging, then she's making a lamp shade from a pair of old knickers. Some people just spring from one thing to the next so easily don't they?"

Ralph smiles. "Really? Old knickers? You'll have to introduce me to this Fenella of yours. She sounds dynamic."

"You don't like dynamic. It threatens you."

He laughs in the way you laugh when something is painfully true and deeply surprising.

"And she's not actually *mine*," she says.

"Whatever," he says.

"Did I tell you that she once stopped a man from jumping off a building by singing a Dolly Parton song?"

"Which song?"

"'Here You Come Again'."

He nods. "That would do it for me," he says.

"Seriously? *That* would tell you life was worth living?"

"For a while," he says, and begins to sing. His Dolly Parton impression excites the dog, which runs in manic circles around their legs. "Never underestimate the mysterious power of country music, Miriam."

She shakes her head. "I'm so baffled by other people," she says.

He pushes a spade into the ground with his foot.

She marks out an area that will be a vegetable patch.

The dog falls asleep under a tree, dreaming wild dreams that make his body shake.

In the distance, all the time—even when Miriam whispers a cautious *maybe*; even when Ralph digs deep while humming the tune to 'Jolene'; even on days full of dirt, fresh air, sunshine and misty rain—something flickers at the edge of things. It dances on the outskirts, a mover and groover, a shapeshifter on the fringes of every life.

Miriam can see it, even when she can't. She can feel it, even on days like this.

Negative space. The presence of absence. The constant spectacle of what isn't there.

ACKNOWLEDGEMENTS

I would like to thank the characters behind this novel, for so many different things, past and present, now and then. For shaping and influencing this story. For supporting me in various ways leading up to this moment. For the hope, encouragement and humour. For being here when you were there. For taking this novel out into the world and accompanying me as I go with it.

My deepest gratitude to Gaia Banks, Elena Lappin, Adam Freudenheim, the team at Pushkin Press and Katherine Stroud, Mum and Dad, Chris, Doris Elliott (1910–1980), Noreen, Nadine, Siân, Esther, Henry (sadly you cannot read, but for sitting beside me while I wrote every word, and scampering ahead of me while I solved every puzzle, I will thank you in walks and fishy flapjacks) and Jacquie (for all your insight and generosity, I thank you).

AN IMPRINT OF PUSHKIN PRESS

ONE, an imprint of Pushkin Press, publishes one exceptional fiction or non-fiction debut a season. Its list is commissioned and edited by the writer and editor Elena Lappin, who selects the best writing by authors whose extraordinary voices, talent and vision deserve a wide readership and media focus.

THREE GRAVES FULL
Jamie Mason
"Incredibly entertaining and suspenseful... brilliant" *The Times*

A SENSE OF DIRECTION
PILGRIMAGE FOR THE RESTLESS AND THE HOPEFUL
Gideon Lewis-Kraus
"A winning blend of earnestness, wit and high-octane intellect" *Observer*

A REPLACEMENT LIFE
Boris Fishman
"Piercing, witty and enviably well written" *New Statesman*

THE FISHERMEN
Chigozie Obioma
"Awesome in the true sense of the word... a magnificent debut"
Eleanor Catton, Man Booker Prize-winning author of *The Luminaries*

WHISPERS THROUGH A MEGAPHONE
Rachel Elliott
"In an over-connected world, a crisp, beguiling voice
observes chaos – and conjures miracles. Elliott is an
inspired observer – fresh, wry and true" Liz Jensen

Forthcoming in 2016

THE MINOR OUTSIDER
Ted McDermott

DON'T LET MY BABY DO RODEO
Boris Fishman

www.pushkinpress.com/one